DWELL HERE AND PROSPER

DWELL HERE AND PROSPER
Chris Eagle

Tortoise Books
Chicago

FOR DICK

Awed have I been by strolling Bedlamites.
— William Wordsworth, *The Prelude*

PREFACE

It's December, and I've just completed one year at a 'personal care facility' in southeastern Pennsylvania. This was the most unbelievable year of my life. A stroke had messed up the left side of my body—leg, arm, and hand. I tried living alone awhile, but you can only survive so long on microwave dinners. I tried physical therapy, but it didn't help too much, so my son and I agreed to try a personal care facility.

We arrived on a Sunday. It was quiet, and a young lady from the facility signed me in and got me settled in my room. It didn't take me long to realize the residents here live mainly on cigarettes, coffee, and soda—nice combination. They are kept in order with various drugs. This staff lady informed me I was one of maybe three who were here for medical reasons. The majority have some type of mental disorder. There are 120 rooms, so it's easy to figure out who's running the asylum.

After a few days, I decided to keep a journal of the crazy and sad events that happen here on a daily basis. Later, my son and I decided a book was a definite possibility. Because of the major cigarette problem, we thought we'd call it *BUTT*.

For the remainder of the year, I worked on observations of people and occurrences. Stealing is another major problem. I personally was robbed twice: money, credit cards, and a new TV. At the year's end, my son Chris and I decided we had enough material to write the book. Chris graduated from Villanova University with majors in English and Philosophy. He will perform the writing from my observations.

— Dick Eagle

INTRODUCTION

When I was 18, my father suffered a major stroke. Overnight, he went from a government employee and scratch golfer to a retiree who was now permanently disabled. I went from a spoiled skater with perhaps too much freedom to a primary caregiver with far more responsibility than I was ready for. What followed was a crash course in the American healthcare system for both of us. He spent the first eight weeks on a stroke ward, followed by another six weeks at a physical rehab facility. For the remainder of my freshman year at Villanova, I wrote all my college essays alongside his hospital bed while he dutifully exercised the hand he'd never use again.

Once he was finally released, we tried out a ludicrous version of independent living where he maintained an apartment, and I handled all his groceries, prescriptions, rehab appointments, rides to my sister's field hockey games, etc. Of course, I couldn't be there round the clock, so one day the predictable happened. He took a fall while I was in my classes, and I didn't find him until several hours later.

The guilt I felt from this forced a decision out of me. We had to try assisted living now. Dad didn't like it, but he didn't put up too much of a fight either. He was no fool, and he could see how overwhelmed I was. Whenever I think back on it from my current vantage point—over a decade's worth of experience as a professor of Health Humanities—I have to laugh at our utter lack of medical literacy. Neither of us had a clue how to access resources, how to squeeze care out of the always-overworked and often-jaded doctors, nurses, and social workers we encountered. In our healthcare system, this also usually requires large amounts of money we didn't have. There was no alternative but to go with the affordable option his social worker recommended—another fateful moment for both of us. The place she sent him to was shockingly filthy, disorganized, full of middle-aged schizophrenics, alcoholics, and addicts. One look around the yard told me Dad was the oldest person there.

I couldn't have put things in these terms at the time, but what I was witnessing first-hand from the second we got out of the car was the downside of the anti-psychiatry movement. For all its triumphalism over the closures of state mental hospitals, a victory I mostly agree with, we've never given much thought in this country to what should have replaced them.

Before Dad was even settled in his room, I promised I'd find him a better place within the week. He gave me one of his stoic shrugs. When I returned to check on him the next day, he said the following to me verbatim: "I'm not going anywhere. This is the craziest fucking place I've ever seen. Get me a notebook."

That was Dick Eagle in a nutshell: able to laugh at anything, especially his own predicaments (which he always saw as self-inflicted), always needing some kind of project to feel like himself. That's why I played along, recognizing creature comforts mattered less to him than recovering his sense of purpose and some laughs after the stroke.

Quickly I learned to love the chaos of this place as well. On an average night, we'd watch the Phillies or the Flyers game together. As soon as he got tired, I'd go hang out in the kitchen or the lounge with all the strolling Bedlamites who had also fallen through life's cracks to end up there. None of the nurses minded. They saw me almost as support staff, breaking up the arguments and handling minor tasks around the building. Lord knows they could use the help.

Eventually we moved on to a second place, a third, a fourth. All were terrible in their own way. Dad kept filling notebook after notebook. He'd been an efficiency expert for the government, and so every page he wrote about these places had its diagnostic side: what was the problem, who had caused it, how to fix it. He even wrote a couple letters to our congressman, who sent him a very nice reply. As soon as he felt this project was complete, Dad took a stab at memoir, filling two more notebooks with every detail he could think of from his birth during the Great Depression up until his stroke. He was planning to revise these memoirs when he died in March 2005.

One month later, I started the first draft of what has taken eighteen years to turn into *Dwell Here and Prosper*. I had dabbled with some sketches, a one-act play called "The Last Supper," even a rough screenplay version before that, but now I'd become intent on pulling off the challenge of setting a whole novel in a building, shrinking the picaresque down to a yard. I do not recommend young writers try this for their first book. With Dad's notebooks plus my own memories of the four facilities where he had lived, I had all the raw materials I needed, but the only way to fit an adequate amount of it into a single novel was to create composites. In several cases, six or seven people I had come to know back then became a single character. Gradually this happened to Dad as well.

My narrator Dick is not Dick Eagle in any simplistic or straightforward sense. Pieces of Dick's backstory come from other residents. He's Dad crossed with three or four or five guys I met walking the halls of his building, sitting outside in the yard with him. Dick is a common type of man you meet in assisted living, and he seemed like the right narrator for this book because I've always felt as much responsibility to tell the larger story of this place and its inhabitants as I did to honor everything my dad went through. This required telling it through types. To paraphrase Ken Kesey, things can be the truth even if they didn't happen.

— Chris Eagle

CHAPTER 1: THE BREAD LINE

Next place they're sticking me sounds permanent. Last place did too until it got shut down. Infestation. Roaches scurried out from underneath my bed in all directions. Lying there, I watched them crisscross the ceiling by the dozens overhead. I heard shrieks coming from other rooms. Magazines kept slapping walls all night. I barely slept.

Three days later, I'm telling the social worker all about it in the car while she drives me to my new facility, fourth in two years. New one's near where I grew up, not far from where my two ex-wives and six ex-kids reside, last I heard.

This isn't what I had been picturing. We're pulling down this bumpy driveway. Four identical brick buildings surround a littered yard. In the center, there's a disused flagpole sticking twenty feet up in the air. A couple dozen residents are roaming aimlessly around the grass. Majority have scowls fixed on their faces. Rest look more puzzled. Every single one of them is wearing third-hand clothes in funny combinations. I spot one guy with dress shoes on under ripped pajamas. Another passes by the car in no shoes yet a decent pinstriped suit. Half the women have on rumpled t-shirts hanging to their knees. Other half are wearing soiled cotton nighties. Way they're milling around, it almost seems as if they put their clothes on in a hurry for some fire drill and are waiting to be told it's safe to return inside.

Ones in the last place weren't this young. I was the baby over there at sixty-four, but everyone in front of me right now is in their forties or fifties. I count two amputees plus several limpers, but I do not see a single wheelchair or metal walker anywhere. Suddenly I'm worried they've shipped me off to one of those Cuckoo's Nests, that is, until I notice the windows aren't barred. People are smoking out of several of them. No barbed wire in sight. Front doors aren't locked. Everyone's allowed to come and go. Those doors look heavy though. All four of them have big white letters—A, B, C, D—stenciled on the front.

When the social worker shuts off the ignition, everybody twists around or lifts their heads to watch her help the new recruit out of the car. Leg's still half shot, two years after my stroke. Arm on the same side is shot as well. She sets a tinted medical waste bag on the pavement. In it, I can see my change of sweatpants, extra golf shirt, socks, cement for my dentures, notebook and pens and paperweight, my standard issue comb and razor, standard issue pisscup (rinsed), along with a washrag which by now resembles a used coffee filter.

I hand her the quad cane first and set my feet onto the tar.

While she's lifting me, I swallow to make sure I don't drool on her nice dress, then I ask the only thing that's weighing on my mind.

"What kind of place is this?"

Once she's sure I'm standing on my own, quad cane secure in my good hand, she lets go of me, a little out of breath, and says, "Assisted living."

■□■

Paperwork's the same everywhere. Name, rank, and serial number. Afterwards, one of the nurse aides lugs my bag to

Building B for me. I've been issued my own lanyard so I won't lose my key. Everybody wears them. New room's on the far end of the ground floor this time which I figure's prudent since it puts me closer to the toilet.

One thing I've learned by now, this is the hardest moment in these places, right after the nurse walks out, and you're all by yourself. That's when your morale is most in danger. Every time, I recall the same corny saying this guy at AA used to love to tell us: Sometimes the bridges burn, but at least the fires light your way.

All I'm doing's taking in the room now. It's much smaller than the last one. There's hardly enough space in here for the twin bed, the narrow dresser, and this little dinged-up nightstand by the door. No tacky paintings on the walls this time. Floor's cement concealed by two blue strips of carpeting, not quite flush to the wall or to each other. One of them oscillating fans is pointed out the only window. Bedspread's gray with maroon stripes across it. No one could possibly call this a cheerful room, but I reassure myself that's also for the best. This way, I'll only want to be in here at night to write down what I saw that day before I try to sleep.

■□■

Getting out of bed's a whole production ever since the stroke. Every morning, my eyes open on their own near 5:00. I've never needed an alarm. I tilt over, let my legs slide off the bed, and elbow myself upright. Next I have to dig my quad cane down into the carpet, tug and bounce a bunch of times in order to gain leverage. Mattress does most of the work, though the bed here is much harder and lower, with less give to the springs than those mechanical beds in the last three places, so it requires six or seven extra tries before I'm standing.

Now I'll venture down the hall. Throat is dry. These places usually have some area with cookies and juice laid out in case you're diabetic. I don't see one here. I'd ask the overnight nurse, but she's snoring roughly on a sofa in some kind of rec room. There's a woman sitting right beside her, smoking, with a blanket wrapped around her in the dark. Least I think it's a woman. All I actually see's the whites of two eyes watching me above the cherry on a cigarette.

I keep walking past a portholed door that leads into a kitchen. Six steps up to the front door. I aim my quad cane at the latch and fight it open.

■□■

First couple mornings go like this. Best I can manage is three laps around the rectangle at dawn. Main goal at present is to be rid of this quad cane in six months, same goal as last year if I'm being honest. Foolish or not, I haven't given up on the idea of myself fully recovered yet: a normal-looking cane, left hand semi-functional, living unassisted in some cheap efficiency somewhere—ground floor, my own TV, one of those shower chairs, worst case having my meals delivered. That's why I do these laps all day. That's why between them I repeat the exercises for my arm and hand that PT guy showed me two years ago.

Same nine pigeons keep me company. They're lined up as usual this morning on the gutters in their designated spots. They sit so still, they seem like mini-gargoyles mounted on the roofs. My route runs from my building, B, alongside the parking lot to A, then down to D, then back across to C. I cheat towards the grass in case I ever trip. Forty paces is about my limit, so I have to break these laps up into halves or even quarters. Anytime my bad leg starts to ache, I lean against whichever bench or tree is handy and wait out the shooting pains in my left shin. Old injury, nothing to do with the stroke.

A few of my fellow refugees are up this early too, or rather are still up because they are the type you find in all these places with no semblance of routine, no discipline, no schedules whatsoever. Today I spot four of them hunched down, inspecting their quadrants of the grass around the benches and the trees, mindful not to crowd each other.

I call this crew the Dawn Patrol. What they are searching for are any and all discarded butts with a few puffs remaining past the filter. No amount of slobber will deter them. It ain't so easy on the stomach watching them degrade themselves like that. Listening to their lighters click soon as they've found another winner is enough to make my lips curl on their own.

■□■

Almost nobody I've encountered here these first two weeks seems capable of planning or remembering more than two days in either direction. I can appreciate therefore why the one I call the Game Warden handles things the way she does. Everybody has to sign their benefits over upon arrival. It's the only way a place like this can function. Green form she slides you first has several small boxes printed on it: SSI, SSD, Veterans, Family Contributions, Children of the Poor, etc. Each week, she deducts your keep then refunds you the difference. That's your pocket money the next seven days. I call this whole part the Breadline.

Warden's office is this stucco annex attached to the side of D. On Fridays, fifteen minutes after lunch, all inmates will start pouring out of all four buildings to line up along the sidewalk, a full hour before necessary, minimum.

Picture upwards of seventy people standing silent but jittery, eyes trained on that iron cut-out of the prosperous family in the horse-drawn carriage that's affixed to her screen door. Certain Fridays bring to mind that mailman's credo, you know: snow, sleet, hail. It could be raining sideways out there. No one will give up their spot.

Myself, I can never stay upright that long. Hip starts hurting if I try, so how I manage normally is I sit on the nearest open bench and proceed through all my stretches. With my good hand—the right—I can bend the left back pretty far and pry apart the fingers. Soon as I let go, everything snaps back into the perfect shape for gripping a beer glass. Nice reminder how I got myself in this predicament. I repeat the same exercises, same order, eavesdropping on anyone around, while I wait for the line to whittle down to two or three, then I stand up and hobble over in my crippled version of a hurry for my bread.

Everybody's turn's the same.

Soon as the screen door squeaks open, you march in and tensely stand while she is calculating your allowance for the week. Warden's got this spiraled ledger where she enters everything. How much you have left depends on what you had coming to you in the first place. Somehow that number varies week to week. She hardly knows who any of us are. That's why you'll hear us roll-calling our last names as we step inside. Ledger has all these columns in it. She lines her wooden ruler up along your row. Everything gets punched into the calculator twice. Procedure takes about a minute. Only other item ever on the desk's a graduation photo of her teenage daughter which is always pointed facing you, not her. Daughter has the same wide phony smile as her mother, same ample perm, same green eyeshadow. Warden announces your amount then turns toward the big cardboard box beside her feet and waits for you to tell her how many packs you want deducted from that, assuming that you smoke. Most every one here does. Word is she lives down in Wilmington. Each week, she sneaks twenty cartons across the Pennsylvania border to resell to us, tax free.

■□■

This breadline system's why it only took a week for me to grasp the rhythm here. Fridays and Saturdays are fairly chummy. Somebody will ask somebody else for something, whether that's a smoke or a quarter, half a soda, and I'd give you even odds they'll get it out of them. By Sunday, half these nitwits have smoked their winnings up already. That's what starts the chain in motion: rampant bumming, borrowing, collecting, stealing. Some guy you don't know is always hovering over your shoulder, kindly offering to finish things for you: tail end of that ciggie, nub off your pretzel, last swig of your birch beer. Trades also get proposed, typically one cigarette for half your coffee or your soda. The boy scouts among us carry empty mugs around all day by the knuckle, just in case.

Remainder of each week, the yard revolves on this slow-turning wheel of half-assed promises to pay you back come Friday, always Friday, everybody's favorite word. That's why you never need a calendar in here. Day of the week feels pretty obvious based on how desperate people act.

Yard therefore can get mighty entertaining by the middle of the week. First month alone, I've seen an adult male unlace a perfectly fine pair of shoes and hand them over to a barefoot man in trade for his fresh pack of cigarettes. I saw another guy get smacked square in the mush one time for refusing someone a sip of coffee to swallow their blood pressure medication. I saw another take his dead father's wristwatch off and hand it over for a pack. I saw a man pay a whole dollar for one cigarette. Another sold his belt right off his pants. Now he has to hold them up all day.

■□■

I've made two friends. There's this cement circle in the center of the yard. I call it the Island. Two good-natured guys who never move from there have made a point of saving me a seat between them while I'm on my laps. Bunyan lives in D. Crutch lives over in A.

Evidently, Bunyan is the lumberjack type: tall, flannelled, overalled, pushing four hundred pounds, a rounder face than Orson Welles. Bunyan's always grinning upwards at the sunlight through his orange beard. He looks around my age. I've noticed he gets winded easy. Apart from that, I can't figure out what's wrong with him.

Crutch is in his early fifties, black, with one of those skunk patches over his right ear and two big shapeless shoulders stretching his ribbed tank top out. Nickname's because he gets around on an old beat-up pair of metal walking sticks, though if he happens to be hurrying somewhere, anyone could tell those crutches hardly touch the ground.

■□■

One Thursday afternoon in June, the three of us are squeezed together in our regular spots when the most obstinate of all the chiselers in this joint begins to bum from bench to bench around the Island. I call this one Cy, short for Cyclops, another black guy, late forties, feather-weight frame, little Sammy Davis mustache. Nickname's on account of the fact that his left eye is missing. Socket is sealed shut. Supposedly Cy's eye got shot out during some bungled robbery. Unlucky ricochet is how I heard him brag about it once.

Around here, Cy and his two henchmen—Popeye and Penguin—are known as our official Go-Getters. That's how I refer to anyone who's willing to perform any errand whatsoever, either for a straight cash tip or portion of the purchase. Runs to the State Store and the WaWa happen all day long. That's the other problem with this place. We're a little too far from town to fend for ourselves.

Hotter it's been getting, more likely these slobs are to pay a Go-Getter a measly dime to run indoors and fetch another soda for them. Change may trickle a little side-to-side that way. Every red cent still ends up in somebody's register by Friday. Couple of the older residents are actually gullible enough to send one of these con artists to town on their behest, either to hock or buy some item for them. Every sixth or seventh trip, the Trio returns empty-handed, hours, even days later, swearing on each other's mothers they got mugged. One reports the details to the chump they're ripping off while the other two stand by as material witnesses.

In the yard, Cy has a repertoire of clever tricks for prying single cigarettes off people too. My favorite is this goofy dance he does sometimes while making his approach. Trotting towards his victim, he will run his palms up and down his purple gym pants, pretending to search for something, even though these are the warm-up kind that button up the sides and don't have any pockets.

I watch him work the bench across from ours.

"Yo, Yo, Bill! King of the Hill! Left my smokes inside."

This clammy-looking fat one I call Dollar Bill is adamant he can't afford to give anything away at the moment because his parents are mad at him.

Cy just spins around and tiptoes up to his next prey.

"Dan, my main man, Dan."

"My name ain't Dan."

"I meant Mike, Mike from up the—"

"His name's Sal," growls this other guy named Paul who I call Swabbie, owing to the anchor tattoo fading on his forearm beneath two women's names—Janice and Laura—both crossed out. His other arm has two dolphins touching noses, curled in such a way to make them look like a pair of lady legs spread wide apart. Swab is hunched forward in a sleeveless Phillies t-shirt and white boxer shorts, alongside Salvy who is leaning back, sniffling and rubbing his knuckles deep into the corners of his itchy eyes so hard I hear them squishing clearly, fifteen feet away. This dynamic duo's maybe forty-five or fifty tops. I've yet to see the one without the other present. Both live upstairs in my building.

Cy claps his hands and starts rubbing them together in a let's-get-down-to-business sort of way. "That's who I meant. C'mon, Sal."

"What, Wes?"

"You got one of them for me? Getcha tomorrow."

Salvy peers down at his half-buttoned shirt. Although it's on inside out, the outline of a pack still gives itself away through the thin powder blue material. His pinky pokes around inside the pack to doublecheck how close it is to empty.

"Sorry, Wes. Can't."

"What you wanna smoke them stale ones for? I'll get you three fresh ones Friday."

"No can do."

Another thing I've noticed is the ones who've lived here longest each have their own version of the thousand-yard stare. Sal's lived here several years. Whenever a moocher's making one of these requests, Sal stares at his big toe, wiggling outside the hole in his grimy tennis shoes. Cy keeps waiting. Sal sniffles violently and spits the oyster he's collected on his tongue off to the side.

"Sal, baby, help me out."

"Holy mother of fuck!" shouts Swabbie loud enough to startle everyone around the Island, "You half-deaf too?"

"This bothering you, is it?"

"He said he don't fucking have any."

"And who told you to listen?"

"To listen? What should I do, Wessy? Stitch my fucking ears up?"

"Or your mouth."

"Your fucking mouth, you one-eyed prick!"

"Fuck you, man!"

"Hey, Wes, what you seal that hole of yours with, a fucking soldering iron?"

Swab grips the wooden plank he's sitting on like he's prepared to stand and settle this. Wisely Cy retreats towards these two lovebirds, next bench over.

This pair has been shamelessly canoodling in front of everybody the past hour. Both are barefoot. Both are wearing jean shorts and black t-shirts. The male of the species lives two doors down from me. I call him Zorro because if you ever step too close to him, he dips into this fencing pose and thrusts an imaginary rapier at your face over and over, mumbling *"En garde!"* until you back away.

His girlfriend Babydoll is this bizarre brunette in her late forties, same as Zorro, with two rows of painful-looking acne bumps along her jaw, a gray bunny tattoo over her left tit. She's always nuzzling this filthy doll with yellow yarn for hair against her chest, making goo-goo talk at it, or scolding it, or trying to teach it things. Last week, I caught her pointing out two squirrels as they were zipping back and forth across the power lines above our heads. Anytime your back is turned to her, you'd swear a nine-year-old was talking.

At the moment, Zorro has his right hand tucked as high as possible between her thighs. Her left hand can't stop stroking his right knee a little frantically. They only cease their smooching when Cy sticks his face up close to theirs and imitates them. Everyone around the Island laughs at this. When they come up for air, Cy taps two fingers to his lips two times real fast. Zorro slides his pack from his shirt pocket and hands over two cigarettes, one at a time, before shushing Cy away.

"What's with the generosity, Don?" Swab calls out to Zorro, "I'll take one too if you're offering."

"What?"

"You hit the Powerball or something? What makes you so fucking nice today?"

"Ohhhhhhhhh," Zorro draws out this evil snicker once he understands Swab's question, "I'm not being nice. I'm trying to give them cancer's all."

■ □ ■

Rest of summer follows this same pattern. Muggier it gets, the end of June into July, the more traffic around the yard increases. Somedays Bunyan and Crutch and I'll witness nasty squabbles over spots, quality cursing, even the occasional shoving match. Anytime a voice is raised, the whole yard twists around to gain themselves a better view, all equally aware that fisticuffs might be our only entertainment for the day.

By 2:00, our daysleepers start lugging kitchen chairs outside. They either carry them where they can hide behind the dumpster, or way over by the row of pine trees past the parking lot, or under those three maple trees clear on the other side. A smarter few will walk their chairs into the gaps between the buildings. Back there's your best bet if your objective is to smoke in peace.

■□■

First week of August is so hot, the air has haze lines in it. One of these trees around us has begun to let off this thick spermy stink which makes the whole yard smell about as pleasant as a peepshow trough. Grass increasingly resembles hay. Middle of my laps on two occasions, I've felt woozy enough to realize I better cut them back awhile.

Nobody here has money to afford an air conditioner, hence this heat wave drives even our most dedicated shut-ins out of all four buildings. Yard looks like some cross between a Hooverville and county fair. Chairs get plunked into the dirt wherever there is any shade. Men mop their brows with hankies every couple minutes. I catch them dozing upright often. Flies have the time to take long walks along their faces before being flicked away.

"You know that expression," I ask my two benchmates, "the one about a lull in a day?"

"Sure."

"Mm."

"Here we got all lull, no day."

They both snicker without adding anything. What's there to add when something's true?

Course it being quiet don't mean there's nothing to observe. I catch people pulling funny junk out of their pockets such as cereal or socks they use as snot rags. Yesterday I caught somebody with his clothes on backwards. I was staring at this clown, not sure what was off, until he turned around and I noticed his zipper on his ass.

This is how I spend my afternoons, studying these dignitaries, monitoring all of their transactions. I eavesdrop on nearby conversations. I sneak harmless-seeming questions in as needed, too. That's always been a tendency of mine. Back in the army, for example, I was the only guy in my platoon to keep a diary with coded nicknames. I used to wonder lots of things about my fellow soldiers. Here I find I'm only wondering two things: how each person ended up in here and what makes them stay.

First part's easy. I've heard four ways how you end up in this place officially:

1. Court declares you incapable of employment.
2. Relatives are sick of dealing with you.
3. VA refers veterans like Crutch or Swabbie.
4. Hospital ships older persons such as Bunyan or myself, soon as insurance stops paying our fare.

Second part is what I've yet to wrap my head around these past three months. I could tell you easy what a geriatric orphan like myself is doing here. I'm just biding my time until my leg and hand recover. Then you got your ones who run their index fingers up and down their bottom lips all day. Those aren't too hard to understand. I assume there's nowhere else to send these fruitcakes now since the state hospital shut down. But what about the rest? Aren't they able-bodied? What's that word you used to hear? Gainful? Gameful? I can't fathom how these younger mostly healthy ones can stand this life. They smoke a pack or two a day and drink ten sodas much too fast for this weather. They end up puking orange on the bushes. One gentleman stands up and pisses anytime he feels like it, right on the grass in front of everybody. Even a dog would have the decency to lean against a tree.

None of the women seem to mind. If they even notice at all, the most they'll do is snicker once or faintly shake their heads. These women only seem to come in two varieties. You have your leather skeletons who weigh no more than ninety pounds and pace the sidewalks all day long. Other kind have bodies shaped like fire hydrants and those pushed-in bulldog faces. Every bench holds one of them. All day, I hear them fart and belch. Often I'll spot them picking at their crotches, just like men.

■□■

Final Friday in August, I'm on the bench as usual with Bunyan, watching yet another payday line begin to form along the sidewalk. Head of the class today is Zorro, seated on the cement with a bottle of peroxide, pantleg rolled up, digging at his infected toe with an unfolded paperclip. Sitting Bull is sitting behind Zorro, observing this operation. Now here comes Patty Cakes, that smiley woman who is always clapping. Next comes the Thin Man. Ben Franklin and Joan of Arc stroll up together. Benny Hill waddles up behind those two, brushing his sandy hair out of his eyes, blinking much more than necessary.

All four front doors keep slamming periodically.

Dozens of idiots are rushing down the stoops, ducking below branches, nearly tripping they're in such a hurry to go wait in line. I'm counting heads when I hear that flimsy metal rattle coming up behind us. Crutch props his walking implements against the bench and presses his left armpit on them. With his free hand, he pats Bunyan on the shoulder first, then me. Bunyan grunts. I arch my head around.

"Sit," I tell him.

He shakes his head. "Doc said stretch it." His thumb begins to fiddle with the wingnuts on the handles of his crutches. "Sposed to try them Canadian ones soon."

"Canadian what?"

"Canadian crutches."

"What's a Canadian crutch?"

"Kind that go around. Not under like these."

"I need one of those for my pecker."

"Not here, you don't."

I redo the head count. Line is over fifty now. Some of their lips are quivering which means their minds are busy guessing how much they will get this coming week. Their index fingers begin doing long division in the air, x amount of dollars or cigarettes by seven. I wonder who they think they're kidding. None of them can plan that far ahead and stick to it. It requires too much wherewithal. I figure I've known my two companions long enough to ask how much they get per week. Both of them chuckle at my naive question.

"Hard to tell. Robin picks a number from her pointy hat."

Bunyan snorts. "Look at them all. You ever seen so much of anything lumped together with so little positive result?"

"Can't say I have."

"Everybody's gonna go out and have a nine-dollar party. They'll still be bumming by Monday."

"Big spenders," adds Crutch, switching his sticks to his other armpit. I get a whiff of raw onion, second he starts wagging his left arm to wake it up. On his right side, this wavy line of burn marks runs along his bicep, shoulder, neck, and jaw.

"Spenders on what?" I ask him.

"Ciggies. Sodas. Candy bars."

"The finer things?"

"The finer things."

"How much are candy bars again?"

"Candy cost sixty cent. So does soda."

Right then the screen door opens. Zorro is standing at the ready with his paperclip and bottle of peroxide tucked inside his trousers. He knows better than to dawdle. The cardinal rule here is never hold up the Breadline.

Minute later, Zorro exits happily with four fresh packs of Lucky Strikes in one hand and a modest wad of singles crumpled in the other. Sitting Bull's the next one out. He hasn't even finished biting off the cellophane from his new pack when the Trio swarms him from three sides. His left hand swats Popeye and Penguin away, while his right gives Cy a couple cigarettes he's owed since Tuesday.

I decide to keep a running tally.

Next one out has eight packs but no dough. I ask some passersby how they made out. Average haul appears to be eighteen to twenty bucks, plus five to seven packs per person. I do some quick arithmetic. Everybody claims Warden ups them fifty cents on us from what she pays in Delaware. Figure four packs a head, average. That makes two bucks profit. Times that by most inmates, say sixty of us, that's $120, give or take, per week. Times that by fifty-two weeks. That works out to an extra six large a year. Off butts.

"How come none of them go halfsies on a carton?"

"She don't allow it," Crutch answers, "Packs only." He keeps watching until the line has dwindled to a dozen, at which point he pries his crutches off our cruddy bench. "Scuse me, champs," he says, "It's time for my reward." He clicks his way carefully off the grass onto the cement, then stops and turns around, grinning with some recollection at the two of us. "You know what the pastor said?"

"Nope. What'd the pastor say?"

"Said it's Friday now, but Sunday coming! Told it to us last month. Easter."

"Easter was three months ago, Dwayne," says Bunyan, wincing as he presses himself off the bench to follow.

I watch them proceed slowly down the sidewalk, side by side, until they've caught up to the tail end of the line.

My eyes tilt past them to the office door. Next one out is Dollar Bill with two balled fists of nothing. Bill's in his late forties with a thick black head of hair covered in rock salt dandruff all the time. He has on some concert t-shirt with a skeleton playing guitar and a peeling list of dates from 1982 across the back. Armpits on the thing look armor-plated from eleven years of sweat. He's pacing in figure-eights across the grass, muttering strings of curses to himself. Fists keep clenching and unclenching at his sides.

"Give me a dollar," he mutters to the nearest group of people. When none of them respond, he moves on to the next group. "Give me a dollar," he repeats methodically, including anybody's name he thinks he knows until he's positive that they are paying him no mind.

Line's down to Tinker Bell, Cochese, Crutch, and Bunyan. I'm twisting my quad cane round to pull myself up when I realize Dollar Bill is looming over me. He rubs his knuckles on his forehead for a moment. His nose has clearly been rearranged a couple times before. It's bent like a letter J across his face.

"Give me a dollar."

"Sorry," I tell him, "I gave at the office."

This genuinely stumps him. I watch him turn around and gawk at the screen door, perplexed. When he repeats himself, I simply wave at him to go away, but he keeps hassling me, convinced all of a sudden I owe him money. I inquire if he even knows my name. His counter-offer is to call it even if I'll give up anything of equal value in a trade.

When I refuse, he makes a sudden sort of joking swipe for my quad cane. Instinctively I mean to grab it with both hands, but only the good one moves. Both of us fumble for the cane until it topples over. As he bends to snatch it up, I kick at him with my good leg. Of course I miss, but he is stunned enough to tumble backwards onto the cement.

Immediately, I feel scores of bystanders looking over. We're the entertainment for the day. We volley a few curse words back and forth. More curious faces fill up windows all around the yard.

With my shoe, I stand the cane back up and aim the prongs in his direction. Remain on the bench, I tell myself, whatever happens, long as you're on this bench, you'll have a puncher's chance. It takes him three tries to regain his feet. I can tell he skinned his elbow pretty good from how he's gripping it. I raise the cane above my head, ready to bash him with it if he charges, but Bill turns around and marches to his building as if nothing happened. All the ones who saw what just transpired start to laugh. Some of the other ones, whose backs were turned and didn't even see, start laughing too at everybody else's laughter.

CHAPTER 2: SURVIVAL, EVASION, AND ESCAPE

Fall's here. Yard's acquired a cidery odor from all the trampled crabapples. Smell reminds me of a ripe dumpster. At night, big piles of leaves get burnt off in some nearby firepit. I can smell them too from bed, even with my window closed. I'm spending every minute indoors nowadays. Cold drove us inside by mid-November. That's when it hit me I'd be trapped within this building until thaw. Main worry is I'll lose the small amount of progress I made over summer with my bad leg, not to mention this near-useless arm of mine.

By October, I was averaging nine laps a day. On my final trot outdoors, I counted how many steps it took to complete one full lap around the yard. Two hundred thirty-six. Next I counted from my bedroom to the rec room. That takes forty-eight steps, door to door. Figure five trips down the hall's as good as one full lap outside. Five times nine makes forty-five. Let's just say I've memorized the walls by now. I could inventory every stain and crack in every piece of drywall for you. Once or twice a day, I'll add a flight of stairs to push myself. I pace like that, all morning and all afternoon, past the same partly-open doors until it's time to eat again.

■□■

Chow ain't all that great. It's not like there's some dedicated chef for every building. Meals are simply handled by whichever nurse happens to be on duty at the time.

Breakfast is cereal left out for us, some pre-sliced bread for toasting, hot coffee in the tall urn on the counter, orange juice from concentrate. Now and then, there'll be a box of powdered sinkers on the table, but those tend to vanish pretty quick.

Lunch is white-bread sandwiches, bologna or tuna, or your occasional burger with some stale potato chips.

Bill of fare for dinner don't vary too much either: thawed-out vegetables with cubes of chicken or pork under an inch of congealed gravy, either that or soup with seeded rolls. Dessert's a pink and orange parfait which resembles molded puke but tastes alright, provided you close your eyes.

Canteen has two large tables in it: a big wooden one positioned over by the windows with twelve pairs of bald spots on the varnish caused by years of elbows, plus a repurposed ping-pong table closer to the door. I sit at the ping-pong table next to Swab and Sal most meals.

■□■

If I'm neither eating nor roaming the halls, you will find me on whichever rubber armchair's empty in the rec room amidst six or seven semi-strangers, all of whom act fidgety whether they're picking at their lips or rubbing crud out of the corners of their eyes. They're rarely more than half-aware what's playing on TV.

Rec room's always pitch dark. There are no windows in here, plus the only lamp is broke. What little light there is comes from the TV or the glow from three machines—soda, candy, coffee—which are set along the left-hand side when you walk in.

While I'm sitting here, I'm always going through those exercises to wake up my arm and hand. I bend the fingers one by one. I rotate the wrist ten times clockwise, ten more counter-clockwise. I tug the arm each way an arm's supposed to go. Highest I can lift it is a foot. Any higher and you'll see me wince.

Now and then, one of my roommates takes note of me struggling beside them. Colonel Klink or Gilligan are talking on TV. Our eyes have adjusted to the darkness of the room. I catch them staring at the arm I'm slowly cranking. They get this sort of pitying expression on their face like they wonder why I bother. It makes me feel like pointing out to them their only exercise all day's to lean over and fart.

■□■

Today's December 8th according to the calendar out on the noticeboard. I don't know how I can take three months of this. My only project at the moment is myself, these indoor laps, these futile exercises. Since I'm stuck in here for now, think what I'll do is make an in-depth study of one of my fellow inmates.

Most intriguing case so far is this Harry guy whose room is one floor up from mine. Harry is slim and early forties with a prominent mole above his brown mustache. All week, he alternates between two tennis shirts: a green one with a yellow stripe across the chest or this black one with white trim along the collar and the sleeves. I call him Thinker. He arrived a few weeks after I did in the summer. I remember how through August and September he would go to fairly great lengths in order to be left alone while in the yard. He owns one of them collapsible camping chairs. Thing is so rusted and worn, honestly, I assume he must've trashpicked it somewhere.

His daily ritual was to carry a book for the day, plus a notebook, plus a screw-top mug full of coffee—the free stuff from the urn they serve at meals—all folded up inside that dumpy chair, way over to those maple trees which line the east end of the property. We would forget about him over there. He sat that still. During my laps, I always spied on him though. Either he'd be reading some humongous book split open across his crotch, or he'd be jotting thoughts down in his notebook. Couple times, I caught him doing neither. His bare feet were propped against the trunk, head back, book closed, just gazing pleasantly up at the leafy branches, thinking. That's when I issued him his nickname.

His general aloofness extends to other things. Not once in five months have I seen him bum or barter. Come payday, he purchases a single pack of Camels off the Warden. He permits himself precisely three a day, which I've noticed he reserves for after meals. Twenty come in a pack, so three times six leaves him two cigarettes come Friday. He smokes the last one while he's waiting in the Breadline, at which point he collects his next pack, plus a couple measly dollars for the coming week. Unlike the others, he seems to have the discipline to stick to it.

Another time he stood out was October. When the Phillies clinched the pennant, Thinker was the only person in our building not to watch the Series. While the rest of us were marching single file straight from dinner to the TV set, this guy kept veering off to go upstairs. Game 5 was that elimination game at home. All of us were nervous wrecks, kicking the floor, hollering, knocking each other's sodas over with our shoes. Schilling pitched that five-hit gem. Game 6 was back in

Toronto. It was tied in the bottom of the ninth. Mitch was on the mound. Schill had a towel draped over his head so he could puke discreetly in the dugout. Mitch kept shaking Dutch off. It was clear he didn't trust his stuff, so Dutch jogged to the mound to calm him down. In total silence we awaited the next pitch. Count was 2-2. Right then Thinker strolled in for a soda. He strolled out sipping it while Carter's skipping down the first base line.

■□■

Two weeks away from Christmas now with half a foot of snow outside, everyone confined together, you'd figure there'd be ample opportunity to chum up to this guy and find out what he's doing here. Problem is I'm fairly certain that he reads in bed all day. I almost never see him except at lunch and dinner, and even then he reads all through the meal.

Today his seat is straight across from mine. Face is covered by some book titled *The Prelude*. Every twenty seconds, his bologna sandwich disappears behind the book and comes out slightly smaller. I've hardly touched my own. I'm too preoccupied with watching him to eat. Soon as he's finished, he sets his book down long enough to light his cigarette, then leaves.

During my constitutional that afternoon, I notice Thinker's door's a foot ajar. From this angle, I can't see his face, but I recognize those brick red moccasins of his in bed. It's the same habit with all these guys upstairs. Every one of them craves solitude, especially this time of day, yet no one ever shuts their door. Peeking in at them, I always feel as if I'm staring at retired circus animals encased in glass, too used to being watched to even care who's going by. Rarely do they bother to acknowledge me.

I check over my shoulder to make sure nobody's in the hall, then snoop through Thinker's door another minute. What I can see resembles the cluttered backroom of some pawnshop. About a thousand books are piled five feet high against the far wall. On his dresser, there's a painted plaster figurine of some old bearded man in a red robe with a tamed lion curled around his feet. Upper torso of a mannequin is sitting in a banker's chair just past the bed. There are blue boxes drawn across its skull.

Suddenly a ruse occurs to me. I dab some drool off on my shoulder, straighten out my twisted sweatpants—my version of presentable—then tap lightly on his door. Second I do, I hear all the other lie-a-beds on the entire floor, six men in total, sitting up at once to locate the disturbance.

"Enterrrrrrrrrrrrr," he calls out like he's impersonating Vincent Price.

"Mind if I borrow your doorjamb? Overdid it again."

I push his door inwards with my cane and lean against the frame. With my fist, I start to tenderize my leg to prove it's sore. As ruses go, it's not ingenious, but it does the trick. Everyone's accustomed to me needing help. Before I have a chance to ask if I can sit, Thinker's already reaching for that mannequin. He sets him on the floor and rolls the banker's chair up to this writing desk I didn't see at first behind the door. Motioning for me to sit, he climbs back into bed and smiles peculiarly, not so much at me as at the ceiling.

I look out the window. It's snowing hard again today. My eyes rove up and down the stacks of books along the wall. I recognize the names of some explorers on the spines, a couple dictators, couple poets, plus a philosopher or two. One stack has big biographies of every president in order. Stack next to that is mostly novels. Stack after that one's full of textbooks: *Kings of Britain, Quakerism, The French Revolution, Tree Identification, The Great Depression, Egyptian Deities, History of Pennsylvania.* Next stack has two full sets of encyclopedias. Final stack's reserved for books about the Amish: *History, Customs, Folklore, Grammar, Superstitions, Recipes, Vocabulary, Shunning, Hexes, Quilts.* The books get bigger going down which makes each stack seem like a little tower. At the bottom, six large dictionaries act as the foundations.

"How often those tip over?"

"Only when my careless neighbor slams his door. You'll find everything from Plato to NATO over there."

"You a professor or something?"

"Used to be." He points at the wall behind me.

Clumsily I swing the chair around and find a diploma from UPenn hanging above his desk. PhD in History. 1984. Harold Jerome Fairless. The diploma looks professionally framed, except for the yellow 99-cent sticker stuck onto the glass. In front of me, there's a pile of those composition books he brought outside with him all summer. There must be over thirty of them. Top one says *Sep-Nov 93.* Three books sitting next to them are titled *Edgar Huntly, Der Zauberberg,* and *Guide for the Perplexed.* Beside the books, there's this antique clock in a glass housing smudged with several fingerprints. I've been staring at it awhile, convinced there's something strange about it, when it dawns on me the clock is missing both its hands. They're sitting right beside it, with this ornate iron winding key.

"Interesting clock."

"It is. That's a pendulum clock. *Drehpendeluhr* in German."

"Don't it work?"

"It works fine. Can't you hear the ticking?"

Listening for it now, I realize the clock's been ticking all along.

"You'll also hear them called four-hundred-day clocks, anniversary clocks, perpetual clocks. They barely need winding."

"What happened to the hands?"

"They were in my way. I removed them."

He reaches up to scratch the bushy ends of his mustache. In his mind, he must be gathering up everything knowable about clocks because, next thing, he's explaining the functions of every gizmo hidden inside: the drum and the thin copper line that coils and uncoils around it, the geartrain and the teeth, the stop, the anchor, the pendulum, and the falling weight, which is most important because it pushes the whole mechanism.

"I was a machinist forty years," I tell him.

"Escapement," he replies, bringing his hands together above his chest. With his thumbs, he demonstrates how the anchor nudges the gear forward enough for a tooth to escape. "A second is just the length of time it takes for the next tooth to catch. And the next...and the next...and the next."

We sit there listening to it tick off several seconds.

"Without someone to wind that," he adds, gesturing for the key, which I lift off the desk and hand to him, "Without someone to wind this, the falling weight is never raised. There needs to be a force applied of some kind."

The clock has fine gold numbers and a grinning moon dial whose face is two-thirds showing. A pair of brass balls keep twisting quickly at the base.

"So what's the big idea with the hands?"

My question makes him smirk. "Well, infinity, obviously. Or Purgatory."

"When's the last time you wound it?"

He ponders this for an uncomfortable amount of time, at least thirty-forty seconds, before simply stating, "I forget."

■ □ ■

Evenings are when medications get dispensed. Don't take yours, and they'll withhold your bedtime snack. It's the only way they can ensure that everybody comes downstairs at some point before bed. No pills, no cookies. The two nurses who split second shift have different systems. The Jamaican one prefers to have us file through the canteen. One who's on tonight, Octavia, likes to watch the basketball while handing us the little Dixie cups with our initials scribbled on the side.

Just after 8:00, she drags the poker table in the corner of the rec room over near the sofa where I'm sitting. She's on the verge of wheezing as she sets the box of happy pills and the three-ring binder on the table. The metal chair creaks as she eases onto it. Ocky is twice the size of anybody here.

"Who they playin'?" she asks, sucking yet more wind.

"The Heat."

Swab flops down next to me. Boxers he's wearing have some kind of luau theme with girls in grass skirts dancing on both sides. Armholes on his POW-MIA shirt are jagged where he scissored off the sleeves. A quart of something blue is tucked between his legs. As he picks the bottle up to take a swig, I glimpse the stretched skin from one of his testicles.

"Want a hit?" he asks.

"No, thank you."

"Not a partaker?"

"Opposite. I partook too much."

"Ah," he says, downing my sip for me, "One of those."

Both teams are lining up for the jump ball. This enormous Mormon kid we drafted steps up by the ref and lifts his arm. I know it's only twenty games, but I've begun to doubt this kid can even play. He can't shoot a lick. Can't dribble. Hands are stone. He's all height, no girth, so all the other centers push him around without much difficulty. Only thing he's good for is the occasional blocked shot, plus a few rebounds, assuming, of course, they fall right to him.

"When'd we pick this stiff again?"

"First round."

"What spot I mean?"

He takes another sip. "Second overall, I wanna say."

"Man."

I return to my exercises. Elbow don't want to bend too far today. I attribute it to this near-zero weather we've been having. Usual buffoons keep straggling in, two at a time or by themselves, to take their pills. If the game is on, the men will mill around the sofa, two or three possessions. If it's commercials, they just ask the score and leave. Women seem to take the evenings harder here. All they do is down their pills without a word and return to their cells.

During halftime, Thinker strolls in and buys himself a ginger ale to swallow his two pills. Then he leaves immediately.

Five minutes later, Ocky summons me back to the table. I take a blood thinner every day. I also take Skelaxin. It loosens up the muscles. Otherwise, this bad arm tightens on me something terrible. As I tilt my Dixie cup onto my bottom lip, another ruse occurs to me.

"Say!" I half-shout at her as if I just remembered something, "What's that pill that Harry takes?"

"Swallow, fool."

I gulp, then show her my furry tongue.

"Good boy."

"What's that pill Harry takes?"

"Who?"

"Mustache guy just now. He was saying that it helps."

"Last name?"

"Fair-something. Fairlane. Fairless."

She flips to his page and spins the binder round. DOB: 9/30/51. Admit: 7/3/93. Allergies: Penicillin, Tea. Rxs: Proscar 5 mgs, Fluoxetine 10 mgs. Emergency Contact: Fred Nietzsche. Number looks made-up. Too many digits. Forty-two years old makes him the same age as my eldest son. I don't understand it. Typically this spells major mental problems with the younger ones, but Thinker's more composed than anybody here, including all the nurses.

"What's Proscar for?"

"Pro-what?"

"Proscar," I repeat, tapping the spot on the page.

"Maybe he got a big prostate. Think that's for that."

■□■

Week later, I'm all out of breath outside the stairwell on the second floor. Leg is throbbing. I decide I better lean against the wall a couple minutes before proceeding any further. Some guy in yellowed long johns steps around me like I'm furniture.

Every few feet, a poof of smoke appears above his head, sort of reminds me of a train. I watch him disappear into the room across the hall from Thinker, who backs out himself a second later, softly shuts his door. I head towards him. He's in such a hurry he don't realize who I am until he's almost by me.

"It's unlocked," he says over his shoulder. From his tone, it's clear he assumes I'm on my way to visit him.

I watch him rush into the toilet. Maybe Ocky had it right about his fickle prostate. I let myself into his room. That *Prelude* book which he's been reading the past week is open on the bed. I decide to take advantage of the time to snoop around some more. Top drawer of his desk is sticking out a couple inches. Inside, I can see the ends of several pens, a lighter, plus this week's pack of Camels. Aware I have another minute minimum, I pull the drawer out all the way. There's two letters hiding in the back. Return address on them says Bill Fairless, 206 Providence Road. Could that be his father? Brother maybe? Doubt he has a son. I pick up each envelope to check the stamps. Older one's dated three months ago. More recent one from last month is unopened. I stick them back and set the drawer just right. His notebooks are in front of me. Top one says *Nov-Dec 93*. I open to a random page and come across this wall of tiny words, two rows squeezed perfectly inside each line to conserve space. First thing my eyes fall on are definitions. *Amphitryon: harassing both sides (Greek). Camarine: a fetid swamp or marsh. Umbrageous: offering shade, easily offended. Malaprop du jour: hunchback whale, overheard during Jeopardy (Salvatore).*

I close the notebook and step over to that mannequin beside the bed. Left arm is missing. Right arm's rotated upwards, index finger pointing at the ceiling like he's making some important point. Words written in the boxes on his head are so small I need to bend and squint to make them out:

Torpor, Pleurisy, Lassitude, Catalepsy, Priapism, Scrofula, Akrasia, Chorea, Strabismus, Phthisis, Gout, Psoriasis, Dropsy.

Door creaks behind me.

Thinker says, "I pilfered that fellow from the Wanamaker's dumpster."

"Just doing my laps."

"That must have been '88 or '89. Two of my students helped me. We had to wait until the middle of the night. They stood lookout while I climbed in and got it. Extra credit."

"Any of these apply to me?"

"I better leave that up to you, monsieur."

"Let's go with lassitude. What is it?"

"Lassitude? It's a type of weariness. Do you feel weary, Richard?"

■□■

Following this second visit, any need for pretext disappears. Signs are obvious he's been expecting me when I reach his room. Door will be two-thirds open. Mannequin's already resting on the dirty laundry in his bushel. Chair's positioned facing him. In no time, things get to where I'm up here four-five nights a week. I call it Night School. Either he will read selections from whatever book's already in his hands aloud to me, as though I'm blind instead of paralyzed, or I'll inch over to his stacks myself and point at ones that sound like they could be my memoirs—*Ragged Dick, Poor Richard's Almanack*—and he reclines in bed and sort of summarizes them for me, all out of order.

Needless to say, we hop around a lot. If Monday's topic is utopias, Tuesday could be anything from astrolabes to Stoicism.

The only topic we return to regularly is the history of Pennsylvania. That's his area of expertise. For nine semesters, he taught two sections of it at the community college, plus some more specialized classes on the Amish and the Quakers.

Question I pose one night about the blue laws makes him roll out of bed and dig this ream of paper from the bottom of his lower drawer. He sets it on the desk in front of me, explaining it's the thesis which he had to write to earn his Ph.D. His name is right there on the title page. Topic is the special rules on how to hold the Sabbath here in Pennsylvania. I start flipping through it. Chapter 1 begins in England: which kings allowed merrie-making, mirth and ale, which kings didn't. Chapter 2 is on some edict called "The Book of Sports," written by King James in 1617. Chapter 3 is all about the "Ordnung." That's the set of rules the Amish rely on to ensure their farms stay small, their pace stays slow, their houses dark at night. Chapter 4 opens with a list of all the things ever prohibited in Pennsylvania on a Sunday. List runs several pages long. I remember half of them from when I was a kid.

Thinker's crouching by his wall of books.

I glance over at him, saying, "It's true. You couldn't take a girl out for a milkshake. What's that old line? I once spent a year in Philadelphia."

He's hardly listening. Because the book he wants to show me next is down the bottom, he must brace his other arm against the stack and yank the book out quick like some magician whipping off a tablecloth. It's some kind of picture book. He holds it open to this painting of a gang of animals, all loafing in a meadow. There's a bull, a leopard, and a bear. A lamb is stuck between a lion and a wolf. One of them kid angels with curly hair and wings is minding them. All the animals seem sort of dopey, way their eyes are open extra wide.

I say, "They look like they've been chewing on the wrong grass."

Thinker taps the corner of the page. Crowded together underneath this amber tree, I count eight Quakers and nine Indians. One of the Quakers is kneeling by an open trunk, holding a blanket out by way of gift. Guy behind him's pointing at a scroll.

"That Billie Penn?"

"Correct."

"Who are the injuns?"

"Those are Delawares. Were you aware this wasn't supposed to be a state like other states? Penn called it the Holy Experiment. This was basically a hippie commune. They were positive they'd found the very site of Paradise on Earth." He runs his pinky along this clean blue river widening out behind them. "That's the Chester Marina where they're standing. That exact spot can't be more than a mile or two from here."

■□■

Night School proceeds like that through January. By Valentine's Day, none of us have breathed new air in over ninety days. Coop up so many skinflints for so long, you're bound to have hostilities. I'd estimate we're averaging ten major screaming bouts per week. Before, these never happened until dinnertime, but first step out the door some mornings, I'll hear two of them at it somewhere down the hall. One party's insisting they are owed something. Other party's equally emphatic *they're* the one who's owed the couple lousy dollars or cigarettes that instigated this. A long barrage of curse words follows. Anyone nearby is doubled over laughing. That includes the nurses. Whenever these episodes occur while all of us are eating, I refer to them as our Full-Contact Meals. With eight months under my belt in here, I've noticed my ability to sense one coming has improved.

Tuesday night, for instance, the very second Cy steps in our canteen while we're wolfing down our pork roll and potatoes, I just know there will be trouble here in River City. I watch him take the long way round both tables to the coffee urn. He picks a mug off the counter and fills it.

Faucet cuts off right behind me. Ocky has to raise her voice in order to be heard over the exhaust fan. "Go eat in your own bildin!"

"I ain't here to eat your slop."

"Well they is, so get the fuck outta here."

Several chewing faces tilt up at both tables. The most grateful-looking one belongs to Swab. Soon as he spots the mug in Cy's right hand, he jabs his index finger at it.

"Did you get our permission to take that cup of coffee?"

Cy shrugs and takes a big sarcastic sip then smacks his lips as tauntingly as possible. Next thing this smart ass does is sashay past the row of windows towards the door. Everyone he passes bursts out laughing at the way his shoulders wiggle, ciggie tucked over each ear, mug held high. Swabbie keeps on twisting further sideways in his chair.

"I asked you a question, jerkoff! Did you fucking ask to drink our coffee?"

"No."

"Well, why not?"

"Never do. Never will."

"You better fucking start."

Ocky drops the pot she was just washing in the sink and stands where she can keep these two apart if necessary. Suds are dripping off her hands. She flings a warning finger at the two of them.

"Keep quiet, Paul. Stay in your seat. And you! Go back to your bildin fore I lay bofe your asses out."

All three begin to scream at one another now. Others are joining in. That guy who only wears the yellowed long johns starts shouting downwards at the table over some completely unrelated matter. Anyone not yelling's laughing. Thinker shuts his book so hard it makes two people flinch on either side of him. That's my cue. It's time for us to head upstairs together.

Thinker always holds my cane for me in stairwells. That way, I can focus on the railing. Otherwise, I have to constantly reach back and forth to set the cane two steps ahead of me. As he pries it from my hand, he always mumbles the same phrase in Latin.

"*Ergo age, care Pater.*"

In reply, I make the sign of the cross in his direction.

By the time we've reached the landing where the main door leads outside, it sounds as though the argument below us spilled from the canteen into the hallway. Thinker shakes his head.

"The mass of men lead lives of noisy desperation."

"They certainly do, Ollie. You realize you don't belong in this place, right?"

"*Danke schön.*"

"*Bitte.*"

"Neither do you."

Soon as we reach his floor, Thinker stands my quad cane on the rug and hurries on ahead, pausing only to unlock his door for me as quick as possible, en route to the toilet.

Watching him shuffle down the hall in his red moccasins, it dawns on me the date is February 22nd, which means Night School has been in session over two months, and yet I'm nowhere closer to an answer to my question than I was back in December. What the hell's a forty-two-year-old former professor doing in this place? No matter my approach, I can't get him to talk about his old job. I've tried priming the guy with flattery about how good a teacher he must have been. I've tried innuendo about coeds. He changes the subject on me every time. Same goes for any mentions of his family.

Here I am alone in his room again. Without a thought, I reach into his drawer and grab that unsealed letter, the thick one from Bill Fairless I first spied months ago. There ain't time to read it all right here. Refolding it one-handed will be tricky too. Sweatpants I'm wearing have no pockets, so I stuff the letter, envelope and all, straight down the front. As I sit down to wait for him, I feel the letter sliding slowly down my bad leg, only stopping when it hits the elastic cuff around my ankle. It's not like I've planned this mission out.

When he returns, I can tell he didn't make it to the toilet fast enough because his pants are damp across the front as if he pissed himself a little and then only made things worse by cleaning them. I pretend not to notice when he climbs in bed and pulls his patterned Amish quilt up to his waist to hide the stain. I hang around another twenty minutes, so as not to look suspicious, then I act like I'm real tired, and I leave.

■□■

Downstairs in my room, I slide my arm inside the pantleg I'm still wearing, fish the letter out, and read all seven pages of it twice. It turns out Bill Fairless is his older brother. I gather from the letter he's the one who found this place, who made all the appointments, who retained the lawyer to have Thinker declared unfit for gainful employment, who detailed every psychotic episode for the judge at that humiliating hearing, who boxed all of Thinker's books along with the other junk, forged the forms for him, packed the sedan, and drove his kid brother over here.

First four pages detail everything Bill ever did for Harold during the three-year period between his firing and his admittance to this place. There are repeated mentions of a ratty couch Thinker converted to a bed down in the basement. Bill makes it sound like Harold laid there catatonic, staring at the waterpipes over his head for an entire year. Weeks would pass without them running into one another. Yet the more invisible he made himself, the more Bill felt the imposition. By pages five and six, the letter boils over with frustration. Bill lets his brother know how much he does not care about the apathetic students. He does not care what epiphanies Harold believes he underwent while skinny-dipping in the artificial pond on campus.

Final page is a long mocking list of all expenses, itemized with lines for rent and Chinese food, lawyer's fees, gasoline, doctor trips, medications, compound interest. The total comes to $8,472.60.

■□■

Next morning, I peruse the letter one more time. It takes me several tries to fit the seven folded pages back into the envelope, one-handed. After dinner, I walk upstairs with it hidden in the waistband of my sweatpants, planning to sneak it back into his drawer. Thinker never leaves the room.

■□■

Sunday night, I walk the letter up again. He's reading some biography of LBJ when I arrive. Enthusiastically he tells me all about this tour which Johnson made through Appalachia back in 1964. When he finally excuses himself, I stash the letter underneath the other still unopened one. Least I know now why he never opened it. Past two days, I've been feeling a tad guilty for stealing that letter, but from the instant I place it back inside its drawer, I feel more angry at the fact that I can't use the information in it. None of this sits right with me: somebody smart as him, witty, halfway handsome, whiling his whole life away in here.

I step over to the window. More snow is coming down. White mounds are building on the benches. Whole yard's blanked out, except for a row of foot holes made by all the nurses trudging up and down the sidewalks. It could be another month before we get to go outside.

I start browsing through the books in front of me. Ten down, I'm convinced I recognize one of them by the khaki-colored spine. I dig my fingers in and slide it out. Sure enough! FM 21-76. *Survival, Evasion, and Escape.* It's the standard Army Field Manual.

I bring it over to the desk. *Sgt Jim Harbin* is inscribed inside the cover. Book's a little brittle, so I have to turn the pages extra carefully: water procurement, cold, nausea, how to wrap a dressing. All your edible plants are catalogued: acorns, bamboo, nettles, nodding onions. There's instructions for building your own hobo stove. Wrong way to right a raft. Internal poisoning. External poisoning. Differences between.

I feel Thinker peering far enough over my shoulder to check which book I've chosen, then I hear the mattress coils squeak behind me.

"That one isn't mine. I requisitioned it from the communal bookcase in the lounge. There was another one with it. A Korean phrasebook. Same name in both. I think this used to be some kind of soldier's dormitory."

"You weren't in the army, were you?"

"God no. You?"

"Affirmative. 2nd Battalion, 31st Infantry."

"You're supposed to say Shakespeare, of course, but if I were shipwrecked and stranded, I'd take the FM 21 ..."

"21-76."

"You could last forever with a book like that."

It didn't help us much in Chosin. He's still talking, but my mind's completely left the room. We were waiting on that frozen ridge, first night of the attack. A flare went off. I thought snow was sliding down the hill across from ours until I heard the mortars thumping. That's how many soldiers there were rushing towards us. Haven't thought about that night in ten or fifteen years, but now I'm seeing Ben get hit again while he was pressing on my leg.

I close the book and spin the chair around.

Thinker is brushing both sides of his mustache with his pinky, lost in thought. Pants look slightly damp again. He only owns the single sweater. Years of wear have made the wool resemble that pink stuffing used for insulating walls. The weekly pack of cigarettes is rising from his chest there underneath.

"Act like the natives," he says, chuckling faintly, "Essential reading around here."

He lets his right arm dangle off the bed. I watch his fingers feel their way along the flattened cardboard boxes neatly stacked beneath the mattress, checking that their edges line up perfectly. Something about the way he's acting makes me even angrier, his mild glibness towards everything. I want to pull that letter out, make him account for every line of it. Why'd he get fired? What did he piss himself in class one day? And what was this supposed epiphany he had?

"So how much longer you plan on staying here?" I ask instead.

As the words are coming out, I'm realizing this is the first truly blunt question I have posed to anyone in here. His eyes let go of the ceiling for a second to glance over at me. From his expression, I can't tell if he's ignoring what I asked or weighing it too carefully. I try rephrasing.

"What I mean's long-term. You got an escape plan?"

He still don't say a word. He just reaches up and twists both ends of his mustache tight enough to pop the whole thing off. His hands let go and start to pat around the mattress for something, up and down his sides, both pockets, until he recalls the cigarettes he's searching for are on his chest. He reaches in and slides the pack out through the collar. He already smoked his after-dinner one. If he smokes another now, he won't have one for after lunch on Friday.

All the same, he takes a fourth one out and lights it.

"Ever think about teaching again? Take a pretty coed on a fieldtrip out to Intercourse, PA?"

He allows himself a long inhale, holds it, exhales it all in one pained sigh, then says, "Auction house of paupers."

"What the hell's that mean?"

"My classrooms. That's what I called them. 'You're like an auction house of paupers. Did none of you read?' Nobody dared to blink. It got awkwarder and awkwarder. I used to ask them if their arms were broke."

"Alright, if not teaching, then name your dream job."

I give him time to think. He don't answer me until his cigarette is finished.

"Man a gas station. At night. Somewhere nobody needs gas. Perhaps the Pine Barrens."

"That's your dream job? They don't let you pump it yourself over in Jersey. You'd actually have to put your book down and pump it for them."

"Good point. Strike that. I've got it. Nightwatchman of a junkyard. Nowhere somebody would ever rob."

"You do that now."

"Touché."

"I think I know what your problem is."

"I don't have a problem."

"Your problem is you think you can live here, and it won't warp you. I ain't faulting you for it. I made the same mistake. I just figured there'd be more laughs in here than in some nursing home. Long as you scribble whatever these morons say in your notebooks, you think it'll keep you separate. You think you can close this door at night."

"What is good for the birds is bad for the gardener."

"Quit quoting people! Look, Harry, I know I'm licked." I lift my dead arm up, let it flop back down to demonstrate my point. "But you...someone as bright as you are, I don't get how you can stand it."

"Now, now, Richard. Listen to what our country has experienced in the past two decades. An inflationary crisis. War. Recession. Natural disasters. Killer bees. Locusts. I believe I am in line with these trends."

"Cut the shit, Harry. You're only forty-two."

"Exactly," he says, sitting up.

"Exactly?"

"Exactly what I realized, what you don't seem to fathom is—"

"Is what?"

"Is how this would buy me twenty-thirty years."

"Of what?"

"Of this. Of reading. Writing. Soon as my brother explained the benefits to me, I only wished I'd thought of it sooner. Look, I understand why you don't understand, Richard, but my being here is permanent."

We sit there silent a full minute. I listen to it tick right off his fancy clock. He slides a fifth cigarette out of the pack, lights it, stares at the ceiling while inhaling extra air in with the smoke. Now he won't have any left come Friday.

CHAPTER 3: OFF, OFF, OFF, OFF

We're into March. First afternoon where I don't fear I'll freeze to death, I head outside. Yard's still a little soggy from the heavy rain past couple days. Leg feels rickety. Something's rubbing wrong inside my hip. I can only muster half a lap, parking lot side, before joining Crutch and Bunyan at home base.

As I'm easing down between them, it occurs to me I haven't spoken to these gentlemen in over four months. Other buildings may as well have different zip codes during winter.

"What's going down, Richie?"

"Nothing but shoe leather."

I scan the yard. Twigs are poking up throughout the muddy grass. There's two downed branches off an oak tree on the sidewalk to my right. All the same pigeons from last year seem to be preening in their same exact positions on the gutters. Bench across from us, some lumpy-stomached woman in a Penn State sweatshirt's dozing with her plastic lighter gripped in one hand, unlit cigarette like a sixth finger in the other. This makes me chuckle. Somehow it all feels proper to me now.

Thirty minutes pass. Ben Franklin joins us.

"Guess who caught one of the nurses in his room again without permission."

"You?"

"Nope."

"Rita?"

"Guess again."

"Wait. Not Crawford?"

Franklin nods. "He made her turn her pockets out and all. Barred the door."

"Unbelievable."

"What's that, the fourth time?"

"Which nurse?"

"Timaka."

"Tamika don't steal," insists Crutch.

"She certainly denied all charges. Sure had a fiver in her pocket though."

"No way, honky, Crawford's always losing stuff."

A pair of no-neck slobs appears from nowhere, interrupting us to plead for cigarettes. Both are balding. Crutch waves at them to go away.

When it's time for my next lap, I decide to take the sidewalk that runs towards D. That guy who tried to snatch my cane last summer, Dollar Bill, is sitting on the first step of their stoop, chin resting on one knee, his other leg stretched out across the sidewalk. He looks up when I'm five yards away and continues eyeing me. As I curve around the blackened bottom of his foot, he smiles in pretend surprise like he's been missing me these past few months.

"Hey, you got a dollar?"

"I sure don't."

"C'mon, I like you."

"Too late, friend. I gave at the office."

He tilts to the side to check around me, but Warden ain't in there, it being Tuesday. Dollar shakes his head and huffs at me indignantly.

"Fuck's that supposed to mean, you gave at the office?"

"It means I'm scrimping by, same as you, buddy."

"Asshole!"

I keep walking. You can't allow yourself to take this sort of comment seriously. Not here. Everybody's always cursing at each other in the yard to make the time go faster. It don't mean what it would mean elsewhere. I've almost made it to the end of his building, about to double back towards C, when Dollar Bill calls out to me again.

"Are you a Christian? Because if you are, you have to give. You can't be worried where it's going. Is that it? It was going towards a soda's all, asshole."

I don't look back at him. It's more important to maintain my focus on my gait. What did that PT guy used to tell me? Heel, toe, cane. Heel, toe, cane. After a few more steps, I hear Dollar yank the front door open and slam it shut behind him.

Ahead of me, I notice Thinker stationed underneath one of the still bare maple trees, bundled in every piece of clothing he owns, determined to read outdoors despite this chilly day. Past few weeks, he's been avoiding me. I tried visiting his room a couple times after our little quarrel. Door was shut. Third or fourth try, I heard his bed squeak when I knocked. I took the hint.

"Reading?" I ask him, fully aware this is a stupid question, but I can't think what else to say. Perhaps I did push too hard. Thinker's life is halfway dignified, I suppose, least for this place. The sunlight's hitting his pale face in patches.

"Indeed. *Mein Kampf.*" Way he's shading his eyes with his right hand, it almost seems like he's saluting me.

"Really?"

"Get a load of this part," he says, clearing his throat, "There is something that comes to one now and perpetually, it is not what is printed, preached, discussed, it eludes discussion and print, it is not to be put in a book, it is not in this book, it is for you whoever you are, it is no farther from you than your hearing and sight are from you, it is hinted by nearest, commonest, readiest, it is ever provoked by them."

"Hitler wrote that?"

After a little snort, he says, "No. It's Whitman."

He lifts the book, certain I'll recognize the mint-green cover which sat on his chest through much of January. He must've recited half the poems in there to me. This silly trick he's played feels like some kind of offered truce. I grin and wiggle my quad cane in front of me to tell him I should carry on.

■□■

Within another week, the old routines return. Benches fill up faster every day. Goat tracks begin to form across the grass. By 2:00, latecomers start unfolding metal chairs under the crabapple trees which have begun to flower white or yellow. Mail truck visits every second or third day. Warden's Buick pulls into its spot on Friday afternoons. There's this two-day window where attempts are made to collect on any debts outstanding from last fall. After that, the slate's considered clean. Nobody owes a single person anything.

■□■

Sunday, I head inside for lunch a little late, only to find ten starvelings gawking at two foodless tables in the canteen. Some of them go check the rec room and the hallways. Day nurse is nowhere to be found. By the time the Warden has been notified and made some calls, Ocky's on her way for second shift already. We have to settle for an early dinner, plus a double share of cookies in the evening.

When the same nurse pulls another no-show the next morning, Warden's forced to fire her. She arranges for Tamika to make lunch for her own building first, then come make ours at 2:00. There's a shuffling of shifts the next few days. That Jamaican girl, Amelia, pulls two doubles in a row. Ocky pounces on the opportunity to switch from nights to days so she can feed her little boy dinner and put him to bed at night herself, instead of relying on her mother's help.

■□■

Late Thursday afternoon, I'm coming from a piss when I run into Ocky taking our new night nurse on a tour around the building. I'm informed his name is Marvin. Handshake's on the limp side. I'd describe him as a slightly pudgy lisper in his early thirties whose complexion is seal-gray and strangely moist as if he rubs petroleum jelly on his face when no one's looking. Also extremely hairy. Forearms are covered in coarse black fur which runs from his elbows to his second knuckles. More fur juts out from his collar, front and back. Minus the apron, I could've easily mistaken him for one of us.

Technically we're supposed to eat at 6:00, but with so much to learn on his first day, Marvin falls behind and doesn't let us in until a quarter-past. I don't detect a pattern until the next day.

Wall clock says 6:11 when I turn the corner on Friday, and yet Marvin is still locked inside the canteen. There's a burning smell. He must be cooking. Half the building's huddled in a semi-circle by the door. Rest prefer to pile on the stairwell at least fifteen minutes early every day. Seeing them crowded together always conjures old time newsreel footage in my mind, those films about the concentration camps I watched as a teenager. Or even better, firing squads.

There's this little nook off to the side. A carved wooden pew, the kind you'd tend to find in train stations or church, is pressed against the wall back there. Most of our furniture's donated.

Sal nudges Swab to tell him to scoot over and make room for me.

The noticeboard is mounted on the wall beside the pew. Left half is where the Warden tacks these typed reminders about regulations. Thou shalt not prop open fire doors with phonebooks after dark! Thou shalt not urinate in corridors! List keeps getting longer. Right half of the board is papered over with obituaries summarizing the accomplishments of every former resident who ever croaked in here. Guess the Warden scissors them out of the paper.

I'm rereading the obituary of some man named John Modesti for the seventh or eighth time when the front door slams suddenly. Zorro weaves down the smoky stairs, palming a couple heads for balance. He's barefoot in black jeans and a t-shirt stained from two persistent nosebleeds suffered earlier this week. I watch him duck into the rec room. In a row, I hear the tinkling sounds of six dimes being fed into a slot. A button gets pounded. A can barrels into the dispenser. Zorro steps back into the hall. From his pocket, he fishes out a sugar packet, tears it open with his teeth, and dumps the contents in the can. After a couple slugs, he presses his nose against the blurry porthole in the kitchen door.

"Let us in," he mumbles, more to himself than to our nurse, "Let us the fuck in!" With that, he slaps his middle finger up against the glass.

Sound of the door unlocking acts as a cattle call. There's this momentary clog when everybody bumps in behind Zorro, same as every night. I've learned to wait back until the hallway clears, let all these steers push through the channel. Nobody gets a chance to knock me over that way.

Zorro never sits down at meals. Instead, he carries a plate over to the windowsill and gazes outside. Because our canteen's on the sunken floor, four feet underground, and Zorro's on the short side to begin with, he's actually looking up at all the droopy daffodils and tulips in our flowerbed.

I take my usual seat.

Marvin's working his way around both tables, handing out the orange drinks and chocolate milks. Tonight the plates have breaded letters on them, plus some roughage doused in vinegar.

"Yo, guy," calls Swab, waving a letter P above his head, "What are these, treats from the land or treats from the sea?"

"What are you athking?"

"Fish sticks or chicken fingers?"

"Oh. Fith," he replies, pretending not to notice all the tittering around both tables at his heavy lisp. "Robin told uth to therve fith tonight."

"Serve what?"

"Fith."

"Why?"

Marvin shrugs. "Cayth you're obthervant, I geth."

"No one looks observant here to me."

One of them two older ladies, Gail or Lolly, who take up the far side of the other table, glances up at our new nurse, confused. They're both in their fifties, with that cardboard-colored skin which lifetime smokers get, same crackly coughs to go with it. I can never tell the two of them apart because they regularly wear each other's blouses.

"What's that man trying to tell us?" one asks the other one.

Swabbie tilts his head back and projects his voice over his shoulder. "You're supposed to eat fish on Good Friday. Don't, you go to Hell."

"These are fish?"

"That's what the man said."

"Fish are disgusting."

"Tell me about it. Sal's Catholic. You observant, Sal?"

Two seats over, Salvy nods, then rubs his forearm so roughly against the underside of his nose I can't tell which side's scratching which. Poor guy's hay fever is back already. Eyes look every bit as bloodshot as they did this time last year. Snotlocker's swollen shut. I hear him breathing through his open mouth. He sniffles loudly, then sneezes directly at his plate and sighs.

"Ain't it April Fool's too?" I ask the room.

"When is?"

"Today is."

"It is?"

"Get out," says Swab, smirking through his chews. "They should make it every year like that."

Now all you hear awhile's the exhaust fan churning, Salvy sniffling, dishwater splashing in the sink, people's pieholes bouncing up and down. As he rinses off each pot and pan,

Marvin spreads them out along the countertop on this pink and orange beach towel he located in the crawlspace underneath the stairs. Nobody seems to know what happened to our dish rack.

Over by the windows, Zorro jabs his fork into his plate so hard the tines snap off. He turns around to survey all sixteen of us. Since mine's the only head facing up, he addresses me.

"Sylvia and I used to go out, back when she was still a local girl. We'd go in the woods after school to swig Beam."

"Who's that?"

From behind some yellow book, Thinker announces, "He's referring to that lady who brought her machine gun to the mall."

"Rifle."

"What lady?"

He lowers the book to answer me. "You know, the one who set upon the shoppers. Shot up Springfield Mall that time, remember?"

"Oh, her."

"Good thing she was a lousy shot," adds Swab.

"Well," Zorro admits, "it wasn't in her nature really to shoot anyone. Now she would shank somebody easy, like she did that counselor that time out at Tri-County. I'm not opposed to something like that either, but she wouldn't use a gun unless you stuck it in her hand." Zorro provides us with one of these Gettysburg Addresses every couple nights, always in the same snickering mumble, as if he don't believe whatever he is telling you and don't need you to believe it either. "I had to go to court with her over that fucking stabbing. It took some doing before they'd let her out after that. I kept whispering, stop laughing at the judge! But then the judge said, you're in for ninety days, ma'am."

Chairs start scraping the linoleum. Half the room is standing up to leave already. Zorro watches Marvin back the first trashcan over to his table, then the second one to mine.

When I stand up, all the food which failed to reach my mouth in transit tumbles from my lap onto the floor, right where Marvin's standing with the push broom in his hands.

"Sorry," I say.

"Not your fault."

I follow Zorro out. He's jabbering again before we hit the door.

"It's wild, ain't it? You're in line for like a pretzel and next thing, *pop pop pop*, this doll in camouflage is fucking firing at you!"

He walks on ahead, overcome with giggles.

From the doorway, I glance back at Marvin, curious if he's listening to any of this, but you can tell he's way too focused on the messy floor and tables to pay Zorro any mind. A single disbelieving laugh at what great slobs we are shoots out of him. I watch him flip the push broom over on the ping-pong table. Wrist up, he slowly steers all the crumpled Styrofoam and plastic forks, the juice cartons, stray napkins, plus the numerous table scraps we have somehow created, all in the general direction of the can. For a second, he reminds me of a midget playing shuffleboard, the way the broom is sliding upside down across the table.

A hand grips my right shoulder. Zorro's back.

"That's why I wanted whoever sold her that gun held responsible. I told them at the hearing. Sylvia didn't even load it. I had to show her."

■□■

Over the weekend, I decide to make this night nurse my next case. I eavesdrop on his every conversation. I even pursue him twice around the building. He sure selected all his favorites right away. First hour of his shift, he likes to gossip through their open doors with them.

On Saturday, I lurk back in the stairwell by the third floor, listening to either Gail or Lolly warn him not to trust the other nurses. She identifies all troublemakers for him, too: Never let Cy into the kitchen during meals. Beware Swab's temper when he's drunk. Don't mind Zorro's middle fingers. He does that to everybody. Watch your step around the hallways because Simon has been known to shit himself upon occasion. Should you ever hear her next-door neighbor sobbing in her room, that's just her daily jags, you can ignore it.

Little after 5:00, Marvin locks himself inside the canteen with this plug-in radio which he lugs in his backpack every day. He seems to have a thing for Motown. You'll hear him humming away in there to the Vandellas, Marvin Gaye, Diana Ross while he's preparing dinner for us.

Soon as everybody's seated, say 6:20 or 6:25, he heats the final urn of coffee for the day then rushes through the dishes while we eat.

For a nurse, he's definitely on the squeamish side. Worst part of the job for him is cleaning the two tables after meals. You can tell from his expression that the sight of our half-finished plates disgusts him.

At 6:50, he drags the two trashcans underneath the corners of both tables. Even if somebody is still eating, he will flip the broom onto the tabletop to let them know it's almost time for *Jeopardy*. It makes no difference to him whether you're done or not. He'll push your plate right past your outstretched fork.

Next task is to padlock the refrigerator plus every cupboard where anything sugary is kept. Housephone also must stay locked inside its cabinet at all times. Otherwise, people sneak long distance calls. Last thing he does is run through his mental checklist, aiming his finger all around the kitchen.

"Fridge, check. Cupboard, check. Phone, check. Oven, check. Burnerth, off, off, off, off."

Guy as particular as him, I figure it's important to get on his good side early before all the spots run out.

■□■

Monday after dinner, I trail him to the rec room. His system for evening pills is pretty much the same as Ocky's was. Only difference is he moved the operation to the sofa. Binder sits stretched across his lap. Box with our pills sits to his right. He fills our Dixie cups during commercials, which means he regularly loses his place. He's set up already when I step into the room. Theme song to *Jeopardy* is playing.

Something lumpy jabs me as I take the vacant spot beside him.

"Think I located Jimmy Hoffa," I say, checking underneath me for an ashtray or a book or something, but there's nothing there besides the sofa cushion.

All he does is grin politely. No one ever gets my jokes. I check around the room. Floor is like a minefield all the time: tangled cords and ashtrays, unfolded newspapers, armchairs tipped onto their sides.

Swab trots in and half-collapses into me. Boxers have little pepperoni pizza slices on them. I smell artificial peaches as he takes a two-finger swig of schnapps then tucks the bottle up against his ribs.

The three of us watch Single Jeopardy in silence. Some Asian lady from Rhode Island's beating a librarian from Indiana and some homemaker from upstate Michigan. Usual buffoons stroll in to take their pills and leave. Thinker arrives right at the start of Double Jeopardy. He swallows his two pills then turns and stares at the TV. Screen goes blue. Category's Economics.

"Who is John Maynard Keynes?" he rushes to say before the answer even flashes on the screen, and yet this still turns out to be correct. Bowing, he hands back his Dixie cup and returns to his room.

Next answer reminds me of another old joke. I tap Swabbie on the shoulder.

"What's the difference between excess and surplus?"

"How the fuck would I know that?"

"Excess is the part of her tit that don't fit in your mouth."

"Alright."

"Now ask me what surplus is."

"What's surplus?"

"Surplus is the other tit."

He lets out a single burpy chuckle.

Topic for Final Jeopardy is Archeology. Trebek reads out the answer.

"This archeological site, located on the island of Pohnpei in Micronesia, is thought to have been built by the twin sorcerers, Olisihpa and Olosohpa."

While the jingle's playing and two contestants are scribbling their best guesses, one of them pondering, Marvin wonders aloud how come archeological sites always need digging up.

Swab shoots him a condescending look. "How else they supposed to get the shit out?"

"No, no, I mean how duth a whole thity get buried in the firth playth?"

"I don't fucking know. Volcanoes? Maybe the wind blows sand over it."

The right question ends up being, *"What is Nan Madol?"*

Only the librarian guesses correctly, but that Asian lady was too far ahead and wagered too little for him to have a chance of catching her. The credits roll.

"Nan Madol," says Marvin under his breath, extending the Dixie cup that's been sitting in his hand this whole time out to me, "Nan Madol."

"You don't say? My turn?"

He nods. As I'm reaching for the cup, he pulls it back and peers inside then doublechecks the binder one more time before rehanding it to me. Initials are correct. Both pills look halfway familiar. I mouth a short prayer then swallow them.

"Whath kuhlakthin for?"

"Skelaxin? It's for my arm. Talk about a wonder drug."

I gesture towards my wrist which remains curled just like a cane hook in my lap. I pick it up and let it drop to prove my point. He smiles sympathetically.

Right then, Zorro startles both of us with an exaggerated yawn. By the soda machine, he dips down into one of his *en garde* poses and proceeds to pulverize a plastic button with his fist.

"Donald! You break that, there won't be any more thodas!"

"There's more buttons," he replies, stepping up behind us, tugging on the front of his shirt to admire the blood stains down the front of it. "That fight three nights ago was bad. Them guys had guns. All we brought were tee ball bats. They weren't even from around here. Dan said they were holed up in some safehouse in Marcus Hook. I heard all this *pop, pop, pop, pop*. I said, shit, they're fucking firing at us!"

"What, are you in a gang?"

Zorro nods at me through a slug of soda. "The Raging Quakers. Gang stuff usually waits for summer though."

"Like any gang would take him," says Marvin, handing Zorro a Dixie cup marked D.G.

Binder's still open to his page. I lean across to read it. Donald Gainer. Forty-eight years old. Admit was eight years ago. Emergency contact line lists someone by the name of Arthur Gainer. I count nine medications, though half by now are crossed out, the rest increased to higher dosages.

■□■

Little later, after *Wheel of Fortune* ends, I ask Marvin to turn the baseball on for me. Tonight's the season opener in Colorado.

Harry begins the broadcast by announcing, *"They're calling for snow in Denver tonight."*

Then Whitey quips, *"They'll be calling this game pretty quick too."*

Bottom of the second, their guy plunks Stocker, so Schill retaliates by plunking one of their guys in the third. You'd think that'd be enough of a deterrent, but it never is. They plunk another of ours in the fourth. Heads shoot up over both railings. For a moment, it looks like the two teams might actually hold an opening-day brawl, but then the Rockies pitcher waves his glove around to blame the wind. In the eighth, their reliever walks the bases loaded for us. Duncan's up. He shudders through a couple foul balls then slaps two guys in on a double. Batboy runs him out a coat like he's the pitcher. Actual snow is falling. The four of us are marveling at it when some freckly guy pokes his head in the room, searching among us for somebody else.

"Anybody seen Wes? Black guy."

"Ain't here."

"I sent him to get me a pizza three hours ago."

"Check under your bed," suggests Swab.

"I'm gonna rip his other eye out when I see him. Rotten bastard. Oh, hey, Simon shit hisself again."

"Oh God, where?" asks Marvin, "WHERE?" But that freckly guy's already gone.

Immediately, Swab and Zorro start to jeer at Marvin, pinching their noses and directing him towards the door. This is the ritual here. As he stands up, a dire smile splits his face in half as though it's inconceivable to him that he's expected to now search around the building for another grown man's soiled shorts, fifth night on the job no less.

"Ever tell you I used to be a pharmacist?" Zorro asks, plopping down in his spot to rummage through the box with our prescription bottles.

"Oh yeah?"

He picks an orange bottle up and squints at it then drops it back. "Philadelphia College of Pharmacy. It's only a three-year degree. I know all about medications. One time when

Octavia wasn't looking, I switched Mikie's anti-psychotics with shit pills. Don't rat me out! The trail ran right from where you're sitting all the way to the toilet."

Zorro keeps babbling like that, both halves of the ninth inning.

■□■

Ten minutes after the last pitch, I'm bent forward with my forehead smushed against my bedroom door, struggling to angle my key into the lock. These lanyards we've been issued are a good six inches shorter than they ought to be.

Because my room is closest to the back stairs, I hear almost everything that goes on in that stairwell. Over winter, we inherited some woman from another building. She sits four steps up and beats her leg all day with her right palm. First month, I thought a basketball was being dribbled. Area above her knee is black and blue most of the time. I'm squatting down in bed, wondering why I don't hear Kneeslapper, when Marvin lets out a howl up there.

"Fuck! Fuck! Fuck! Fuck!"

"Good God," answers Kneeslapper.

"How the fuck am I thupposed to clean thith?"

"Pour water down the stairs."

"Won't it get all over?"

"It already is all over."

Stairwell goes silent. He must have gone to get supplies. Unvelcroing my sneakers, I think how much simpler a hallway cleanup would've been. Protocol in that case is to cut out the affected part and glue a new strip of carpeting in its place. Every building keeps a roll on hand for such occasions.

I lie back and drag the blanket over me. Hopefully I get some sleep tonight. Nights can be awful noisy here. There's arguments. I think this new guy in the room above mine stomps on purpose. Doors slam unexpectedly. Smoke alarm goes off so often we ignore it. Toilet across the hall is loud.

I shut my eyes.

In lieu of sheep, lately, I've gotten in this unwise habit of counting all the two-handed activities I'll likely never do again: tie my shoelaces, putt, butter bread, drive a car, cut a steak, fondle two tits at the same time. Stroke struck two years ago last Friday. Arm's a worse conundrum than the leg. I've tried a thousand times, but I can't figure out how I could manage on my own with only the one functioning hand. Out of habit, I reach down and drag this dead lump closer to my chest. I pry apart the fingers. They're curled even farther inward than they were at Christmas. I jam my other fingers in-between and stretch them to the count of ten, three times. Next I start rotating the wrist in little circles. I'm on the verge of feeling sorry for myself when I hear this splashing sound. A bucketful of water's rushing down the steps.

■□■

Marvin has off the next two days. Place is quiet.

Amelia makes Jamaican food for us on Tuesday night: some sort of chicken in red syrup with these miniature bananas. It's not bad at all.

Phillies beat the Rockies, 7-5, on Wednesday night.

■□■

Thursday morning, I decide to rise an hour earlier than usual. I want to try doing a full lap without stopping once. I don't mind this chilly air. Pigeons zip by me as I walk. It's hard to tell them all apart, but I keep noticing this extra-scroungy green-and-silver one in the same spot down by the end of A.

By 9:00, there's thirty more lined up along the gutters with him. You have to watch out then. They do these sudden coordinated divebombs straight to any spot where they sense food's been dropped. They peck away until the food is gone, then scatter. I never used to notice pigeons much. They're more agile fliers than I realized. Squadron leader is this charcoal-gray one who sits fourth from the left on D. He'll take off sometimes and veer under the branches of those crabapple trees. All the others follow. If you're not careful, one of them will knock the hat right off your head. I saw it happen to some dope last month.

■□■

It's 4:00. I know because our nurses are descending from the stoops, their purses swinging from their chubby elbows. They always meet up by the parking lot and march together to the bus stop, jawing back and forth, laughing off the incidents of that day. I blow a kiss to Ocky. She blows one back. As I watch the four of them disappear together down the driveway, it occurs to me I have just passed an entire day observing pigeons by myself. Not exactly what I envisioned for my golden years. I should have finished off a round by now, be teeing grass out of my cleats behind my car.

Here comes Marvin up the driveway. None of the other nurses seem to like him. I half-expected him to quit after what happened Monday. I shoot him a friendly wave. Normally he'd come and talk to me for ten or fifteen minutes, tell me how his mother's treatment's going, remark on some crazy woman he sat next to on the bus or something, but he only waves and climbs the stoop defeatedly.

■□■

Hallway's packed when I arrive for dinner. So's the stairwell. Near the top, both Gail and Lolly have their nighties bunched around their thighs. Saggy hosiery they're wearing is the color of Vienna sausages.

Wall clock says 6:19 when Zorro begins banging on the door. Next thing, the smoke alarm goes off inside the canteen. Everyone covers their ears until it stops. Swabbie flops against me, laughing. Today his words smell more like pineapple.

"Pot pies last night. Remember how I said, hey everybody, hey, look at my massive bowl of fucking food! What's it Thanksgiving already? They're in the aluminum foil, right, like the Swansons. You were there. Pot pies are this fucking big." He holds his fingers apart the diameter of a very small pot pie. "For a grown man? A fucking kid maybe!"

"Amelia didn't appreciate it when you asked her for the antidote."

"Fuck her."

"How was the grub in the Navy? Worse than here?"

He don't answer. Somehow his mustache is sun-bleached a full shade lighter than the stubble on his jaw. He starts scratching at it violently.

"Weren't you in the Navy?"

"Fuck the Navy."

"So you were, then."

"Eight years." Using my shoulder for balance, Swab gets himself standing and staggers over to the door. Boxers have snowmen on them. "It's 6:42 out here!" he shouts, slapping the porthole with his free palm, "Open up! I can smell it's burnt already, whatever the fuck it is."

When the door eventually opens, Swabbie and Zorro barge in side-by-side like Moe and Curly. I wait back until the stairwell clears. By the time I've claimed my seat, Swab is already complaining to the entire room.

"Cold peas. Cold gravy. Man, why can't you let us in before you set shit out? Least then it wouldn't be halfway back to frozen when we ate it."

Marvin ignores him. He's waiting for the sink to fill so he can start the dishes. There's cremated meatloaf on my plate, plus peas, plus lumpy mashed potatoes. The bottled gravy drizzled over everything does in fact look frozen solid.

"Cold motherfucking peas!"

By the window, Zorro picks a lone pea off his plate and flicks it at the table.

"Here," he says, "This one's warm."

Swabbie's eyes follow the pea as it rolls past him to the floor. He picks a corner off his meatloaf and whings it back at Zorro, who ducks for cover then flicks a few more peas in his direction. One hits Swabbie in the chest. Shouting commences at both tables.

"Kathie, get your fingers out of my food!"

"That's my plate!"

"Quit playing with your pud."

"Fuck you..."

"Fine, here, take it, you fucking cheapskate."

"...and by you, I mean ALL of you!"

It's so loud I barely hear the tap turn off behind me. Marvin stomps across the room. Cheeks are flushed in spots. His jaw is quivering. He lets the shouting build to a crescendo before shrieking at the lot of us.

"THILENCE! All of you! Thut the fuck up! I've fucking had it with you thycos! Try being thilent for a—"

"Try learning how to talk," Swab snarls back, "Thilence? Kuh-rist. What did you bite your tongue too hard as a kid or something?"

"Fuck you, Paul! You're the no-good alkie here. Not me."

Swabbie upends his chair by standing up too fast. Marvin points down at the table.

"Back in your fucking theat!"

"I don't have to sit down."

"And eat your fucking—"

A handful of meatloaf hits our night nurse, mainly in the apron, also the neck area. Some of it works its way inside his collar. He stands completely still a moment. His demeanor strikes me as both stunned yet unsurprised. He's feeling around his apron for the ring of keys.

"Go ahead, 3-0-2 me," Swab says, watching him unlock the cabinet where the phone is kept. He has to crouch to dial the number. Swabbie picks his chair back off the floor and sits. "Grub's way better over there anyway. I could use a break from your slop."

Everybody quiets down to listen to our nurse explain the situation to some dispatch operator. He names our facility, the resident, the nature of the crisis he or she is having. After he hangs up and locks the phone away, he turns and hisses "Reported!" under his breath before storming out. Front door clangs open a moment later. Zorro's watching him out in the yard.

"What's he doing?" I ask.

"I ain't a bad drunk. I've always paid for my booze. Okay, my fucking mom changed her number on me. Okay, my stepdad slips me a few bucks now and then. So what?"

"What's he doing out there?"

Zorro shrugs and says, "He's definitely hyperventilating. I'm a doctor."

Everyone but Swabbie crowds around the windows. It's two rows deep. I have to squeeze in down the end to witness Marvin zigzagging across the grass. Bad as I felt for him on Monday night, bad as I'm feeling for him now, I also cannot shake this opposite feeling he belongs in here as much as any of us. He steps up to one of the oak trees, wraps his arm around the trunk, and doubles over in convulsions. Either he's sobbing out there, or he's laughing uncontrollably at us. I guess a week is long enough for either to be possible.

CHAPTER 4: YOUR CONSUMMATE CREEP

Bench spots are set by May. Longtimers know to keep a seat map in our heads. Any one of us could tell you which spot's owned by Benny Hill or Patty Cakes, whomever. Three's a comfortable limit per bench. Four abreast is pushing it. If someone goes inside to relieve themselves and buy another soda, they expect their seat will still be waiting for them ten or fifteen minutes later. But name me an unwritten rule that always works. Problem is the newer inmates. It isn't like our names are etched into the backrests. Rookies think they can sit anywhere they want until whoever's seat they're in comes back outside and wedges roughly in beside them. Both start elbowing. Eventually they stand and throw ten feeble swings apiece. Yard's good for six or seven of these fracases per week. One of the nurses calls the Crisis Center. A pair of paddy wagons come to cart our pugilists away for seventy-two hours.

■□■

Crutch and Bunyan guard my spot for me. We face the parking lot. By squinting, I can make out a few chalky headstones through the tree line. Past the cemetery's town. Some of the lower branches have been snapped to make a shortcut over there.

It's a good twenty-minute walk up to the State Store. On Saturdays, Swab dons pants and marches up the hill for his supplies, one bag clinking in each hand when he returns. Liberty Steaks is up there too, next to the WaWa. Warmer the weather, the more inclined people are to hire themselves a Go-Getter. All day long, I watch men disappear into those trees. Hour later, they return with somebody's hoagie or cheesesteak cradled in their palm. Whoever it's for'll wave them over.

■□■

Twice a day, this newer guy named Al emerges from the shaded shortcut with a giant Styrofoam cup and a brown bag of pretzels rolled at the top into a makeshift handle. He wears an olive drab military jacket all the time. Weekly cycle never seems to affect him. Even Wednesdays and Thursdays, when everybody else is flat broke, unable to afford a simple soda, not even split four ways, Al still cuts up to town around 1:00, again at 7:00, to purchase four pretzels plus one extra-large flavored coffee. Aware of everyone's predicament, he makes a point of sitting somewhere near the center of the yard where as many onlookers as possible are forced to watch him guzzle down his coffee with his pretzels.

Nobody here can compete with Al for sheer rottenness. He's the one whose room's directly above mine. Keeps very late hours. I'm still convinced he stomps around up there on purpose to annoy me. I know for a fact that's why he slams his door so often. Four in the morning once, he slammed the thing so hard, it woke up the entire building. People started hollering from all three floors. It sounded like he got a running start. I could hear him laughing at the lot of us, right through the ceiling. That's how I knew it was intentional.

All of this is why I call him Creep.

■□■

Tuesday, I'm halfway through my fifth lap when I spot Creep ducking underneath the branches, guarding his coffee from some falling pine needles. I watch him stride across the parking lot and squat down on the bench across from mine to eat. He's gnawing the shoulder off his second pretzel by the time I reach the Island. All the regulars are watching him intently.

"Where he get the cash for all that?" Crutch wants to know. His thick hand grips my bicep as I'm easing down.

"From his parents," replies Swab, "They set him up a tab at the Wa, the fat prick."

Salvy nods resignedly. "It's true," he says, "His mother knows the manager. It all gets added on her bill."

In silence, the four of us watch him steadily devour the second pretzel, followed by the third. With both hands, he lifts the giant coffee to his lips and downs at least a quarter of it in one drawn-out gulp. Now he reaches for the fourth pretzel.

"What, do they write it down?"

Salvy nods again. "He won't add anything on for you. I went with him one time."

Last pretzel down, Creep balls up the now-empty paper bag and chucks it over his right shoulder as he's marching towards us.

No greetings are exchanged.

He stands there gawking at us, sort of equidistant from both benches, using his tongue as a toothbrush to dig the remaining dough out of his molars. Creep is short and extra-tubby at the waist. His skin has the puffy texture of an uncooked pie. You can always tell when he's about to speak by the sound his upper lip makes as it unglues itself from his front teeth.

"They changed the name of the bank again."

"What was it before?" asks Sal.

"Lincoln something. Now it's just initials."

"What they change it for?"

"To keep idiots like you talking about it."

"Who's the idiot? I don't keep my money there."

"Your money!" Creep snorts, sucking down more coffee. "Hey, what's my hat say?"

All four of us look up, only to remember he isn't wearing a hat, which appears to be the joke because he laughs immediately and points.

"I got you fuckfaces."

"You got *oogatz*," says Sal, wagging his hand at him to go away.

"What's my shirt say?"

"Can you believe this fucking *stunad*?"

"Get lost, honky, fore I stick this crutch up your ass."

"Al, why don't you go play in traffic?"

Creep's giggling too hard to drink his coffee now.

"Hey Al! Go climb a tree with that cup, and I'll wave at ya, ya fucking Polack."

"Just ignore this *stunad*. He'll go away."

"No, I won't," Creep says.

■ □ ■

Rec room same evening, I'm seated beside Marvin with the binder open on my lap. I was getting sick of sneaking looks at people's pages all the time, so I suggested I could help out with medications. New system is for me to call out every name followed by their prescriptions. All Marvin has to do is stick the proper pills into the proper cups. He keeps them on a cafeteria tray in front of him. I've noticed this one pill pops up for almost everybody.

"What's Diazepam again?"

"Valium," he says, raising the humongous bottle from the box to shake it at me, "I with they gave theeth out before I got here."

Creep's page turns up next. He's over in the corner at that poker table, playing chess with Thinker. Last name is Musnicki. Sheet says he's forty-nine years old. Admit: 3/5/94. He only takes two pills, one for indigestion, another one for hypertension. Allergy line lists dogs and cats. Emergency contact line says "Mom" with two phone numbers, one labelled "Work," the other "Home." I keep glancing at him from the sofa.

Those two have taken to playing one long game of chess per night. Monday through Saturday, they alternate sides. Whoever's behind plays white on Sunday unless they're tied, in which case they flip a coin. Often these games stretch out for three-four hours. On my way to bed, I'll stop to tally up the pieces. They seem to be a pretty even match. Zorro likes to lurk around the board and heckle them. Tonight the topic is his clothes.

"You know what they did to me, day one? They made me give all my fashionable duds to George. I had $100 shoes, calfskin, $100 pants, $100 belt, $100 shirt. Belt was alligator. Shit was sharp. Now I'm dressing in clothes for the compound. Look at me. What did I join here, some kind of junior birdbath brigade?" He pauses to delicately scratch this scabby sore at the corner of his upper lip which has been festering for days. "You two'll see. Once you're a homicidal maniac and snap the fuck out in here, eight or nine years from now, that's when you'll really see the kind of shit this place can pull."

Thinker makes a move, then sighs back against his chair and grips his forehead with both hands as if he needed to make this move in order to realize he was definitely losing. He lets his arms flop to his sides and shakes his head.

"Mommy, the bad man hurt me," whispers Creep. His eyes are focused on one sector of the board.

With one of his knights, he takes Thinker's last bishop away. By take, I mean he carefully tips the bishop on its side, then weaves it slowly by the horse's nose right through the field of battle off the table into his crowded lap. Thinker's too accustomed to this to find it either funny or insulting. He takes back the knight. Creep immediately takes one of the checker pieces which they have to substitute for missing pawns.

Now they're considering the board again. After a couple minutes, Zorro taps Thinker on the shoulder.

"Do you know about schizoid defective disorder? I have a master's degree in psychology. Ever hear of it?"

"Schizoaffective?"

"Right. Schizoid effective."

"And by that you mean?"

"Your move," says Creep, sipping his coffee.

"By that, I mean one half of my mind is so evil it drives me to shit."

"That's probably not a cognitive problem."

"Exactly. That's why I say schizoid defective, because I have an imperfect mind, which is to say it's broken. Half anyway. The other half is good pure honorable love."

"Just because a mind's imperfect doesn't make it defective."

"You're always quibbling."

"Your move."

"There's a difference between arguing and quibbling."

"No, there isn't."

Salvy steps in for his pills. He grips both knees, groaning as he lowers himself down beside me. Marvin hands him his Dixie cup.

"Schill pitch tonight?" he asks, knocking three pills back dry, jutting his chin out at the TV set while he hands back his cup. Salvatore Poverelli. DOB: 5/1/41. Admit: 12/24/83. Allergies: pollen, grass, mold, dust, cat dander, dogs, perfumes. Rxs: Coated aspirin (2), Diazepam 20 mgs (2x daily), Clonidine .2 mgs. Emergency Contact: Maria Poverelli. Area code is 215, so that must be the sister that he mentioned in South Philly.

"Still hurt," I tell him.

Commercial playing's for those two brothers who sell diamonds down on Walnut Street.

"Schill being Schill, right?"

"Schill being Schill."

"Who's it, the Spanish guy then?"

"Valenzuela?"

When he nods, I nod back and say, "Gave up four. Slocumb's in now."

We watch the next inning, the fifth, with our view repeatedly obstructed by the stream of inmates stepping by us to take their pills so they can have their cookies. Slocumb gives up a leadoff walk. Runner gets to third on a single. Wild pitch scores him. I feel my head start shaking on its own. So far, this season's been nothing but injuries. Krukker got cancer of the privates. Larry has a bum shoulder. Schill ripped both his elbow and his knee on the same pitch. Each night during pregame, Harry announces which player tore which obscure muscle or cartilage the game prior. Anytime we happen to get a little hot streak going, you can bet it'll cost us a groin or two.

During the seventh inning stretch, we hear this loud metal crash come from the canteen, like someone hurled a chair straight at the fridge. Hollering ensues. Marvin rushes out to handle it. All the others follow him to watch. Only Sal and I stay put. It sounds like Swab got ripped off by one of the Go-Getters. An unfamiliar voice is swearing he got mugged. Swab keeps demanding either his fifteen dollars or his vodka. Another chair slams into something. Sal sniffles and shakes his head in the direction of the door.

"Everybody gets pissy middle of the week."

"I hadn't noticed."

"Least in the hospital you could go somewhere to get away from them. Trouble here is everybody comes out of their rooms to smoke. Guess they're afraid they'll burn the building down."

"There's a thought."

"I'm still waiting for this place to make the paper."

"It won't be long."

More chairs topple over. The big wooden table groans across the floor. From what Marvin's screaming, I figure Swab must have that Go-Getter cornered by the windows. Everybody else is cheering.

"Someone'll go missin. You wait. It happened to a girl over at Elwyn. I was sick, so I had to go to the hospital first. But then I was at Elwyn about six weeks before I came here, and you're sorta committed there. It's not like this place. One day this girl left out a window."

"Leapt?"

"Left. Left all her stuff even."

"Took to the road, did she?"

"Took to the road. I got her comb. Think Elwyn used to be a nuthouse, matter of fact. They'd watch you take your pills there. You had to open your tongue and all. Places like that tell you when to smoke even."

"Set times?"

"Yeah. You can't just go out anytime you feel like one. It's every hour like. Don't go out at 7:00, you gotta wait til 8:00."

"Least you know what time it is that way."

■□■

Remaining week is uneventful. So is the week after. Rest of May is warm enough to loosen my bad leg a little. I'm able to raise my laps to twelve some days. Encouraging. Being outside so much, I notice we've added a new pair of all-day walkers, type who roam our perimeter compulsively from morning until night.

First one's this bony woman in her fifties with brown clumpy hair who speeds along the sidewalks so fast, she must do twenty laps for every one of mine. Her slacks change on occasion. Top never does. You'll always find her wearing the same black sweatshirt with a snarling wolf emblazoned on the front. Cuffs stay scrunched up in her fingers while she walks. I've yet to see her speak to anyone, but now and then she'll come to a sudden halt, bend at the waist to pick a used butt off the ground, stuff it in her pocket for later, hurry on. I call her Roadrunner.

Other all-day walker is this chunky guy, also fifties with a warty sunburnt nose and squarish glasses held together by scotch tape. This one likes to investigate the trunks of trees, the area around the dumpster, and the flowerbeds for any interesting debris. I call him Three Bags because he's never without these bulging plastic shopping bags which he's continually switching back and forth from hand to swollen hand. Three Bags is completely bald. A patch or two of skin is always peeling off his pate. Whenever he passes me, I try to make out shapes inside them bags. First one's full of old prescription bottles. Second one is crammed with twine, some magazines, a few other plastic doodads. Third bag's reserved for his transistor radio which plays the Oldies station at low volume all day long. Anytime some object interests him, he'll pick it up and scrutinize it carefully on all sides, completely mesmerized, as though it fell from outer space. Then he'll either stash it in one of his bags or set it right back on the ground, same position as he found it.

■□■

First week of June, the temperature climbs in the nineties. That stinky tree's kicked in again. Yard smells like laundry in a cathouse. It's so muggy, I feel dangerously woozy every afternoon.

Monday, all I manage is one lap, split into quarters.

Tuesday, after everyone has filed out from lunch, I slide over to a seat where someone left behind their copy of the paper. On the front page, there's a large color photo of three wrinkled vets at some important ceremony off in France. First one's wearing a drab Ike jacket, leaning on his cane. Second one's saluting in a khaki coat that's weighted with about two dozen medals. Third one's eyes are cocked off to the side. From his expression, you can tell he's remembering something awful. Above their picture, it says, "*50 YEARS!*"

I start flipping through the paper: movie times, the horoscopes. Ocky's cleaning up around me.

As she reaches for my plate, I ask, "How's little James?"

She beams. "He good," she tells me, walking my plate and somebody else's over to the trashcan, "He ain't little anymore. I can't hardly lift him."

"How old now?"

"Four."

"Good age."

She stops hauling plates a minute to complain about her back problems. Doctor recommended breast reduction surgery. He's convinced it'll reduce her pain, but she can't afford to take a week off work for that right now. I turn my head to size her knockers up. They're shaped just like artillery shells. She's squeezing her lower back in front of me.

I hold my palm out towards her, wriggle my eyebrows like Groucho Marx.

"What?"

"Would you like a second opinion?"

That got her good. She lets go of her back to grip the table.

"You ain't no doctor!" she snorts at me. "You's just a titty man."

"I don't deny it."

"I knew you was dirty."

We go on yapping for another half an hour, then she leaves to watch her shows with Gail and Lolly. I read the obituaries next. No one I knew. I can tell I have no laps in me today. I head to my room instead to rest awhile. Shoes still on, I shut my eyes in bed. Hallway's silent. Everyone's outside. I doze off right away.

I don't wake up until the school bell goes off down the road like some air raid siren. That means it's 3:00. Same school my sons attended is two blocks from here. St. Francis High. Second wife was Catholic. Some of these black kids who live in the half-houses around us go there now. Last fall, I saw them carrying their helmets and their shoulder pads from football practice. Couple of them used to cut along our parking lot each day. They kept their distance, shot us funny looks at most, but never spoke a word.

I hear some of their voices approaching my window now. When I sit up to check, I see five of them under the trees: two checkered skirts, three pairs of pants.

One of the boys undoes his belt and begins chasing a second one around the trees, whipping the leather end at him until they both run out of breath, and one calls time. Third boy's busy taking off his shoes. He knots their laces tight together and lobs them up toward some power line. I hear them hit the ground a second later.

One of the girls yells, "You'll get athletic feet!"

"Athlete's feet," the boy corrects her, lobbing them again.

Shoes must've caught this time because I never hear a thud. They're only ten feet away, however, they can't see me at this angle. I assume the boy's a senior. It must be the last dress day of school for him to throw away a perfectly good pair of shoes like that.

■□■

With how my energy's been lagging this past week, I can tell I need another case to solve, some project besides pigeons to propel me up and down the stairs. Figure I'll monitor Creep for now. He skips most meals. Yesterday I passed his room two times, planning to use the same old chair ruse I used on Thinker, but his door was shut. On my second pass, I heard him snoring loudly, so I banged on the door five times to get revenge for all his late-night stomping.

Today we're on my bench all by ourselves. Crutch is inside, and Bunyan has been AWOL past two weeks. We've been sitting here almost an hour without speaking. One bloodsucker after another begs us for cigarettes or odd amounts of change— eight cents, thirty-four cents—however much their palm is missing for a soda. We take turns waving at them to go away.

I'm trying not to make it obvious how I am watching him more than the yard. He giggles periodically at passersby. Sneer never leaves his upper lip. Suddenly he turns and looks me up and down, entertaining himself openly with my appearance.

I can't entirely blame him.

What hair I have left shoots straight up like two spools of cotton candy. Drool's always accumulating on my shirt by my left clavicle. My sweatpants have eleven months of stains by now. Tops of my shoes are coated with this lovely peanut-butter-jelly-dandruff mixture. I've tried rubbing one shoe off against the other. All that ever accomplishes is to smear the stuff around.

Creep points down at the arm curled in my lap.

"Don't your arm work?"

"Not yet," is my reply.

"So you expect it to work again?"

"Absolutely."

He smiles skeptically. "Stroke? Bet it was."

"You guessed it."

"You know it looks like you're holding a beer glass."

"What?"

"Your fingers. The shape," he says, imitating my hand with his own.

"Yeah. Right. I asked them to put it that way."

He shakes his head at me like I'm the idiot. Maybe I am. Sit next to someone of his caliber too long, you start to wonder whether you're the fly or the turd. Another half an hour passes without either of us speaking. I'm waiting for some opportunity to get him talking about himself.

On the bench across from us, three men, all neighbors from A, get into a disagreement over the day of the week. The middle one, a flabby shirtless guy in a white fiddler cap, shoots up in disgust, convinced today is Friday, when in fact it's only Wednesday. Creep watches this Fiddler go inside to check the calendar.

"Can you believe some of these losers?"

"Pathetic," I say, "How long you lived here yourself?"

"Months."

"From around here?"

"Where else?"

When I try asking where he went to high school next, he cocks his head at me, lets out this moody chuckle.

"What's with all the questions?"

"No reason."

"Well, I ain't a shit shooter, alright?"

"Alright."

"It's not that I dislike you. I just prefer not to shoot shit."

"Alright," I repeat, "Long as you like me."

This makes him howl with laughter. "I'm just pulling your leg, Dicko," he says, "I went to Interboro. Where'd you go?"

"Ridley."

"Figures."

Yard's emptying. It's almost dinnertime. I twist around to check our window. A silhouette is darting back and forth which must mean Marvin's setting out our plates. I spin my quad cane wrong way round to get myself standing. Legs push. Arm pulls. Creep lets me fail four or five times before he presses me down by the shoulder.

"What's the hurry? You going in for a blowjob?"

"What gave it away?"

"Hold on a second. Let me show you my latest trick first."

He pulls an empty pack of Marlboros from the leather pouch he always wears around his waist and wiggles it at me like some vaudeville performer. Now he circles the Island, snatching every used butt he can find off the cement. Once he has a handful of them, he gets down on his knees and sets the empty pack beside the flagpole. One by one, he slides the butts inside, filter end showing, to make it look like a fresh pack, just dropped there accidentally.

"Watch this," he mouths, sitting back down. He rubs his fingertips excitedly against his linty corduroys.

"All you need's a string."

I stick with him for five more minutes, but nobody happens on his trap. Zorro's face is in the canteen windows now. Somebody's yelling something at somebody else behind him. I get up to go.

"I'll be in in a minute," Creeps calls out to me, as if I even care, "Someone'll take the bait. They always do."

■□■

Evenings the Phillies aren't playing, some of us have gotten in the habit of bringing our ice cream sandwiches out to the Island after dinner, so I end up right back in the same spot, hour later. Dusk has begun descending. There's a million crickets chirping, plus about a thousand lightning bugs blinking on and off around our faces.

At least one delegate is present from each building, therefore this becomes our chance to catch each other up on all rotten developments: guess whose turn it was to shit themselves right in the middle of the sofa, guess whose valuables went missing, which nurse is suspected this time, who puked all over the dining table, who caused another fire drill at 3 AM by smoking in their bed, who has a stowaway hidden in their room this month, who got themselves arrested for shoplifting or for flashing kids in town.

Right in the middle of one of these stories, Bunyan sits down extra-gingerly beside me, wincing at the end.

"Where you been?"

"You don't wanna know. My colon went on strike."

"What?"

"I was in the hospital. Roto-Rooter job."

"Oh no."

"Yeah. All cleaned out. Should be good til New Year's."

He nods over at Ben Franklin, the one with the stringy hair and rounded spectacles, who's in the middle of updating us on what happened with some guy named Albert, Monday night. Apparently Albert got himself 3-0-2'd for yanking all the books down off the bookcase in their rec room, after which he went around unplugging every lamp and box fan he could find, yanking on doorknobs from both sides to try to snap them off.

"What's this 3-0-2 stuff?" some new guy inquires.

Five voices jump to answer over one another. "Involuntary removal!"

"They say go. You say no. They say 3-0-2. Hour later, two nice men help you into the van for your three-day getaway."

"Cops?"

"Them or the guys in the white coats."

"How many you up to now, Paul?"

Swab arches his chin. "Shit, I lost count at twenty."

One by one, they slowly head inside to watch TV, dropping the wrappers from their ice cream on the ground behind them.

After an hour, it's down to me and Bunyan. Across the parking lot, I notice Zorro lurking by the shortcut, peering inside as if he's scared to set one foot down there. Something about this time of evening makes him even squirrelier than usual. His head keeps darting side to side. Right foot is stomping on the dirt. That twitchiness keeps building until he starts barking curse words straight into the trees.

Bunyan comments, "That guy's wound tighter than a kamikaze pilot."

"You're telling me."

From the bib part of his overalls, he pulls a pouch of loose tobacco out, followed by a slip of rolling papers, gets them situated on his belly. I watch his withered fingers sprinkle the tobacco inside the paper.

"Think he buys his own bullshit?" Bunyan asks, looking up from his task to check my expression.

"Who, him?"

"Twenty years he told me he was in the FBI. I told him your pension must be pretty good if you're borrowing phone call money offa me."

"Who'd he need to call, Hoover?"

"Uncle. I think he mails him money. Don rooms with you guys, don't he?"

"Three doors down," I say.

"We got one just like him in my building. Crazy stories."

"What about?"

"They range. There's this one he likes to tell about a magic beer, made specially for him. He let me have a sip one time. I didn't feel anything. Guy's some kind of Mormon or Jehovah, I forget."

When Zorro charges full tilt at this pigeon near him that's minding its own business, the two of us crack up.

Bunyan licks the rolling paper up and down. He folds it gently over and pinches both ends of the cigarette he's made. Now he offers it to me.

"No, thanks," I say. "Save money that way?"

"I do."

"Smart."

"It is."

"Wonder why nobody else here does it."

"Too lazy. I bet you remember when they sold loose ones."

"For a penny."

"Your pops smoke em like that, did he?"

"He did. It killed you cheaper."

"It does. What year were you born, Richard?"

"Twenty-nine."

"Month?"

"October."

"Jeez. Your pops lose his job, did he?"

"Week I was born."

"What did he do?"

"Automobiles. Ford put him on short time awhile first."

"No, I mean after."

"Oh. He became an ice cutter. My uncle ran an icehouse. Got him on there."

With my good hand, I draw the dimensions of the standard block of ice my father used to cut, couple hundred times a day for six or seven years. I share how my mom took me to that icehouse where my old man worked one time. It was a wooden pyramid, painted white to reflect away the sunlight. I remember how it had these rubber flaps over the entrance. My father came out to greet us in a leather apron.

"Can't afford a Ford," he mumbles while he lights his cigarette.

"We didn't have it so bad," I add, "He always made sure me and my sister ate. Never missed school."

Bunyan nods. I keep him company while he enjoys his smoke. Only noise is crickets. At one point, I check the parking lot again, but Zorro's vanished. Soon as Bunyan finishes his smoke, he pats me on the arm and wishes me goodnight.

■□■

Next day after lunch, I'm straightening my sweatpants on the stoop, surveying the whole yard, deciding where I feel like walking first. Place looks like a Hooverville again. Shaded spots are packed with chairs. There's all kinds of litter. Everybody's either slouched back on a seat or napping stretched out on the ground. I head left then right along the parking lot this time. For some reason, all four daynurses are convening over by the dumpster. Way they're arranged, I get the impression three of them are ganging up on the other one whose arms are folded. Ocky's talking at her while the two on either side keep nodding in agreement.

"You gotta call your rep. They gonna hear your side, then they gonna hear her side. I had to go for a hearing when bitch pulled this on me."

"But you—"

"But me shit! I got my money. Thing's this. You gotta keep coming in though and filling out your sheets. And you gotta let them reps know you and soop-bitch don't get along."

They don't notice me go by.

I stop at the nearest bench in front of A. I could really use a hat. Bald spot keeps getting scorched. Ben Franklin's on the other bench. I wave across the stoop, but he's staring off at those maple trees where Thinker's reading. I've been seated less than thirty seconds when Popeye and Penguin descend the stairs together.

"Hey buddy, spare fifty cents?"

"Yeah, got fifty cents? It's for a phone call."

I'm about to answer when I realize that they're asking Franklin first, not me.

"No way," he says, "Out of the question."

"Quarter?"

"Yeah, just a quarter?"

Franklin's gray hair hangs down his head in such greasy strands you'd think he had combed pine tar through it. He scoots his glasses up his face by wriggling his nose and glares at both of them.

"No, you can't have a quarter. You can't have a cigarette either. Let's see. You can't have my pants. You can't have my socks. You can't have my glasses. You can't—"

"Alright, alright," says Penguin, "Don't get carried away."

"Yeah, don't have a period about it, Christ, it's only a quarter."

Franklin gives them a second glare as they retreat back up the stairs.

Standing, I can tell I don't have a full lap in me yet, so I cut down the diagonal sidewalk towards home base where Creep is stuffing yet another pretzel down his gullet.

"Fancy seeing you here, Dicko," he says, mouth full, while I'm lowering myself onto the bench.

"Al. Catch any bears lately?"

"Bears?"

I point over by the flagpole where he left his trap the day before.

"Oh!" he snickers, "Not bears. Ready for my next trick?"

"Can't wait."

He pulls a straight piece off the pretzel he is holding and starts nibbling the crust off with his front teeth, stopping an inch before the end. Thing's about three inches long. He starts to knead this lump of dough between his palms until it's slender as a pencil. Next he bites both ends flush and runs his tongue over the whole thing twice. Now he holds it up for me to inspect.

"Resemble anything to you?"

All I can do is shake my head. The genius even thought to leave an inch of crust to simulate a filter. Gleefully he sets it on the grass about twenty feet from us. His teeth are grinding with excitement when he sits back down.

"One of them'll try to smoke it. Watch!"

"My money's on the pigeons."

"How much, Dicko?"

"Dollar," I tell him.

He nods twice to confirm our bet then rubs his palms real hard across his linty corduroys. I count eleven pigeons lined along the gutters. Five more are bobbing through the grass. I wonder what pigeons rely on when locating food, their eyes more or their nose? Sometimes I catch them pecking at nothing, pebbles, clumps of dirt. Occasionally, I'll even catch them pecking at used butts, mistaking them for something edible.

Hour passes. Not a single human or a pigeon ventures anywhere in the vicinity of his trap. As I stand to do another half a lap, Creep lets me know that he will hold me to our bet.

By the flowerbeds in front of C, I pass Three Bags picking something red and nozzle-shaped out of the mulch. Frankie Avalon is singing faintly from his radio. Some woman's sleeping stretched out on the bench, elbows, tits, and knees all hanging off the side.

I turn and head back towards the Island.

Roadrunner zips around me.

Creep has relocated to the bench across from mine. He's talking to some guy in swimming trunks and an unbuttoned dress shirt. Under the shirt, the guy's got some kind of colostomy bag affixed to his gut.

Past them, I notice Crutch is laboring along the bumpy driveway. He struggles up onto the sidewalk and pauses three more times to catch his breath before he reaches me.

"How you, Richie?"

"I'm fine. You alright?"

He grips his crutches as he lowers down. "Pretty beat."

"Heat getting to you? Radio said ninety-three today."

His head shakes. "Just got my blood money."

"It ain't Friday."

"Nah. Over at the blood bank."

"Blood bank?"

He wags a finger at the driveway, then points at the crook of his right arm. A cotton ball is taped there. "You give them some blood. They give you some money."

Creep is clearly eavesdropping on us. Something possesses me to raise my voice and see what happens.

"What's the going rate for blood these days?"

"Ten a pint. Platelets they give ya twenty. Only take those monthly though."

"What are platelets?"

"Same as your blood but thicker. It's got the plasma in it."

"Very clever, these Americans."

"Looks like barbeque sauce to me."

Creep's still staring at us.

"Did I just hear you say you can sell your blood?" When Crutch pretends not to hear him, he walks over to repeat the question. "Did you say you can sell your blood?"

Crutch tilts his head off to the side. "I can. You can't."

"Horseshit, I can't. Where?"

"They don't need no more white blood. Full up."

"C'mon, who buys blood? The hospital? Where'd he say it's at, Dicko?"

I shrug and point straight at the cemetery. Crutch keeps turning his head this way and that, doing his utmost to avoid eye contact, but Creep won't let him. He shuffles his feet as much as needed to stay even with him.

"You sick at all?"

"Nope."

"They can't use sick blood."

"Nothing ails me."

"Yeah, well you ails me, muthafucka." Crutch fumbles with his walking sticks, all flustered now, rising to go. "Pardon me, Richie. Spose to get ribs with my daughter tonight."

Creep watches him hobble all the way across the yard, remaining ready for that moment when Crutch will undoubtedly turn to scowl at him again. He does. Creep acts like he's injecting himself with a syringe right as the door slams.

"I'm a hard stick," he says, reclaiming the empty spot beside me.

"What do you mean?"

"When it comes to needles. I'm a hard stick. They can never find the vein."

CHAPTER 5: GO-GETTERS I HAVE KNOWN

Some year. Today's my anniversary in this dump. I realized a moment ago when I turned to my own page in the binder. DOB: 10/29/29. Admit: 6/24/93. Allergies: none. Rxs: Skelaxin and Ticlopidine. Emergency Contact: Richard Junior with a made-up phone number.

After twelve months in here, I could really use a few provisions: shaving gear and change of clothes for starters, some bars of soap, shampoo, a cap to keep my head from scorching in the yard, one of them clock radios you can read in the dark, new pisscup if possible. A coat can wait, but those clothes the hospital discharged me in are no longer what you'd call presentable. Sometimes I'll glance down at my sweatpants only to recognize a chunk of food encrusted to them from four days ago. White golf shirt they issued me looks even worse. I stick them in the laundry bag each Tuesday. That's our day. They come back looking pretty much the same.

Added problem is my pisscup has these ochre rings growing inside it. Frankly I'm scared to slide my pecker in there anymore. Pisscup's mainly for the middle of the night, or times the toilet's occupied and I don't feel like I can hold it all the way upstairs. Lift it off my nightstand. Smell is strong enough to numb your nose. Burnt butter. Ammonia. I catch whiffs of it already as I'm bending to unlock my door. Twice a week, I walk the cup across the hall and tip the contents down the drain. I try my best to rinse it out, but even when I blast it with hot water, those cruddy rings stay put.

For obvious reasons, I'm reluctant to approach one of the regular Go-Getters for help. Some of these suckers send them up to town on simple errands, like for a hoagie or a six-pack on a Friday night. Eight times out of ten, those transactions happen smoothly, but none of them could be trusted with the kind of job I have in mind. Normally the tip's negotiated in advance. What am I supposed to do, hand Cyclops fifty dollars and a shopping list? He'd relocate to Florida and change his name. Part of me wishes the Warden would open some kind of company store herself. Least that way we could buy some basic items on the premises. Even if she marked them up on us, same way she does with cigarettes, I'd gladly sell my soul for that.

Night I mention my predicament to Marvin, he nods supportively but then changes subjects so abruptly I figure he's afraid I'll ask him.

"Whoth next?" he says, meaning in the binder.

"Donald's turn. Let's see. Thor-a-zine. Two of those. Di-lan-tin, three of those. Ci-met-a-dine. Just one."

He locates the Dixie cup marked *D.G.*, shakes the proper pills inside, then summons Zorro over from the poker table where he's lurking next to Creep and Thinker. They've been playing chess almost two hours.

"All these great options," announces Creep, "Check."

I glance over at the board. Thinker's lips are moving, and his index finger's wiggling in the air right near his nose. He moves his king out of harm's way.

"Check."

Thinker moves his king again.

"Check."

Thinker sits there frozen for another minute, calculating, then he grimaces and tips his king onto its side.

"Never in doubt."

"Good game."

"You trapped your bishop."

"I know. I forgot you could just play c6."

"Total patzer move."

My attention returns to the baseball. It's the bottom of the fifth. Glavine's pitching to Incaviglia. He just walked Kruk. The Braves put up a five-spot in the fourth, so we're down 5 to 3.

I'm still mulling over my predicament.

There's this new kid arrived last week. Think I'll ask him. He seems more trustworthy than the others. He's only twenty-six years old. Name's Jack. I refer to him as Gums because he has no teeth. He's every bit as scrawny as the kid in them old Atlas ads, you know, the one who gets the sand kicked in his eye. I'd describe his face as chiseled, though not particularly well. Anytime he speaks or eats or musters up a grin for one of us, his bottom lip curls down into the hollow where his teeth should be. It reminds me of those train-hopping winos from the Thirties. I flip to his page. Family name is Porter. DOB: 4/27/67. Admit: 6/18/94. Pills are for depression and anxiety. Allergy line says antibiotics with an exclamation point. Emergency contact line lists a Colleen Sullivan with the word "Sister" in parentheses. At the bottom of these entrance forms, there are five dashed lines for any important notes about the resident each nurse should know. They're almost always blank, but his has two words written there which I'm surprised I haven't seen before, come to think of it. Suicide Risk. Admit date's six days ago.

Last Saturday, there was some confusion over who was moving in with us when he arrived. Cars being such a rarity here, every single resident looked over at the dusty station wagon pulling in the parking lot. All talking ceased. We were so focused on the older man who climbed out the driver's seat that we ignored the kid who hopped out the back.

We watched them slide a couple boxes from the trunk and set them on the sidewalk. Soon as the older man we all assumed was moving in with us went and slammed the trunk, a baby began to wail from the back seat. That's when this pregnant woman, several months along, climbed out and opened the back door, annoyed, desperate to soothe the baby while Gums and the older man carried a box apiece, one loose pillow, a skateboard, plus a duffel bag in the direction of my building.

Murmuring picked up around the yard after the man came out alone and got back in the driver's seat. With that baby still screaming, it was impossible to hear what he was saying to the woman, but I sensed sharp words coming from both of them. Something he uttered at one point made her turn and stare at our front door for several seconds. After that, they drove away.

■□■

Near 6:00 on Saturday, start of his second week, I locate Gums awaiting dinner in the hallway with the others. He is seated on the bottom step beside this other new guy who's hunched over coughing horribly into his palms. I call this cougher Redbeard, even though his facial hair's a whiteish blonde, because I've watched him cough up blood right down the front of it two times already. His coughing fits persist for several minutes. At the end, he spits however much has broken free into an orange mug with a black Flyers logo on the side. Either Gail or Lolly reaches down and takes the liberty of pounding on his back. The others seem too used to it to notice.

I squeeze in between Swab and Salvy on the pew.

"Time to put the feedbag on, or what?" Sal asks, flashing one of his filmy yellow grins at me. When I don't bother answering, he repeats himself at twice the volume. "We ready to put the feedbag on, fellas?"

"Left my feedbag upstairs," says Swab.

"Well, I'm friggin famished." Sal's forehead furrows as he checks the clock. He's squinting too, unable to make out the time for some reason. Finally he waves across the hall at Gums and says, "Hey kid, what time's that say?"

Gums springs up to check for him. Lips part like he's about to answer, then they shut again, and he looks over at us in complete befuddlement.

"What's it, twenty after?"

Now he's staring at the clock again.

"Can't you read a—"

"It's only got one finger," he tells the three of us.

"Hand," I remind him.

"One hand."

"Whaddaya *stunad*? They're just on top of each other."

"No, there's only one hand. Look."

All three of us tilt over on the pew to see the clock face better. It looks like it says 8:00, or forty minutes after something, neither of which can be right. Gums reaches up and rotates the only hand forwards and backwards a few minutes, or hours, to prove to us no other one is hiding there behind it. Sal looks at me for help while Gums is searching all around his sneakers for the missing hand.

"Leave it," I tell him, "We'll know in five minutes."

"How?"

"Yeah, how?"

"Is it ticking?"

Gums nods.

"Point it at the six."

I let what feels like three-four minutes pass, listening to Redbeard gasp for air. When I check the clock again, that hand has hardly moved. I'm explaining to them how I know the hour hand is missing just as Marvin unlocks the door.

■□■

Dinner's minestrone tonight. All the uneaten hamburger from lunch has been crumbled up in it to make the meal seem slightly heartier. Marvin also diced the leftover raw onion and tomatoes, dumped them in as well. It ain't so bad. Everyone is eating quietly. Even Swab seems to enjoy it. A plate of saltines is getting passed around, six apiece.

As I slide the plate to Gums, I ask who those two people were who dropped him off last week. Everybody at our table has been sneaking glances at him. They must be wondering what someone half our average age is doing here, same as I am.

"That's my sister," he answers, gumming some kidney beans around his mouth, "and my in-law brother, Ken."

"What's your sister's name?"

"Colleen."

"What was that in the back?"

"In the back?"

"Howling away back there. That your nephew?"

"Niece." He takes a moment to mush up a scrap of ground beef before swallowing. "My nephew don't get here til September."

■□■

I pal up to Gums the next few days. First opportunity outside, I make a point of introducing him around to all the guys. He grins at each and every one of them—Swab, Ben Franklin, Bunyan, Crutch, Zorro, Creep—repeating their real names twice so they'll sink in better.

■□■

Next couple nights, soon as he steps into the rec room for his pills and cookies, I insist he stick around and watch the baseball with us. There've been all these inklings lately about a labor strike, possibly calling the whole season off, no Fall Classic for the first time in a hundred years. I don't buy it.

Right as Valenzuela lets go of his final warmup toss on Tuesday night, I plop five quarters in his palm and gesture at the soda machine.

"Grab two birch beers for us, Jack."

Gums cracks my soda open before handing it to me along with my nickel change. He sits cross-legged on the floor in front of me. Between pitches, I keep staring at his scalp. He has bright orange hair which he buzzes rather than letting it grow out. He's been watching every play intently, yet it only took a couple innings for me to realize he don't even know the rules. Twice now, he has tapped me on the leg to ask me questions any little leaguer ought to know. What's a force out? What does ground rule double mean? He didn't even know the different movements on the pitches come from how you grip the ball. From the sounds of it, his father never taught him how to catch or throw.

"Wasn't your old man into sports?"

"Not really."

"Football neither?"

"Nope."

"Angler?"

"What's that mean?"

"Fisherman."

He shakes his head.

■□■

Come Friday when the breadline forms, Gums remains on the bench across from mine while everybody else is rising up around him. Deaf Mike is first in line today, followed by Sitting Bull, Lazy Mary, Zorro, then Babydoll. Last two are engaged in some kind of lovers' quarrel because her mother's moving her to South Carolina in a month. She keeps pressing her groin into his backside, sliding her free hand in his front pocket until Zorro finally spins around, fed up, and gruffly mutters something inaudible to us but meaningful enough to her to make her cry.

Next comes Dot, short for Dorothea, this moody old black woman who got transferred to our building back in May. Dot has on her favorite dress, a liver-colored velvet number which is stretched in several places like it's learned to fit her over time. Hair's tugged upwards by a dozen bobby pins around her scalp. She rolls her head in figure-eights three times then gazes skyward.

"Just wait. Neckbone stew. Mmmhmmm. Knuckle collards. Mud pie. De-fricken-licious! Can't get none of that here. Nine hundred a month. I oughta plant a lawsuit on this place."

"Praying all morning," I say.

"Cursing all afternoon," replies Crutch, "She worse than my Uncle Ray. Jesus Christ and a dollar."

"Her two closest friends?"

"You got it, Richie."

"Get a load of this next one."

Guy traipsing up the sidewalk behind Dot is wearing blue-striped socks, pulled up, red running shorts, and a white linen jacket. He can't stop running his left hand through his blonde hair.

"Looks like recess let out at the zoo."

"Wouldn't you throw that back if you caught it?"

Bunyan chuckles. "That's that Jehovah I was telling you about, Dick."

"Which Jehovah?"

"The one who drinks the magic beer."

"Oh. Why's he dressed like an alternate for the Mummers Parade?"

Bunyan shrugs. The three of us watch Three Bags struggle slowly up behind the Mummer. Limp is new. He sets his bags down on the ground and lets out this exaggerated sigh which makes the Mummer giggle.

"What a day to skin my knee!"

His fingers are wiggling at his sides now to regain feeling. Even clear across the yard, I can tell how plump and discolored they are, a permanent purple from the constant weight he lugs around all day. Another loud exhale pours out of him. Although his jeans aren't ripped, there is a sizeable dark stain by his left kneecap.

"All that stuff!" declares the Mummer, still giggling over his shoulder at him, "Don't you have a room?"

"I have a room."

"Well, why don't you leave your stuff in there?"

Three Bags shakes his head at such a naive question. "Because they'd steal it in twelve seconds flat if I did!"

Mummer grants him that with two long nods. Three Bags flexes his sore knee a couple times to test it.

"Great! Now I can't even run."

"Go put your knee up," Mummer suggests next, but Three Bags sneers at this suggestion too. Give up his spot, what with three others on their way to get in line?

Raggedy Ann steps up behind him, picking at her scabby elbow. Friar Tuck walks up next, followed by Chaplin.

Half an hour passes.

I count the line again, well over fifty souls when the shadow of the Warden's hand undoes the latch on the screen door. Everybody inches forward. Deaf Mike yells his last name extra loud as he is let inside.

Each time the line advances, Three Bags has to relift his possessions. As he sets them down again, his radio retunes itself a little. Ricky Nelson's singing now, "Travelin' Man," garbled up with some commercial for deck remodeling from the next station over on the dial.

Same old Trio—Cy, Popeye, and Penguin—are waiting in the grass off to the side. They've developed a new switcheroo this season. I call it the Double Play. Say Cy talks you into lending him a dollar. When you approach him to collect, he sends you off to Popeye for it, who then sends you off to Penguin, who informs you that he paid that debt already. By then, Cy is nowhere to be found.

Today they keep on swarming everybody as they're exiting the office. We watch them pick this older lady clean when she walks out.

I say, "Tinker to Evers to Chance."

"Last shall be first," says Crutch.

"Fucking bums!" yells Swab on top of him, "You open up a pack. Give someone you know one. They hear the wrapping. They're on you like killer bees."

"Or leeches."

"By Monday, they're all broke again. Just sit around holding their cranks all week."

"You drink, Dick?" asks Bunyan, groaning upwards from the bench.

"I've been known."

"Fifteen dollar party in Joe's room tonight. Lorraine's gonna strip. Pass the word."

Swab and Crutch rise with him. They go get in line. Everybody's left the Island except me and Gums. I wave at him and pat the flaking wood beside me.

"Don't you get an allowance?" I ask as he's changing seats.

"Nah. I still gotta apply."

"Robin just let you owe her?"

He shakes his head, not understanding I was kidding. "My sister and her husband pay it."

"They slip you any spending money?"

He shakes his head again then grins at me and shrugs.

"Feel like making ten bucks?"

Now he sort of nods and shrugs at the same time.

■□■

Later that evening after medications, I borrow pen and paper off Marvin and, leaning on the binder, write out a fairly extensive list of bare necessities.

I don't give the list to Gums until breakfast, following morning. I'm seated at the ping-pong table by myself, listening to Redbeard hack into the nearest trashcan when Gums walks in, barefoot and groggy. There's still some sinkers on the table. He stuffs one in his mouth and mushes it while staring at the list I've handed him.

"What's zinc powder for?" he asks.

"For my balls."

"What's a pisscup?"

"It's a cup you piss in, has a neck handle. That's important. Lid's optional."

He aims another powdered donut in his mouth and keeps on reading.

"Big shirts?"

"Big as you can find," I tell him, tugging on my arm, "Can't get them on otherwise. Or off."

"That black store in Morton sells t-shirts to your knees."

"Not long. Big."

"Gotcha."

"Girth is more important than length, my son."

"Gotcha."

I slide the kid three crumpled twenties I've kept hidden from the nurses this past year, reminding him to spend ten dollars on himself. I figure it's a good sign he don't bolt right out the door. He's mushing up another donut, squinting at the sunlight coming through the window, mapping out his route I guess.

All of a sudden, Redbeard doubles over retching. We look over. His hands are gripping both sides of the trash can. Throat sounds like the engine on an eighteen-wheeler turning over. He coughs determinedly a couple minutes until he gags, which causes him to vomit the entire contents of his stomach—dark brown deposits—likely coffee since I've never seen him eat before. Done, he staggers to the sink, all out of breath, sips some water, swishes it around his teeth and spits it out, then rinses his beard thoroughly.

Soon as he leaves, Gums fills me in on his whole plan. That medical supply store in Woodlyn must sell some pisscups. He'll skateboard there first, then he'll ride over to the discount store in Morton. From how he describes the route, I figure it must be right near this helicopter factory where I used to work after the War.

"You were in a war?"

"Korea."

"When was that one?"

"Fifties. I was only over there a couple months."

"How come?"

"Some asshole shot me in the leg."

"A Korean?"

"Think he was Chinese. I never got a chance to ask him. Is there a big hangar near that clothing store?"

"It is a hangar. That store's gigantic."

Gums wipes the donut powder from his chin onto his sleeve, then leaves to grab his skateboard from his room. I turn and face the window. Light's casting a bar across the other table.

There goes sixty bucks, I think, pulling the final donut from the box.

Some woman closer to my age inches around me in a pink house robe, followed by a younger woman in a shiny red pajama top and pale blue shorts. As they take the two seats catty-cornered from me, I notice they have virtually the same lumpy nose, same tripled chin, same shade of heavy luggage underneath their eyes. Older version smiles one of those sleepy partial smiles at me, three teeth short of a set along the bottom row. Younger one seems shyer. They sip their coffees without speaking to each other. I'm deciding how to broach whether they're mother-daughter when I hear the skateboard smack the sidewalk and depart in the direction of the parking lot.

■□■

Rest of the day, I lug a sixty-dollar knot around inside my stomach. I've never been someone who thinks it does you any good to trust your fellow man. Returning a nickel change without needing a reminder's one thing. Sixty smackers is another. What will I do if this kid pulls a fast one on me? After each lap, I sit where I'm able to monitor our driveway.

By lunch, Gums hasn't showed. I eat a quarter of my ham-and-cheese and leave the rest to wait in the same spot outside.

Around 2:30, I remember there's a day game against the Padres. Only Swabbie's in the rec room, drinking beer. Boxers have four-leaf clovers printed on them. Commercial for that correspondence school is playing.

"You watching the game or O.J.?" I ask, squatting down.

"Game." He's got this smirk from the commercial. "TV/VCR Repair. Now there's a noble trade."

"Seen Jack around?"

"Jack who?"

"The kid."

"Not my week to watch him."

It's the top of the second. Schill's pitching today. He came off the DL just a week ago. He's hitting his spots alright. He even works out of a jam. Nothing about his delivery seems that off to me. Schill's always been my kind of pitcher. What I like about him's how he relies more on control and savvy than velocity. Whitey starts going on about these notebooks Schill is known to fill with first pitch tendencies, two strike tendencies, any little edge he's ever found on every single hitter in the league. Fregosi pinch-hits for him in the bottom of the fifth. By then, the game is barely holding my attention. We're too far behind the Expos and the Braves. Plus with this strike looming, it's hard to get too worked up about another losing season.

When Swab wonders if I'm old enough to have seen Whitey play, I tell him about those doubleheaders I used to attend down at Shibe Park when I was young. Opposing players rode the trains in those days. We would guide them up to 30th Street in exchange for autographs. I got Duke Snyder that way. Musial. Sissler. Pee Wee. Bobo Newsome. All three DiMaggios. Pete Gray. I hope my son held onto them. They must be worth a couple bucks by now. I can still picture this long plywood wall of peeling War Bond posters where the players used to line up, waiting for their trains to board. Pete Gray had me climb under the railing and hold my program up against the wall so he could sign it.

"How the frig did he hit?"

"Gray? He slapped singles mostly."

"Any of em not sign your book?"

"Ducky Medwick," I say without hesitation. "Ducky Medwick didn't. Giants needed one of two to win the pennant. They lost both. I stuck with him from 21st and Lehigh all the way to 30th Street. It meant extra pay in those days if you won. They paid them by the game."

"How do they pay them now?"

I shrug. "Think they'll really call the season off?"

"Nah. They're all bluffing. It's just greed." He points the neck of his bottle at the TV set. We're down four in the eighth now. Kruk's out of breath on second, hands on his hips. "All these fucking slobs. Why don't they try a hunger strike instead? It'd do more good."

■□■

First thing I do after we lose is piss. Then I head upstairs to check if Gums is in his room. I press my ear against the door, but I don't hear a sound over Creep's snores across the hall.

Hallway's packed already when I head downstairs. I ease down on the pew and wait.

"Anybody seen Jack?"

Nobody's seen him.

By dinner time, I'm fully convinced the sixty that I gave him is a goner. Marvin opens my drink carton for me. I'm debating whether to bring up the matter when I hear our front door scrape against the cement lip.

Ten seconds later, Gums comes striding in with rings of sweat around his armpits from the weight of the two shopping bags he's lugging. He plops down and opens the first bag to let me see inside: pile of toiletries, same kind of notebook Harry uses, new pens, and a fresh pisscup. From the second bag, he pulls an Eagles hat and lowers it onto my head to check the size before adjusting it for me. New sweatpants are maroon.

Phillies t-shirt he holds up is twice my size. I don't recognize the player's name.

"Thanks."

"Oh wait," he says, digging in his pocket.

"What?"

"Change." He sets a five, two singles, and forty-six cents next to my plate.

■□■

Gums hangs around more often after that, helping me in and out of chairs, righting my cane whenever it tips over, opening the heavy door for me whether I'm coming or going.

I think the kid has lacked affection in his life. Say we're on one of the benches together. He's always finding excuses to pat my shoulder, always repeating my one-liners back to me. Often he'll tag along during my laps. He takes the inside path so as to block anyone from bumping into me. At the slightest indication I might trip, his hand shoots out and grips me by the elbow.

These walks are very slow.

In bits and pieces on them, I begin to gather how a twenty-six-year-old could end up in Assisted Living. Unlike some here, Gums can legitimately claim to be unlucky. Both his parents died of cancer by the time he was twenty. He dropped out of high school after Ridley held him back the second time. Wisely, I suppose, his parents left the half-house they nearly owned outright in Collingdale to his big sister. Colleen married a much older man and quit her job when she got pregnant. Ken handles sales for some big HVAC company. Things went fine awhile. Gums was bagging groceries part-time down at the Acme. Larger room upstairs went to the newlyweds. Smaller room next door became the nursery. Gums was content sleeping downstairs on the long sofa. But once Colleen got pregnant with their second, she and Ken decided it was time to work through the courts in order to put him somewhere like here.

When I turn the topic to his missing teeth one day, he shrugs and looks me in the eye like he was hoping I'd tell him what happened to them. This is late July. We're passing through the shade from D to C. Thinker's underneath his favorite tree, reading a book with orange trim around some man smoking a pipe in glasses. He smiles at us. Along the way, Gums has been picking maple seedpods off the ground to pass the time. He starts tossing them over his head, one by one, then watches them spin to the grass with no reaction. I keep walking.

"The first one fell out when my mom died. Well, a month after."

I thought he forgot my question, but he goes on explaining how the doctor didn't understand it. Tooth looked healthy. He declared it grief and sent him home. When the second one felt loose a few weeks later, the doctor put him on antibiotics. Gums had some kind of bad reaction. Hair fell out. So did more teeth, two to three at a time, the way they would in a bad dream. Six months later, there were only four remaining. Colleen arranged to have them pulled.

■□■

By mid-August, once the baseball strike's been made official, season cancelled, no World Series, all anybody wants to watch on TV day and night is this new O.J. Channel. Trial hasn't even started, and yet the yard's been noticeably emptier.

Somedays it's me and Gums alone out on the Island, Roadrunner roaming past us every couple minutes, Three Bags exploring, Thinker reading over yonder. It's more peaceful and I'm not complaining, though I won't pretend to understand how nearly a hundred idiots could skip this mild sunny weather, arguing indoors over pre-trial motions as if this connects them to the world at large.

Evenings, Dot and Gail and Lolly walk into the canteen, elevate their plates, and walk them right back to the rec room where they sit in the same order on the sofa, so engrossed that they forget to eat whatever's cooling on their laps. Rest stuff themselves too quickly, bump their shins a bunch of times lugging unfolded chairs across the hall. Gums and I have gotten in the habit of remaining in the canteen, keeping Marvin company while he shuffleboards the tables, wipes the stove, and so forth.

I've put Gums in charge of helping me with all the PT exercises I can't manage on my own. He stands a little to my left, two feet behind me, and he turns my bad arm like a crank, fifty times, as wide an arc as I can take. After that, he bends my wrist back until all my knuckles are about to crack, holding to the count of twenty before letting go.

"You could be a PT man, you know," I tell him, between winces, Wednesday night. Marvin's scouring the sink behind us. "Whaddaya think?" I turn to ask him, "Wouldn't Jack make a good physical therapist?"

He gives Gums a hurried smile. "Thure hath the paythence for it."

■ □ ■

Wednesdays are my shower night. I need assistance with that, too. Our shower room has sea-green tiles with gray grout around them. There are three curtained stalls to choose from on the left-hand side, and on the right two urinals, a toilet, plus a grimy tub nobody ever touches. My plastic safety chair stays alongside the sinks on the far wall. Gums sets the chair up in an open stall for me. I sit there staring at the tiny orange freckles on his scalp while he removes my shoes and socks. I let him lift the lanyard off my head so he can rush down to my room to bring my toiletries and towel. I attempt to take my t-shirt off, one-handed, until I'm completely tangled up inside it like Houdini with one ear folded in half. He always snickers while untangling it for me.

Next he pulls the curtain.

I stand up and tug my sweatpants inch by inch, right side, left, right. Once they're past my hips and knees, I ease down again on the cold plastic. Last thing left to do is sneak the cuffs over my heels. Anytime I try this part myself, my pants end up all damp, so I extend both legs beneath the curtain.

"Alright," I say, as usual.

Gums drops to one knee. He's sliding them off my two heels right when the door squeaks open. I hear feet slapping the tile. They stop.

"You two need a little privacy?" Voice sounds gravelly. Think it's Swab.

"Fuck you, sailor."

"Sorry, I don't do three-ways, Dick."

His shadow passes by the curtain. I hear the clink of his bottle on one of the urinals. Prick's laughing at us over there.

I turn the valve to two o'clock. A blast of arctic water hits my neck. I grumble through it.

Gums hands in my shampoo upside-down and squeezes some onto my palm. I rub it roughly all around my head and leave it there a minute. I'm watching the water run off my bad arm down the hairy drain. Swab snaps me out of this.

"Finish up, Dick. You're missing one helluva speech out there. Dotty's practicing in case they call her in to testify. The Juice would never do a thing like that. He's too nice and handsome. Man, they sure stick to their own kind, don't they?"

"Don't we all?"

Door opens and shuts. I close my eyes and lean my head under the water.

"Ready for soap?"

"Alright."

Gums hands in my bar of soap.

"How's your sister?" I shout, lathering myself. Trick with these one-hand showers is to soap your clean parts first. Otherwise, you'll just be shifting crud around. "She shoot that baby out yet?"

"Almost," he shouts back, "Due in a couple weeks."

"You say a couple weeks?"

"Yeah."

"Maybe she'll have it on Labor Day. Get it?"

"Labor Day, I get it." He takes the soap from me. "You have any kids yourself, Rich?"

"Six, that I know of."

"Six!"

"They tried to pin a seventh on me, but I beat the rap."

"You beat the rap. I guess they all live far away?"

"Yeah. Pretty far."

Holidays seem like the only time when anyone does any pitching in around this place. Every nurse but Marvin requested off for Labor Day. That puts him in charge of feeding seventy of us himself. He must've needed the extra pay. Minute ago, he ordered every able-bodied male to follow him across the yard up to the shed. He's crouched inside there, handing out the items we will need for our big annual cookout.

Six men from A and D set up the three long folding tables in a row across the grass. Popeye and Penguin carry the two grills into the middle of the Island. Swab and Sal are lugging bags of charcoal. Creep is trailing them with lighter fluid. Zorro drags the plastic tub with all our recreational equipment to the sidewalk near the parking lot. He dumps it carelessly, the way a child would. Amidst the mess of shuttlecocks and baseball mitts and tennis balls, he locates the mallet and the two stakes, and he hammers them into the ground, ten paces apart.

Several women I have never seen before are streaming in and out of all four buildings. Without being told, they know to bring the bags of ice, the yellow cooler, the six cases of free soda, rolls and buns and popcorn, pretzels, paper towels, potato chips, the plastic cups, and plates. Raggedy Ann and Betsy Ross are busy arranging things around the tables, dumping snacks in bowls, etc. Marvin's back inside, preparing all the meat. Sal and Swab are dumping in the charcoal right in front of us. They rip large pieces off the bags and jam them down inside. Creep empties the lighter fluid on the grills. There's a sudden whoosh as Swabbie aims his lighter at them. He jumps back and checks his arm hair hasn't singed. Him and Creep and Sal are standing there, admiring the fire for a minute.

Over my shoulder, I hear Three Bags shuffling up behind us. Static from his radio is slowly growing louder. He eases to a halt, not setting down his bags as yet.

"What the hell is going on?" he asks in a nervous tone as if all this commotion is upsetting him a little.

"Honky, what it look like?"

Bags don't answer. Knee's still bothering him. He keeps shifting his weight from one foot to the other.

"Circus is in town," I tell him.

"Circus?"

"I'm just kidding, Chris. Everything's fine. Today's the cookout's all."

"Cookout? What for?"

"For Labor Day. Why don't you turn your music up for everybody? Make it a party for them, Chris."

"What if my batteries run out?"

"Marvin'll get you more. Turn that song up."

He lowers all eight of his bags down on the grass, fishes out his radio, and twists the volume button. Dion's singing "The Wanderer." Instantly I notice grins break out on several normally dour faces. Even some heads begin to bob.

In no time, the yard is full of happy hobnobbers, their chairs arranged in circles randomly around the tables. Some are passing bottles back and forth. Some are sharing cigarettes. Sam Cooke starts singing next. Soon as Dot recognizes his voice, she jumps out of her chair and does this clumsy version of the Twist which makes the polka dots across her dress stretch into ovals. I can't take it. I start laughing uncontrollably. When Crutch and Bunyan turn their heads to check on me, I gesture with my hand at the entire yard as if to say: behold this spectacle. There's Chaplin and Dollar Bill tossing the football back and forth. Those two had a fistfight not a week ago. There's Popeye and Penguin holding a friendly catch with the two mitts. They weren't on speaking terms just yesterday. Horseshoes has commenced. Several onlookers are gathered around Franklin as he's eyeing up his toss. Out in the middle of the parking lot, Zorro's playing one-man badminton, whacking a shuttlecock upwards as violently as possible, then trailing underneath it with his head arched back, adjusting to its course, racquet at the ready.

A cheer ripples through the yard when Marvin and Thinker emerge in matching black aprons, bearing two large trays of hotdogs and hamburgers. It's almost 7:00. Ones full of alcohol are getting rowdier. Some yell at them to hurry up. The grilling smells turn everybody rabid. Some start making for the tables. They're tiding themselves over with potato chips and pretzels.

Better get myself a spot. I stand, adjust my sweatpants, and steer my way around Marvin, who's perspiring over our burgers while Thinker rotates the hotdogs. On the grass, I veer around this older pair slow-dancing out of step to "Wildwood Days."

Host comes on. *"We'll be right back after we pay our electric bill with a few commercials. This is W-O-G-L. Rocking Oldies in the Cradle of Liberty!"*

Near end of the table's full already. I head for the empty spots around that mother-daughter duo, Peg and Mimi, ones who moved upstairs from me last month. They're sitting by themselves, both frowning at their sodas. When that piano for "Earth Angel" starts, I let go of my cane, extend my arm, and hit them with the high stuff for a couple verses before drool reverses down my throat and I begin to wheeze. Whole yard's laughing at me. Peg and Mimi set their sodas down to clap and snort just like a pair of circus seals.

"I've never been serenaded before!"

"I don't believe it," is all I get out before another cough takes over. I start pounding on my chest.

"Mi, help him!"

Mimi pulls one of the chairs away so I can step up to the table.

"How's the bursitis?" I ask hoarsely, easing down.

"Bring Dick a soda."

Everyone without a seat's converging on our table from all sides. Franklin takes the spot across from mine.

"How goes the struggle, Richard?"

"Slow and sloppy."

"You hear the latest?" He checks over both shoulders. "Any of you hear what happened to Wesley?"

Sal and Swab squeeze next to me.

"Yo, Dick!"

"What?"

"Is no one aware what happened to Wes?"

"Yo, Dick, where's the Boy Wonder?"

"Has no one heard?"

"What he do now?"

"Who?"

"The kid. Where's Jack?"

"You won't believe this. Actually, you will."

"Oh, he's on French leave."

"What?"

"Wes got arrested, folks. That's right. We've graduated to full burglary now."

"He's at his sister's."

"Who?"

"Jack."

"That jackass actually attempted a hot prowl a few blocks from here. Man of the house saw these two hands feeling around his desk through his back window and—"

"Yo Marv! C'mon!"

"Whammo! He slammed the window right down on his wrists. Pinned him there like that while his wife was calling the cops."

"Good riddance."

"Riddance? He'll be back."

"C'mon! We're fucking starving over here. Bring over what's ready. If that fairy brings us a pile of frozen hamburgers, I swear to Christ I'll kill him."

Marvin's heaping meat onto the serving trays now. Thinker's running them back and forth. I've never seen him move so briskly. Swabbie pounds our table when he realizes we'll be the last ones served.

"Yo Harry! Har! Us first. I'm fucking starving, you fuck."

Since I'm seated down the far end, I can see a hundred hands reaching over one another, snatching buns and jamming hotdogs in them, shaking ketchup bottles upside down while we sit waiting. In the very middle, there's a giant bowl of strawberry Jell-O which keeps jiggling each time somebody bumps the table. Flies are hovering above it.

Thinker finally brings a tray of meat to us, extending it towards Swab for a second then pulling it back. "Cloven or uncloven?"

"What?"

"Fatted calf or fatted hog?"

"What the fuck are you talking about? Man, put that fucking tray down."

Swab snatches two hamburgers before the tray is fully resting on the table. Sal lunges for a hotdog. Franklin helps himself to two.

I elbow Sal and ask if he can set me up a hotdog when he gets a chance. He pauses for a second then slides the one he just made down to me and makes himself another. After two bites of his, he grunts approvingly and holds the hotdog up to everybody as evidence of what he is about to say.

"This ain't chopped liver."

Franklin and Swab nod in agreement.

"I mean it ain't sazeech and peppers, but I've had worse."

"So've I."

"Yeah. Food's alright here."

Swab nods through another bite. "Hell. This place is the Taj compared to last one I was at."

"Which one?"

"Something Pines. Tall. Short. I forget. Navy found it for me."

"That the one that used to be a Catholic school?" someone halfway down the table wants to know.

"The one in Darby?"

"Yeah. I was there too."

"Yeah. I got along with everybody there. Only thing is it wasn't that clean."

"Dirtier than here?"

"Much. Lot of people lost their legs in there."

"Nam?"

"Diabetes."

"That's rough."

"Man, have I slept in some bad places."

Swab laughs off some memory he's having, finishing his burger. Marvin and Thinker distribute seconds now. The pair look like exhausted coal miners, faces glazed with sweat and streaked all over with stray charcoal marks. They flop down on the grass to eat. It's beginning to get dark. I didn't even notice when the radio died. Yard is silent except for crickets.

I scan the mess along the tables: dozens of beer and soda cans tipped over, not to mention all the napkins and the dirtied plates and empty liquor bottles too. A bit of breeze picks a lone napkin off the table and sails it way up into one of the trees. Ground's even worse. Pigeons have begun to work around us, pecking at the hotdog nubs and ends of rolls. I'm watching this gray one stick its head inside a plastic cup when I notice the station wagon pulling in the parking lot. That brother-in-law is giving Gums a lecture while he parks the car. Gums leans up to the windshield like he's wondering what all of us are doing in the yard. I don't see his sister anywhere. She must've had the baby.

CHAPTER 6: THE HIBERNATION PERIOD

We've officially re-entered hibernation. There ain't a whole lot else for me to do besides pace the halls or watch the O.J. trial with the other inmates. Leg's making progress at least. At present, I am averaging eighty indoor laps, plus six to seven flights of stairs per day. There are no windows in the halls, and none of these nurses can be bothered to replace the lightbulbs, so it's generally pitch dark unless somebody leaves their door open. Whenever I hear footsteps barging up behind me, I press against the wall and wait for them to pass. For the most part though, I have the hallways to myself.

■□■

Every Friday after lunch, I watch a row of anxious onlookers form at the windows. They're weighing two forms of waiting in their heads: go outside now and shiver in a shorter line, or wait inside for longer where it's relatively warm. We've had no snow as yet, but by Thanksgiving, temperature was in the upper thirties. Next day, the ones in line had no choice but to march in place in all the clothes they owned. I spotted Zorro fending four guys off with his imaginary rapier. Dot was two spots ahead of him with an old afghan wrapped around her shoulders. She wore so many pairs of white stockings that it looked like she had broken both her legs.

■□■

Saturday nights, some of us go in on a Chinese order while we still have spending money left. Most weeks, it'll be me and Gums, Sal and Swab, Peg and Mimi, plus whoever else has deemed whatever Marvin cooked unappetizing. He lets us use the cabinet phone to call Dragon Garden, which is the only restaurant that's willing to deliver here. Mimi writes our orders on a corner of the Friday paper.

"Put me down for two eggroll," Sal tells her.

"Okay."

"Better add one for Paul. He's in the toilet. I'll eat it if he don't. Remind them hot mustard too."

"Okay."

"Moo goo gai pan!" yells Zorro in a fake Chinese accent.

"Got it."

"Moo shu pork," says either Gail or Lolly.

"Pepper steak," mumbles the other.

"Moo goo gai pan!"

"I heard you."

"Kung pao chicken," I say, "Wonton for Jack."

"Where is Jack?" Sal asks me.

"Asleep again. He'll eat it later."

"Large shrimp lo mein," Peg reminds her daughter, "Shrimp!"

With all the orders taken, Mimi hunches down to dial the number in the cabinet. Every single week, she reprovides them with detailed directions: the quick left you take after the red light by the hospital, first building on your right when you pull in the parking lot, first door on your left downstairs. Hearing the route described reminds me I have not laid eyes on anything beyond this building or that yard of ours in over eighteen months.

My eyes keep hopping back and forth from Mimi to her mother. Both are wearing wrinkled floral dresses that the other one will wear tomorrow. Neither believes in bras. Hairdos are identical. Only difference is that Peg's is gray all over, whereas Mimi's hair is black with a gray strip along the middle where she parts it.

Mimi confirms the total with the Chinese lady, hangs up the phone, and makes her way around the tables, accepting dollar bills and change from everyone who ordered anything. As she counts the money up beside her mother, Salvy waves across the table at the two of them.

"Don't you ever mix it up, Peg?"

"Mix what up?"

"You always get shrimp lo mein."

Mimi snorts. "Tell him why, Ma." She starts counting over.

"Why what?" asks Sal.

"Why she always gets the exact same thing."

Peg giggles guiltily at all the eyes on her around the room. In her most sheepish voice, she says, "Because they can't make cat look like a shrimp."

■□■

Back in June when these two nincompoops arrived, Warden moved somebody over one so they could have adjacent rooms on the top floor. Peg got rather adamant about it. I call that floor the Convent because it seems to be an unofficial policy to house all female residents up there. I've heard they do the same in other buildings. Here in B, six women occupy those rooms at present: Peg, Mimi, Gail, Lolly, Dot, and Kneeslapper.

Evenings, I've gotten in the habit of doing laps along their hall. It's cleaner and brighter than the lower floors. These women don't expect a man to be up there, therefore their doors stay open. They have nothing to conceal from one another. Dotty mutters constantly at night. Often I find her agitated in the middle of her room, berating some imaginary nurse for stealing all her valuables. Last week while passing Gail or Lolly's room, I saw whichever one it was rear back and spit on her own floor. Kneeslapper's usually hiding in the stairwell, beating herself black and blue. Before I pass her on the steps, I need to rest awhile. Two floors all at once is hard for me.

Wednesday night, I'm leaning against the wall outside Peg's room, not meaning to peep or anything, simply waiting for the throbbing in my shin to cease. I can't avoid seeing the pairs of corrective stockings airdrying on the doorknob, the parachute panties draped over the lamp, her partials stationed on the dresser.

Peg's weighing herself on a bathroom scale. She notes the number with an annoyed sigh, steps down, and nudges the scale under her dresser with her toe. Soon as she notices me in the hall, her cheeks scrunch up into a dopey grin.

Covering her mouth, she says, "Why don't you use the chair in here?"

"Don't mind if I do."

I only plan to rest about ten minutes, but ten quickly turns to thirty. I can tell she appreciates the company because she slips her partials in so she can give me her life story. As it turns out, we attended the same high school fifty years ago. Born 2/6/29 makes her eight months my senior. Neither of us remembers knowing one another back in those days, but we discover we had several friends in common. Peg don't recall meeting my first wife ever, and her husband was from Iowa. I never met the man. She waited on him at the Folcroft Diner until he proposed.

On my way into her room, I noticed these three shoeboxes lined up along the dresser. One had sewing gear. Next one was full of sugar packets, lipstick tubes, loose change, stool softeners, and such. Third box had maybe forty musty-looking letters lined up in a row. Way they were slanted, I made out a few return addresses: Topeka, Kansas; Tulsa, Oklahoma; Twin Falls, Idaho.

"Those are from Roy," she says, catching me eyeing them again, "My lovely husband. You can read some if you like. Roy couldn't write a love letter to save his life."

"What did he do?"

"He was a long-haul trucker. He was gone ten months a year."

"Teamster?"

She nods. "Some of those letters are just lists. Motels he stayed at. Diners. What he ate that week. What he wants to eat when he gets back. Hardly ever mentioned missing me. He never mentioned Mimi. Roy was an odd man."

"How long ago he pass?"

She's been sitting on her mattress angled towards me this whole time. Her eyes roll upwards.

"What's it, '94? Twelve years. 1983. No, eleven. It'll be twelve in March."

■□■

Unwise or not, I decide to continue paying evening calls to Peg. I hope she doesn't get ideas, but I must admit I find her entertaining. New case should make another winter trapped inside this building go by faster, too.

Occasionally, we'll glance at one another and just laugh at being old. I'm sinking so far down into her armchair that my cane brushes my chin. She's crushing her mattress in the middle like an elephant on its hind legs. We're at that age where you accept there will be trace amounts of piss and shit marinating in your clothes. Some nights my nose can't tell which of us smells so bad. Horse radish. Lemon and clams. Long as she don't appear to notice, I assume it's her. Peg takes long baths at 9:00 to help her sleep. If she's not decent or is in the tub already when I'm passing by, I rest on the armchair in her daughter's room instead.

■□■

In my head, I file Mimi next to Thinker, meaning I can't understand what she is doing here. True she is depressed, but she is also able-bodied, semi-intelligent, a little overweight but halfway pretty, with dark eyes and decent knockers. My sense is she's never had a sex life. I asked her one time if she ever considered marriage. She shook her head and told me never. Binder says she's forty-one-years-old, allergic to more things than Salvy, takes a heavy dose of Depakote, plus Tramadol as needed for her migraines and her monthly cramps. I suppose those pills explain the slightly slurry way her words come out and why her eyes never seem truly focused. On the emergency contact line, she put her mother, who put her in turn. She's the most quiet person in our building, though she's gotten comfortable around me, sets me up at breakfast, even helps me with my PT now and then. I reward her with a can of soda.

Tonight Mimi's lying back in bed in her pajamas underneath this hat collection which she hung herself on four-inch nails across the wall. There's eighteen of them, ranging from a baby's bonnet to a French beret. Birthday presents. I've yet to see her wear any of these hats around the building. They just hang there on the wall.

I'm staring at the skipper's cap with the gold anchor on the front, number sixteen, when her flat voice perks up a little.

"Should we watch another movie?"

Black-and-white classics seem like her only joy in life. Prize possession is this thirty-inch TV set which sits on her dresser with a VCR. There's several cardboard boxes by her bed full of old screwball comedies, detective pictures, and those sappy melodramas she recorded off the Turner channel years ago. Under her window, there's four stacks of movie magazines, trivia books, and glossy biographies of all her favorite actresses and actors.

Without intending to, we've sort of started up a movie club together. Lately we keep choosing these Depression-era ones where poor people get rich all of a sudden, or vice versa. Sunday was *Splendor in the Grass*. Tuesday was *God's Little Acre*. Last night, *Sullivan's Travels*. Tonight she puts on *Our Man Godfrey*.

We're about twenty minutes in, right at the part where Godfrey takes his old pal Tommy on a tour of the Village of Forgotten Men, when two hard thuds come through the wall at us.

"WHAT, Ma?"

"I'm calling you, that's what!"

Mimi makes a noise between a sigh and groan. Peg acts like such a harmless simpleton around the rest of us that I forget how she can get sometimes. Often she invents little errands to interrupt us, which makes me wonder if she's jealous. Right away she needs her medications or her cookies, or she needs her heels pumiced, whiskers tweezed, laxative mixed, arthritis cream rubbed in her knuckles.

As Mimi's scooting off the bed, a bit of popcorn spills from her pajamas to the floor.

"Want me to pause it?" I reach for the VCR.

"Nah. I've seen it fifty times."

Godfrey and Tommy are seated on this wooden plank outside some clapboard shack. There's laundry strung above their heads, a lantern. Some pots and pans hang on the wall as well.

"Pretend you're peeing," I hear Peg tell Mimi through the wall.

"What, and just sit on the toilet?"

"You know how Lolly hogs the tub."

"It's freezing in there."

"Exactly. I don't want to get out of my hose and all for nothing."

■ □ ■

Week later, I'm downstairs resting in the rec room between laps. All morning, I have paced between this rubber armchair and the folding chair which I had Gums set up beside my window. We just finished lunch, which means there's five more hours to kill until dinner. Dot is bundled in her afghan, hogging two-thirds of the sofa to my right, however, it's apparent she believes she's alone with the TV. This has been going on since summer. Finally they've finalized the jury. Now they're selecting alternates. Dot has been grumbling at this Asian judge for twenty minutes straight.

"Think it's news you don't like me? Look like I give a damn? Going down check the housing authority. Tell em move me out of here fore I cut your throat too. Robin know she took sixty-four dollars off me. Let her. Bitch better give me back my crochet needle too. Do the black side right for a change!"

Either Gail or Lolly pokes her head in from the hallway just to gawk at Dot, amused by what she's overhearing. She lifts her sweatshirt sleeve up to her mouth right as a cough jumps out of her.

Dot glares in her direction.

"Fuck you looking at? This ain't slavery time, white witch. If it was, I'd kill you, and they'd hang me. Kill the ministrator too. It's a good thing I raised up. There three white people in here hit me. Went to her about it, didn't I? She ain't done nothing. Got a sinking suspicion she ain't even called nobody."

Gail or Lolly risks a little laugh at first, then backs away when Dot lurches forward like she's willing to stand. She keeps shouting threats straight out the doorway.

I can only bear the noise a few more minutes. I stand and take the long way round the sofa to be safer. There's always a few inmates in the canteen sick of staring at their ceilings too. Thinker and Creep have moved their matches to the afternoon. Salvy's turned sideways at the other table, flipping through last Sunday's paper.

Thinker glances up at me as I pull even with the board.

"What's Dorothy soliloquizing about now?"

"The trial. What else?"

"I thought maybe Marie Antoinette."

He's playing white today. Looks like he's one pawn up on Creep. I sit beside them. Ten minutes pass without a single move. Exhaust fan's churning. Salvy's squinting at some article in the paper.

I look over at the thinning garland Marvin tacked onto the wall two nights ago. He also took the glossy cut-outs of the Pilgrim and the Indian down, replacing them with ones of Rudolph and of Santa. A single string of lights is blinking on and off above the windows. Why's he bother? By the trashcans, he went to the added trouble of setting up this Nativity set which he discovered in the shed back in September. The three plastic wise men are propped up on orange milk crates, making them about as tall as us. Their robes glow different colors. It's hard not to stare at them during our meals.

Now Dot is screaming at somebody else to go away. She hollers out a phone number with area code, all ten digits of it, twice.

"That's the Governor's direct line," I say.

Creep retreats his rook four squares then folds his arms across his gut. "I wish she'd go croak in an alley somewhere."

"Agreed," says Sal, flipping the paper over to the Sports.

Swab appears in the doorway. "Careful," he warns the four of us, "Dotty's crying rape again." He gestures over his right shoulder on his way upstairs.

■□■

Later same afternoon, I turn onto the second floor to check on Gums. I'm worried about him. Kid's gone nocturnal on us, regularly misses meals, skips his medications often too. He'll still assist me with my showers if I ask, but I let Mimi handle all my PT now.

I knock on his door and wait.

My theory is that second baby did a number on his head. Colleen and Ken have only had him over once since it was born. I think he must've realized on Thanksgiving what that meant because he didn't say a word through the entire meal and exited before the pumpkin pie was served. On second thought, I bet he realized it sooner, back on Labor Day. After the station wagon disappeared, he turned and stood there in the parking lot two minutes like some kid dropped at an orphanage.

No answer. I knock three more times.

Kid may be sore at me. Last week, I tried reading him the riot act, much like I tried one year ago with Thinker. Little good it did. I warned him these vampire hours he was keeping are the dumbest kind of trap. Place like this is no life for somebody twice his age, which makes it twice as bad for him. He should be making eyes at broads across some bar somewhere. What about joining the army? Least they'd issue him some teeth, and a routine. When he stopped nodding suddenly, I got nervous and slapped him on the shoulder, way men do to prevent open sobbing.

He's not gonna answer. I've been on my feet over an hour. I keep going.

Thinker's door's ajar. I knock and ask to sit. I haven't been here for awhile. Stack of notebooks seems two inches taller. Absolutely nothing else inside his room has changed.

"*Natürlich*," he says, "How many laps you up to?"

"Thirty-six. Long night ahead. I'm behind schedule. My heel keeps acting up."

"Miles to go before you sleep."

"That Whitman?"

"Frost."

"Right. Who won your match?"

"We drew again. Al keeps using this Hedgehog defense. It's impenetrable."

"That the pawn thing?"

"Yes, a6, b6, d6, e6. I made the mistake of telling him I hate it. Now it's all he wants to play as black."

"Whatcha reading?"

He tilts the beige book on his chest in my direction. It's a biography of Jakob Ammann, fellow all the Amish are named after. He's come up a couple times before. Thinker starts summarizing the chapter he just finished on this famous meeting Ammann held three hundred years ago with all the other elders in his church where he informed them they were growing lax and needed to shun the unrepentant sinners in their flock. A few of the other elders tried reminding him that Jesus ate and drank with sinners all the time, but Ammann couldn't be persuaded. Either they agree, right then and there, to commence shunning or they could expect to face shunning themselves.

"Shun or be shunned, huh?"

"That's the gist of it. Let him be to you like a heathen and a tax collector. Matthew 18:17."

"Adultery get ya shunned?"

"Assuming you don't seek forgiveness. The term for it is *Meidung*. You don't share a meal with them. You can technically speak to them, but that's mainly to remind them that they're shunned."

"How bout drinking?"

"You don't drink with them either."

"No, I mean does boozing get you shunned?"

"Oh. Definitely. Proverbs 23:20."

"How's it go with the kids on something like that?"

"Well, they're supposed to shun you too. Matthew 19:29." He flips back until he finds this passage which he reads in a proclamatory voice as if he's in some town square with a rapt audience gathered around him. "If anyone, either through a wicked life or perverted doctrine, has so far fallen that he is separated from God, and, consequently, also separated and punished by the church, he must, according to the doctrine of Christ and his apostles, be shunned by all the fellow members of the church, especially in eating, drinking, and other similar intercourse, and no company be had with him that they may not become contaminated by intercourse with him, nor made partakers of his sins, but that the sinner may be made ashamed, pricked in his heart, and convicted in his conscience unto his reformation."

I hang around another hour.

On our way to dinner, we hear Sal and Swab griping back and forth across the hall from their respective beds about the Eagles game last Sunday, even though today is Thursday, and we're closer to the next game than the last.

"Too many men on the field," sighs Sal.

"Twice!"

"Thirteen the second time."

"How do you fumble a field goal snap?" asks Swab rhetorically, "Catch the fricken ball. Put it down. Turn the laces. Give me a day to practice, I could handle that. Hell, an hour even."

These two have been working themselves up like this the past four weeks. Seeing us go by, they both perch up in bed.

"Feedbag time already?"

I nod.

■☐■

Next night, I'm resting in Peg's chair while she mends the shoulder of her favorite dress, all nice and situated with four pillows Mimi fluffed and stacked behind her. Even with her glasses on, Peg has to hold the fabric right up to her nose to see what she is doing.

I watch her make a couple passes with the needle, then my eyes drift up to the four paintings hanging right above her, amateur nature scenes done on real canvas but unframed. They're so similar I figure that they must've been for practice. The same creek is rushing through the middle of all four of them. Same stone mill is built beside it. In the background, there's a small red cabin with four different curls of smoke leaving its chimney. The same man is fishing in all four in different spots with slightly different postures, different style hats, but always wearing light blue dungarees. I wonder if her husband is responsible for these? Initials at the bottom say *R.H.*

"Roy liked to paint, did he?"

"He did," she says, tugging the needle through its hole, "Those are the last ones he finished. That's this river he fished at in Oregon one time."

"They're awful similar."

"I told you Roy was odd."

"A painting trucker. That is odd."

I'm on the verge of asking how Roy died when Gail or Lolly yells something incoherent from her room.

Peg clucks her tongue three times. "There goes the call of the dingaling."

"Say that again."

"That dingaling down the hall. Gail. She keeps calling for the nurse all week. There's nothing wrong with her even." Peg's lost her place. Realizing, she retreats the needle and reinserts it. "Some ladies in here are gems," she says, "They can teach you things. Ones like her they ought to lock up."

About a minute passes before Gail lets out the next distress call. This one's higher-pitched and longer, held until her lungs run out of air. Peg starts taking her annoyance out on the poor dress, yanking the thread through each hole roughly. Once the seam looks fixed, she knots the thread and bites it off, jabs the needle back into the purple pin cushion. When Gail calls out for help a third time, Peg jams the cushion in the shoebox.

"Feel like a cream soda?" she asks, thumping on the wall.

I shake my head.

"Here, put this away," she tells Mimi, instant she steps inside the room.

As instructed, Mimi puts the shoebox in its spot, gently lifts the mended dress off her mother's lap, and hangs it on the metal garment rack that partly blocks the window.

"Need anything else, ma? I'm gonna start a movie."

"I guess not."

"What's showing at the cinema tonight?"

"*Robin Hood.* You seen it already, Rich?"

"With my mother about sixty years ago. She had a thing for Errol Flynn. I suppose that's long enough to watch it again."

"I don't know how you two can take those corny movies. Mi, come here. Do I feel warm?"

Mimi turns and presses the back of her hand against her mother's forehead, long enough to be believed, eight or nine seconds. Then she mutters, "You're not warm, Ma."

■□■

Peg must've drifted off to sleep because we get through the entire movie without being interrupted. I always hang around to do my PT afterwards. This room's so small, she has to stand in front of me, left hand on my right shoulder, right hand on my left wrist, which situates her knockers no more than a foot from my face. I watch them swing in little circles as she cranks my arm. Sometimes an urge will grab me to reach up and touch the nearest one with my good hand. Nipple's visible. What would she do? I can't imagine she would curse at me and order me to leave. Would she pretend to ignore it? Pry my hand free with a gentle smirk?

Since she's not saying anything, I share the only Errol Flynn story I know. Think I heard it on the troopship to Korea. 1950. I have no clue whether it's factual or just some bullshit legend, but the story goes that Errol Flynn was at some café on the Riviera, drinking martinis with some chum of his. All these gorgeous women kept on passing—one after another after another—until Errol's friend looked over to commiserate. When he did, he noticed there were tears streaming down Errol's face. He asked him what he was crying for, and Errol's answer was he knew he'd never be able to sleep with all of them. I expected a grin at minimum, but all she does is numbly state she never heard that one before.

"He was genuinely broken up about it," I add.

"It sure sounds like him."

On my way downstairs a little later, I have to switch sides around Kneeslapper which always makes me nervous since my good hand's nowhere near the railing. I survive. Over her whacking on her thigh, I can hear Redbeard coughing somewhere far off in the building. It's past midnight, awful late for an old man to be returning to his room.

As I'm coming out the stairwell, I spot the naked silhouette of my next-door neighbor, guy named Foster, rushing towards me in the dark. I call him Jiggles. Day we were introduced, he grinned at the ceiling overhead, which I took to mean hello. We have exchanged exactly three cold grunts since then. All I know's his name, his age, how he's receiving treatment for cirrhosis, and takes seven showers minimum per day.

Jiggles slams his door right as I open mine. While I'm unvelcroing my shoes, I hear one of his dresser drawers squeak open through the wall. Like Dot, he has developed this sad habit of berating people who aren't there, usually some woman by the name of Martha. That's another thing I know about him. I've had four months to figure out this Martha is the mother of his only grandchild.

■□■

Almost a week now, I've been forced to do my laps barefoot, no stairs, reason being I've developed blister problems with my heels. Right one got infected. Band-Aids Mimi has tried sticking to it keep on falling off. I just passed one of them on the carpet.

What happened is the padding wore away inside my shoes. Some shard in there tore all my socks and cut into the skin. Guess I'll ask Gums to pick me up a new pair once it's warmer.

Damn cold keeps making parts of me cramp up at random too. Shoulder. Big toe. In the mornings, my left foot feels so rubbery you'd think I'd stored it in a meat locker overnight. I have to bang it on the floor three times to wake it up before I set out for my day.

Lap 27 on Friday, I'm passing the shower room around 1:30. I hear Jiggles hosing off again. I hear Redbeard coughing through his door. Word is he has emphysema. Marvin informed us all at dinner other night after one of his worst coughing fits.

Turning the corner by the pew, I hear the TV blaring in the rec room. I don't know the context, but Judge Ito's chewing out that Jewish lawyer.

"What would you respond to the argument that the parties chose not to avail themselves of a system for private communications?"

What's his name, Shapiro, answers, *"It is disingenuous for the Court to even suggest that privacy was provided."*

"Take a deep breath," Judge Ito answers back, *"and understand that I said I was posing a question. I participated in the creation of this system. When you argue that the Court is disingenuous, I would suggest that you think about that."*

At the noticeboard, I rest a minute. Heel still stings.

Lap 28. As I near Zorro's door, I overhear him mumbling to Kneeslapper. I'm sure it's her from the familiar whacking sound of palm on thigh inside his room.

"You fighting it, Kathy?"

"Oh, I'm fighting it alright."

"Attagirl. One day at a time."

"What they say."

"Hey, you got that dollar, Kathy?"

The whacking stops.

"Friday."

"It *is* Friday."

"Jack owes me. Ask him."

"He owes me too. C'mon. You can bum it up. You have ways."

"Don't make me get hoarse."

The whacking resumes. Zorro lets out a yawn.

By then I'm passing Jiggles' open door. A dozen empties have accumulated on his dresser. He opts for the flavored stuff like Swab: pineapple, raspberry, piña colada. All his allowance goes to that. I hear these trotty little footsteps coming up behind me. I wait to turn around until his door has slammed. Last thing I need is to see his bouncing pecker for the second time today.

Lap 29. I'm nearing Redbeard's room when his door opens, and that segment of the hallway fills in with his shadow. He's got on that Temple sweatshirt, the white one with red lettering Sal traded him for cigarettes. Hand shoots up like he's some crossing guard.

"Excuse me. You got change for a five?"

"No."

"How bout five ones for a five?"

"Still no."

It looks like he's about to formulate the question some third way—twenty quarters, fifty dimes—when we're both startled by Dot's sudden shouting in the rec room.

"FIX IT, BITCH! FIX IT! FIX IT! FIX IT!"

I poke my head in there. Dotty's standing with the channel changer gripped between her palms. Ocky's down on one knee by the TV set, pressing all the buttons on the front. Gail is seated on the sofa, watching with her mouth agape. Their lunch plates are on the floor.

"FIX IT, BITCH!"

Ocky twists around. "Bitch, call me bitch again!"

"What I gotta cross the yard? FIX IT!"

"I look like a TV repairer to you?"

"Call one then!"

While Ocky's getting off her knee, bracing her arm against the TV stand for leverage, Dot waves the channel changer like a wand then jabs the power button ten times in a row. Picture stays blank.

■□■

Repairman don't show until a little after 6:00, when we're all crowded near the kitchen door awaiting dinner. Zorro escorts him down the stairs, acting in charge. The man is in his fifties with a slicked head of hair and sloping beer gut. He's swinging an old rusted toolkit, chewing loads of gum, as he passes by the pew into the rec room. All but me and Sal follow to watch this operation.

Hallway's empty when Marvin unlocks the door, two minutes later. He looks over at us, palms up in the air.

"Where the hell did they go?"

We point to our right.

He steps up to the doorway. Moment ago, I heard a toolkit clicking open, some screws unscrewing, and a squeak like the repairman had removed the housing from the TV set. Next I heard a spark.

"Anybody smell smoke when this went out?" he asks.

Dot answers, "No, sir. Just a pop."

"A popping sound?"

"Yes. Like a rubber band. It went blank after that. We tried every button. We tried replugging it."

"Looks like your horizontal output transistor shorted."

"Is that bad?"

"It's not good."

"Can you fix it?"

"Sure could. If I had a transistor on me. I can bring one by on Monday."

"MONDAY?"

"I'll try to come tomorrow."

Marvin points suddenly at someone in the room. "Donald, put that down!"

In his news anchor voice, Zorro says, "Good evening. We have breaking news. Five nuns died in a shootout with some priests in the St. Francis section of Chester. Also the jury in the O.J. Simpson trial has unanimously agreed the former football star definitely, without a shadow of a doubt, murdered his sexy blonde wife."

"Donald! Take that off your head."

"I need to put that back," says the repairman blandly.

"Donald!"

"You know what we call visitors around here?" asks Zorro, dropping back into his normal voice, "We call you people worldlings, you know?"

"Is that so?"

I hear the housing squeak in place.

"Worldlings, yeah. Most of the time when you guys come in, we split. We can't deal with people from the outside. But I believe it's more and more important that some of us actually communicate with you, converse and stuff. As much as possible."

It goes quiet for a minute. Repairman must be putting back the screws. Toolkit clicks shut.

"I'll try tomorrow, ma'am. More likely, Monday."

"Please come tomorrow, sir."

Repairman steps into the hallway. Zorro follows him.

"You know we're closed in here. Shut away every fucking night. I mean prisons ain't that hard. They'll give you a lot more breaks than this place ever will. They'll write you a check. You'll be in debt, but they'll pull you out of it."

Zorro stops in front of us and watches him ascend the stairs. His voice keeps raising, farther the repairman gets.

"In there, it's no you can't come in. No, you can't have this. Here they kill you with yes. Set it right in front of you. It makes it worse in a way, that you can leave whenever you want. Thirty days. Walk anytime. It makes it worse."

■□■

Sunday morning, I've been in the canteen half an hour, staring out the window sipping lukewarm coffee by my lonesome, when Peg stumbles in, followed by Lolly. Those two are the slowest wakers in our building. Mimi's right behind them. She slides the chair next to mine out for her mother. Lolly takes the chair across from us. I've been sitting at the women's table lately so I can see outside.

"You just missed the pancakes," I tell them, "Begs and achin. Strawberries."

"I don't smell eggs and bacon."

"Don't believe Dick. He's pulling our leg again."

Mimi sets their two coffees down, then brings the box of cereal and plastic bowls. She makes a second trip to bring them milk and spoons. Peg humps her chair forward and puts her glasses on to read the fine print on the cereal box. Wording may have changed since yesterday.

"You want a waffle?" Mimi asks me.

"Why not."

While she's waiting by the toaster, Sal and Creep stroll in together. Sal slides his arm around my shoulder, sitting on my other side.

"You got a quarter?"

"Nope."

"Who you like today?"

"I like us."

"You always say that. He always thinks we'll win. Even after we keep losing every friggin week. Never loses faith, this *stunad*."

Creep makes a scoffing sound while pouring himself coffee. These two love to pester me on game days.

"How many they lose now?"

"Five straight. We were 7-2 five weeks ago."

"They're gonna choke again. Bank it."

"We're not really benching Randall, are we?"

"That's what Eskin claimed."

"Talk about desperation."

"So who's gonna start then?"

"Brister."

"Brister!" repeats Creep, "Bubby Brister? That guy kills more worms than a lawnmower. Might as well not watch if I were you. The Giants just have too much heart, Dicko."

"Hey, how we gonna watch the game?"

"They didn't fix the TV yet?"

Sal shakes his head. "Guy never came. Anybody got a TV we can borrow for three hours?"

Lolly pulls her coffee from her lips and smiles. "Mimi has a TV."

Sal swings towards Mimi, who looks down uncomfortably. He folds his hands in prayer, about to beg her, but Peg intervenes.

"Out of the question!"

"C'mon. We'll put it back."

"Not for loan," Peg declares sternly.

"C'mon. It's just three hours."

"Absolutely not. I paid for that thing. You klutzes'll drop it down the stairs."

"Fine. Forget it. We'll just go across the yard."

■□■

At 3:15, I'm decked out in my Eagles sweatshirt and my Eagles ski cap, banging on Gums' door. He's putting on his pants in there. Game's at 4:00. I went easy on the laps all afternoon to save some strength up for this trip across the yard.

"Let's go."

"We're early."

"Exactly. I don't want to have to fight some guy for a seat."

"I'll fight him for you."

I get a head start down the hall. Thinker's reading in bed. Sal and Swab sit up in their beds as I pass by.

"Time for the game already?"

"You got time."

I descend the stairwell. Door sticks when I try to open it myself, so I wait for Gums who shoves it open with his shoulder, at which point a frigid gust of wind blows in at us. We hurry down the stoop. His arms stay folded as we march across the grass towards A together. It's so cold my cane is shaking like some old divining rod in front of me. We climb the other stoop.

■□■

This is the first time I've set foot in any of the other buildings. Layout seems identical to ours, apart from there being no door on the hinges to the canteen, and the sofa and TV set being flipped in their rec room. I count ten inmates crammed around the beat-up coffee table in the middle. No one objects when we take the two empty chairs closest to Bunyan. He doesn't notice us at first because he's watching Brister warming up. Summerall's explaining how we're not mathematically eliminated yet. Long as the Eagles win their two remaining games and get a little help, we can still make the playoffs.

When I tap Bunyan on the shoulder, his mouth drops open for a second like he should know who I am but cannot place me. A grin forms. He pats me on the forearm. Words come out a little garbled like he just woke up.

"When they move you over here?"

"I'm still in B. Our TV died is all."

"Oh. Annoying. You brought Jack too. Help yourselves to some snacks, compliments of Robin." He gestures at the plastic bowls of cheese doodles and pretzel rods in front of him.

Scanning the room, I am surprised the only ones I recognize are Popeye and Ben Franklin. Rest I've never seen before. Several cannot stop themselves from shuddering or muttering. Some don't seem aware a television's on in front of them. Enough are smoking for a cloud to fill the room around our heads.

When the camera cuts to the field, Franklin mutes the TV and turns the volume way up on a radio plugged in beside it so that we can listen to Merrill Reese call the game. Players are lined up. Our fans let out the loudest boo you ever heard right at the kickoff. It's nothing but punts at first. Neither side can do three things right in a row. When Zordich intercepts Brown, most of the rec room breaks into a cheer. That sets us up around the Giants' 40. Four plays later, Brister hits Bavaro for the score.

Second quarter, we tack on a field goal. That makes it 10-0. Right before the half, Meggett fumbles it to us, but then we end up punting it right back to them which lets the Giants get that field goal back, 10-3.

During halftime, everybody hurries down the hall to piss, then gets in line for sodas. Hands keep passing cigarettes or change around my head. Bunyan reaches for the bowl of cheese doodles and offers them to Gums.

"Got any Christmas plans, Jack?"

Gums nods. "I'm having dinner at my sister's, Christmas Eve."

"That's nice. How bout you, Dick?"

I shake my head.

"My nephew usually stops by. Last year he couldn't make it. His kids came down with something which meant they came down with something too. They spent all Christmas puking. Guess he'll come this year." His beard is flattened on one side. Face seems a shade redder than normal. He grins and looks me in the eye. "Why don't you give one of your kids a call?"

I clear my throat. "I don't know, Joe. It's been years. What's the polite word? We're..."

"Estranged?"

"Yeah, that's the word."

He pats me on the forearm. "It don't have to be perfect, Dick. Long as you have some relationship. That's something. Give that son of yours a call. Trust old Joe."

Start of the third, we kick off to them. They punt it back to us. We punt it right back. We're still up 7, but Brister can't figure out how to put them away for good. Too many of his throws either sail high or skid along the turf. He almost never picks up the free blitzer in time to avoid the sack. Camera cuts to Randall, helmetless, pacing the sidelines in his full-length silver coat. Our defense holds again. It's first down at our 40.

At the snap, Brister bootlegs to the right and underthrows Barnett by several feet. Their corner, Randolph, intercepts it easily.

Now we sit moodily through muted commercials which don't match what's coming from the radio. There's a picture of a Chevy truck in an open field, but the voice is advertising Medford's Meats.

Giants take over at midfield. It only takes them a few plays to tie the score. I curse under my breath.

A close-up of the full moon fills the screen while Merrill's rehashing all the worst mistakes of this long losing streak. Camera cuts back to the field. Giants kick off, and Sydner fumbles it too fast for us to tell what even happened. Five Giants pounce on the ball. During the replay, we can see that Sydner rammed into the elbow of his own lead blocker, thereby causing his own fumble. Giants take over on our 45. Somehow we hold them at the 1. Daluiso drills it down the middle for the lead, 13-10.

There's still a minute left. We're only down 3. We've got the ball. Brister moves us to the Giants' 40. Ten more yards, and we can tie it. He spikes the ball with 22 seconds left on the clock. Next play, the Giants jump offsides which moves us to the 35, but then Kotite decides to run an extra play we can't afford. Brister hits Barnett in the flat. Couple Giants grab hold of him and won't let go. He can't make it out of bounds. We have no timeouts left. Seconds are ticking off. Every single one of us is screaming at the TV. A Giant grabs the ball and takes off downfield with it, forcing the ref to blow the whistle as the clock is running out. The Giants storm onto the field to celebrate. Some Eagles storm on too in protest. Fans start hurling cans of beer and food down on the turf. Camera zooms in on this loaf of bread that's lying on the 40-yard line, whole. Ref runs to the center of the field and waves his arms above his head, announcing there should be two seconds remaining on the clock.

The Vet erupts into a cheer.

Merrill's shouting, *"One more play! We got one more play! They can tie it here. It's all up to Murray now."*

The players are still shoving one another. It takes the refs another minute just to clear the field to hold one final play. It'll be a 45-yarder. If Murray makes it, we'll still have a chance in overtime. They line up to kick. Snap is fine. Kick's no good. Murray hooked it left. No good.

■□■

Outside, I'm huddled underneath the awning next to Gums, both of us shivering with all this sleety rain pouring around us. Poor fool and I have waited over fifteen minutes in the hopes the rain would lessen enough for us to walk back to our building without getting soaked.

I see the others got sick of waiting. Creep and Swab and Sal are dashing through the grass from D to B. Rain's too loud for me to hear what they are yelling at each other. What's the use of waiting any longer? Way this wind is blowing, rain's already hitting us.

I hand my cane to Gums and hobble down the stoop. Shortest path is straight across the grass. Gums steps sideways alongside me with his hand tucked in my armpit.

At the halfway point, I lean against one of the trees and catch my breath. Our hovel still looks far away. I squint up at the rows of windows. Mimi's shadow fills the one. Thinker's a floor below her. I can't tell if they are watching us or not. Without its leaves, this tree we're hiding under is completely useless as a shelter.

"C'mon," Gums pleads, tugging my arm, "Inside's this way!"

Look at the pair of us. My hair is whipping back and forth. Water's running down his cheeks. Our clothes are drenched. Our shoes are waterlogged. Something in me gives way. I laugh so hard, I have to grip the tree to keep from falling over. Anytime I get like this, I always wheeze. Gums knows by now to pound straight on my back. He gives me four good ones in a row between the shoulder blades. When he bends down to check on me, I nod a bunch of times to tell him I'm alright.

CHAPTER 7: THE DAYS OF WINE AND CIGGIES

It's March again. Here I am weaving around little slushy mounds of ice on my inaugural lap of spring. Air's crisp but not too cold. Green buds have started forming on the branches overhead. None have opened into leaves as yet. By mid-afternoon, it's warm enough to station myself on my bench an hour comfortably. I like having the yard completely to myself. The squirrels and pigeons keep me entertained. It's so quiet that I register each passing car out on the road.

Around 3:00, Crutch emerges from his building. Soon as he's done groaning down beside me, I hold my palm up for him to pinch two fingers into it like it's an ashtray, then we bump fists, then shake.

"Dwayne."

"Richie Rich."

"How's the Juice?"

"The Juice ain't loose. They gonna question that detective next." He stares straight ahead at the row of evergreens in front of us a minute. "Hear about Joe?"

I nod twice. Bunyan died last month. Ticker stopped while he was napping in the rec room. They only realized when somebody tried to wake him up for dinner. That's how Marvin relayed the story to me anyway, after their nurse relayed the news to him over the housephone.

Four days later, a copy of the paper got passed around during dinner.

Obituary stated Joe Campbell died at sixty-six and was survived by one younger sister, one nephew, and two nieces. Also it mentioned the fact that Joe had been a master bricklayer for twenty years in Yeadon prior to some injury. I would've never recognized him from the photo they included. Beard was missing, as well as a hundred pounds around the waist. He was squinting at the camera in some fishing vest, kind with twin rows of pockets down the front.

"That other guy died too," I say, groping for the man's real name.

"Who?"

"Uh, Andy."

"Andy who?"

"One with the bum lungs."

"What?"

"The one with the cough. He had emphysema."

"Oh."

"What?"

"I owed him five bucks."

He stares off past the parking lot. I stare at the sky through the bare branches on one tree so long my eyes go all unfocused.

Fifteen minutes pass before he asks me, "Think that's custom-made?"

I have to blink to make out where he's pointing. Near the parking lot, Three Bags is leaning on some brand-new metal walker with four tennis balls for feet. A canvas basket's fastened to the front with handles of shopping bags protruding from it.

"Oh how the mighty have fallen."

"I like that setup. Could stick my soothing syrup in there. Little guilt basket. Whatcha think, Richie?"

"Stick your ass in there too when it needs a rest."

"I'm gonna ask the VA to get me one of those."

"Looks friggin heavy to me."

"That's what them yellow balls is for."

We go back to staring.

Twenty minutes or so later, Franklin joins us in a white windbreaker, navy-blue pants. Hair's clumped together in multiple spots.

"Gentlemen."

"Where?" I ask.

"Hear about Mike?"

He means the Mummer.

"What he do now?"

"What did he do? Only offer Steve a blowjob during dinner. How'd you like me to suck your cock? That's what he said verbatim. Came out a little louder than intended."

"Bone man, huh?"

"Most of the room heard."

"What did Steve do?"

"Steve? Steve wasn't pleased. He said ask me again, and I'll smack your fucking face. Mike backed off."

"Wise."

"Nothing wrong with a good blowjob."

"Oh and remember Wes?"

"One-eye guy?"

"Yeah. Jail."

"No shit?"

"Dave too."

"What Dave do? Expose hisself again?"

"No, he caught William in his room, red-handed, going through his dresser. Will has been quite the mess of late. In arrears with almost everybody. He tried the old mistaken-room act. Dave didn't fall for it. Boy did he kick the shit out of him! Needed stitches. He's back of course. We always expel the wrong ones."

Franklin continues talking. I tune him out. My attention's on this tall man beside the dumpster with a wide black cowboy hat. Sweater he's wearing is so lumpy you'd think he had a cat hiding inside it. He keeps reaching down inside the dumpster, pulling objects out, and walking them across the parking lot to toss them, underhanded, at the row of trees. Back and forth. One item at a time.

I interrupt Franklin to ask, "Who's the Lone Ranger?"

He looks over and shrugs.

Lone Ranger's on about his fifteenth trip when a piece of crumpled newspaper slides out from the bottom of his sweater to the ground. He stops to pick it up and stuff it back inside his collar.

■ □ ■

Yard remains peaceful the next couple weeks.

Most of the pigeons have returned to their spots on the gutters.

One by one, I shift my laps outdoors, some before lunch around 11:00, then 10:30, 10:00, 9:30, and so forth as the warmth stretches earlier into the day.

Very early one such morning, while the Dawn Patrol searches the grass for butts, I happen to run into Gums, coming from God knows where on his skateboard. We're face-to-face there on the sidewalk. All I can think is how I failed to straighten him out. Kid didn't listen.

■□■

Late April around 3:00 one day, I'm resting with Crutch and Franklin on our bench. Zorro, Swab, and Sal are seated next bench over. The six of us are ogling this woman in the grass who's sunbathing about as naked as someone can get while still technically clothed. Name's Lorraine, but everybody calls her Rainy. Warden relocated her from D to B about a week ago.

Rainy just strolled around the grass for several minutes until she found a sunny spot she liked, coincidentally where all of us were facing. First she slipped her flipflops off, then rolled her t-shirt up real high so that the sun would hit her stomach. As she lifts her right leg up and crooks it to the side, that bruisey crease peeks through the frayed end of her cutoffs at us. Swab lets out a groan.

"Catch that?" Zorro asks.

"Why's she always trying to prove what a slut she is? I mean, we get it."

"Lady's got a right to be comfortable, don't she?"

"You know I walked into the lunchroom, other day, right as she's taking a big bite out of something."

"What was it?"

"Cheesesteak, I think. This was Friday. So I say, can't you say hello? She says, I got food in my mouth. So I say, something different for a change!"

Zorro giggles. "What she do, she deck ya?"

"Nah. Half choked from laughing. She took my meaning."

Rainy rolls over on her stomach now and scoots her t-shirt even higher. Skin's the color of an overripe banana. Torso's dotted everywhere with moles. Hair's bleach blonde. She stretches her arms and wriggles through a yawn.

She knows what she's doing.

Crutch starts to mumble in my ear how things went when Lorraine was living in his building. Nude strolls around the halls. Late-night parties with however many men fit in her room. Rivalries developed. Two suckers actually believed she was their girl exclusively. Both were supplying her with wine and cigarettes. All this largesse ceased soon as sucker number one recognized her moaning in the second sucker's room at 4 AM. Big brawl broke out. Half the floor got 3-0-2'd. That's why Warden moved her to my building.

"She got a daughter too," Crutch adds, five minutes later.

"Who does?"

"Lorraine there. Teenage. She came to visit round Christmas. Ain't like her mother though."

"How's that?"

"She acted grown, for one. Lorraine just went on talking and talking, showing off like, introducing her around to all the men. Daughter didn't say a whole lot."

"Here comes your mascot, Dick," says Franklin.

I have no idea what he means until I spot the station wagon pulling in the parking lot. Colleen picked Gums up by herself just a few hours ago. Ken must be working. Birthday was Thursday. Last week, I gave him twenty extra bucks on top of money for these velcro shoes I'm wearing, plus new socks.

Gums don't seem happy over there. I bet he expected dinner, maybe spend the night on the old sofa. Colleen meets him in front of the car. He keeps gesturing towards the Island. She keeps glancing at the backseat. Engine's idling. There's a small box under his left arm. Abruptly she initiates a hug so she can go. He waves a bunch of times while Colleen backs out and drives away.

Everybody's eyes are on the cardboard box when Gums steps on the Island.

"Hiya, Jack."

"Hi."

"Go home today?"

"Yeah."

"How's Colleen?"

"Fine."

"What's in the box?" Swab wants to know.

Gums unfolds the flaps and tilts the box for him: tapioca bottles, butterscotch krimpets, lollipops, and an assortment bag of saltwater taffy.

Sal honks his nose and spits over his shoulder. "What's it, your birthday or something, kid?"

"Thursday was."

"No shit? Happy birthday! Three days late."

"Happy birthday."

"Yeah, happy birthday! Gonna share?"

Without a word, Gums surrenders the saltwater taffy. Swab helps himself first, then hands the bag to Zorro. Rainy's coming over. When Crutch hands me the bag, I hold it out to Rainy, gesturing for help untwisting one.

"What'd they go down the Shore?" Sal asks.

"This shit pulls my teeth out."

"How bout yellow?"

"What's yellow?"

"Banana."

"Gimme a striped one then."

"Last week. Ken's mom rents a place in Wildwood every year. They like April cuz it's not as crowded."

Rainy helps herself to a pink one then returns the bag to Gums. We're all making sucking noises.

"Was that your girlfriend?" Rainy asks.

Gums snickers. "Nah, my sister. I wanted her to bring the baby over for you guys to see. He's much bigger."

Rainy nods. "It's the same with my daughter," she says.

"What's the same?"

"You know," she says.

■□■

At dinner later, Rainy ends up in Swab's usual seat. Everyone moves over to accommodate her. Mug she's holding has one of those bearded monkeys swinging from a vine with *America's First Zoo* printed across the top. She rubs a circle on my back and sips her wine.

Tonight's Salisbury steak with some reheated string beans and the potato skins off last night's mashed potatoes. Top's so burnt, my plastic knife can't even dent the steak. I put the knife down and try jabbing at it with the fork instead. All that does is turn the whole thing into mush.

"That's a sin," Rainy says, soon as she notices me struggling. "Gimme that."

She confiscates my knife and fork and cuts the meat up into manageable bites. When I thank her, she flashes two rows of rotting teeth at me. It's no fun having your food cut up for you like you're some kid. She must have sensed this because she rubs another circle on my back a moment later.

Between sips, she's glancing quizzically at all the chewing faces. Nobody returns her gaze. None of them seem to like her. I don't understand it. She may smell like a French whore and act like a French whore, but at least you can kid around with her. You can't deny she's added some vitality into our building.

"Like a funeral parlor in here," she announces to break up the dismal silence.

"Indeed."

"Another friendly evening among strangers."

"Yep."

"How's your...whatever that is, Dick? Wait, do you prefer Dick or Richard?"

"I prefer Dick."

"So do I!"

"So I've heard."

This earns a medium guffaw.

She looks at Sal next. "How do, Sal? Did I steal your seat?"

"Lousy," he wheezes at her from the other table.

"Lousy? How come?"

"Allergies. Gotta have my lungs heard in a couple days."

"How do, Paul?"

"My shit ain't had a tip on it in months. But other than that—"

"Glad I asked. How do, Peg?"

"So-so. Supposedly I have a goiter."

"I don't see one. Dick, you see any goiter? She looks gorgeous to me."

This forces Peg to smile. "What about you, Lorraine, you well?"

"Who, me? I'm diamonds. Got my mammos done last week. Everything came back good. You got yourself a boyfriend in here yet?"

"Not in here."

"That's alright. They all run around anyway."

"Mine can't run. He's six feet under."

"There you go."

While those two go on complaining about their former husbands—one deceased, one across town—Marvin is busy gathering the empty milk crates from the previous week. He has to set them on the curb each Sunday night for the delivery guy to pick up in the morning. Collectively we burn through seven of them crates per week.

Corner of my eye, I see him raise the stack of empties, swinging them around at the same instant Rainy rocks back in her chair. There's a solid thud from crate on skull. Top one crashes to the floor and skids exactly halfway underneath the table. Rainy grimaces, palming the back of her head.

"Owwwww! Why don't you knock my fucking head off next time!"

"Try remaining in your theat," he tells her, setting the stack down on the floor. He has to crawl under the table until all that I can see of him is the grooved bottoms of his sneakers.

"Alright, I'll remain in my *theat*," she replies, waddling her hips to amuse the rest of us, "if you *inthist*."

"Fuck you, Lorraine."

"Take it easy, faggot. I'm just pulling your teensy little chain."

"FAGGOT?" He's still scooting backwards with the crate. From his knees, he tells her, "You're the no-good hooah here. Not me."

Rainy snorts. "The no-good what?"

"You heard me. The no-good hooah."

"What's he trying to call me?"

Marvin is trembling with rage when he stands up. His whole face contorts itself in preparation. What comes out of him sounds like some elaborate birdcall.

"A HOOAH! Thath what I called you. A HOOAH!"

"You ain't even got a dick, do you?"

"Everyone here knowth what you do for thigarettes, Lorraine."

"Oh yeah? And what do you do for em?"

His face has gone completely red. I'm struggling to hold my laughter in while everybody else is laughing openly at him as he storms out with all the crates. Front door slams.

Once the laughter's finally died down a little, Rainy proclaims, "That faggot don't speak proper English. If you're gonna call someone a whore, say it right at least."

■ □ ■

By 7:00, things have settled down. I'm in the rec room next to Marvin. Don't get me wrong. He's still stewing over Rainy calling him a faggot. I can't ever remember seeing him this furious, not even that time Swab hit him with the meatloaf. My fellow inmates love these opportunities to gang up on our night nurse. They heckled him straight out the door, but he showed them. Revenge was no dessert.

"Next," he says, eyes on the TV. *Jeopardy* is on. Some prep school teacher from Nebraska's in the lead. Travel agent from Louisiana's gaining on her.

I lift Zorro's page and curl it over the three binder loops, revealing Gums.

"Porter," I say.

"Whath with him lately?"

They got in an argument as well. Because Gums has gotten in the habit of sleeping in all day, he keeps showing up to dinner in the mood for breakfast. Yesterday he demanded oatmeal during dinner then grumbled out the door with his request refused. Skipping medication is a major issue with him too.

"Flu-ox-e-tine."

"How many?"

"Two."

Marvin shakes them in the Dixie cup marked *J.P.*, then aims his mouth towards the door and screams.

"JACK! GET IN HERE!"

"Quiet!" snaps Creep, "Can't you see I'm concentrating over here? Queen a8. The bad man hurt me."

"Jack stays out skating half the night," I inform Marvin, "Any idea where he goes?"

He shrugs. "GET IN HERE NOW OR NO COOKIETH!"

"Quiet!"

"This place oughta have a curfew."

"I can't hold him down and make him take theeth."

"He's gonna get in trouble one of these days. Imagine him in jail."

"He'd be popular," says Swab, "No teeth!"

Zorro starts to giggle right behind us.

"That's true. He'd have to beat them off with a stick. I never had that problem. Always had protection down at Graterford. Those jailbirds knew I was in with very serious people."

"Next."

I flip the page. Lorraine Reynolds. DOB: 5/22/53. Admit: 12/30/93. What's that make? Twenty months. Room 206. Warden moved Gums downstairs last week and let her have his room upstairs because the Convent's full, so that was closest they could put her to the ladies toilet. For an emergency contact, she began to write the letter T or P, then scratched it out and wrote *Amy Reynolds* in its place.

"Whoth next?"

"Your favorite. Flu-co-na-zole. Two."

"LORRAINE! Come get your penithillin!"

We hear her laughter from the canteen. As she's stepping through the doorway, suddenly she sticks two fingers in her mouth to whistle at somebody down the hall.

"Who's the nudist?" she asks, pointing behind her.

"That's my neighbor."

"We need to buy your neighbor a towel."

"I agree. Let's take up a collection."

Zorro leans over the sofa to give her one of his drawn-out winks.

"What is that?"

"What is what?"

"You look like you're trying to bite your own ear off."

"Come back here, buttercup!" he yells as she turns to go.

"Buttercup?"

"Yeah, bring that buttermilk over here."

By the vending machines, she slides a dollar from her pocket and flattens it across her thigh. There's a whirring sound. Her bare foot's tapping on the carpet. She presses a button. A candy bar lands in the dispenser. Zorro tiptoes up behind her, shirtless in black jeans. When she turns around, he pretends to be counting all the change in his palm. She aims the Mars bar Zorro likely paid for in his face.

"Reach for the sky!"

His hands shoot up into a stickup pose, spilling a bunch of dimes and nickels on the carpet. With his hip, he tries to corner her against the machine, but she just shoulders her way through him.

"Bye bye, buttercup," he calls out, bending down to pick up all the coins, "Let me know when you make up your mind. What mind you have!" Returning to the sofa, he addresses all of us in a pensive sort of voice. "Most girls here in the afterlife either love me or eternally hate me. I've spent more money on that cunt than anyone else has, fucking every day this week, and she gives me…you know what she gives me? Two lousy dates, a pair of blue balls, and I'll see you around after you get beat up, and your forehead's caked in blood."

"Careful," cautions Swab, "She'll have you writing bad checks before you know it."

Creep bursts out laughing. "Checks! What's he gonna sign them with, crayons?"

"You gotta keep em third, Don."

"Keep what third?"

"Broads."

"What's first and second?"

"First is work. Second's friends. Broads come third."

"That's sound advice," I say, "Wish somebody told me that forty years ago."

"Bet they did," Swab tells me.

Soon as *Jeopardy* ends, we put the game on. Strike ended last week. We're playing the Braves. Greenie's command looks good. We go up 6-0 in the fourth. We win. I stand up quietly. Swab's snoring with his arms folded over his Dokken t-shirt.

Before I've reached my room, I know that Zorro won't be heeding Swab's advice. I can hear him trying to impress Rainy in there.

"That's for my street gang. Matter of fact, you know what it started as? It started as a softball team. That's the truth. We had this softball team called the Quakers, and one of the guys, this guy named Rick, Rick said hey, this is a real neat jacket. How bout we make a gang?"

Coast looks clear behind me. I rearrange my twisted sweatpants and lean back against the wall to eavesdrop on these lovebirds for a minute.

"We had this book where all the new members put their worst secrets. Say you're madly in love with your grandmother or something. You write that in there, and nobody can use it against ya."

"Bet yours was sick."

"You did time though, you were out. That was ironclad. I got my jacket off a guy in Graterford, day he got pinched. Not that the laws ever made any sense. They'd give you the electric chair in Wyoming, but you'd win the Medal of Honor in Vermont."

"How long you had this room, handsome?"

"Nine years, buttercup. Next year, I'll be a ten-year dealer."

"Robin know about all this?"

"About what?"

"About what? About the walls!"

Zorro giggles. "Octavia finked on me. They'll never move me now. None of these people realize I'm in with very dangerous—"

Rainy shushes him. He tries to say something else, but she shushes him a second time, a third, a fourth, until it takes. Next thing, I hear a metal object, probably the buckle on his belt, land on the floor. Next sound's a chair shoved out of someone's way. Zorro emits a rather high-pitched moan.

"Why don't you take your bra off?" he suggests, but Rainy scoffs.

"What are we gonna make a project out of this?"

■□■

It sounds like Gums has finally had his breakdown. Padres game is in the fifth, Mulholland's on the mound, when we hear howling down the hall, followed by something being smashed to pieces. Marvin rushes to investigate. I trail behind. Assuming it's him, this has been building up for months. Winter was rough on Jack. The obligatory Christmas Eve away from here. That's it. I hoped that spring would kinda sort him out somehow, but his depression's only gotten worse. Habits aren't helping any. Besides all the late-night roaming, he's begun to bum off everyone except for me.

Marvin's still banging on his door when I catch up. He ducks around me and sprints down the hall to call the ambulance as if he's scared that Gums might take a shot at hara-kiri on his watch. Zorro's observing from his doorway, smoking, unperturbed. Soon as I yell Jack's name, the smashing stops. Five seconds later, he unlocks the door but makes me turn the knob myself.

Room's in shambles. Bottles smashed. Ken and Colleen's yearly Sears portrait has been ripped in tiny pieces. He cracked the front wheels off his skateboard beating on the dresser. Wrists aren't cut. I talk him into sitting down in bed. I put my arm around his shoulder. Kid sobs on and off until we notice sounds of walkie-talkies in the hallway. Cops. Crisis Center. He seems relieved. Seventy-two hours. Who knows? Maybe a 3-0-2 is what he needs. Everybody swears the food is better.

■□■

Canteen's been quieter this week. Many are missing meals. Ten eaters tops. Unattended plates of food all go to waste. Straight in the can.

Friday, the chairs on either side of me are vacant for the third night in a row. Gums should return tomorrow from his 3-0-2. Where's Rainy though? I've been so preoccupied with him, it didn't dawn on me I haven't seen her in a week.

Climbing the stairs two hours later, I decide to detour past her door. I knock. No answer. I search around the rim for any light, none, so I continue on to Thinker's room. A giant textbook's open on his chest with colored diagrams and charts.

"Yo Har, you seen Lorraine around?"

He chuckles with surprise it's me who's asking.

"Day or two ago, why?"

"No reason. Ain't seen her's all."

"Try Paul's room. She was coming out of there the other night."

Swab's door is shut. I don't hear them going at it in there. Across the hall, Sal's seated sideways on his bed, staring intently at the fingernails on his right hand.

"Yo, Sal."

"Yo."

"Where's Paul?"

"He went to buy some beer. Hey, Rich, I hate to ask again, but you got a quarter?"

"No."

Back on the rec room sofa, I inquire whether Rainy happened to get 3-0-2'd or relocated to another building. Marvin's head shakes very slowly.

"Do I theem that lucky?"

"You don't."

It's almost 10:00. Phils are still on this road trip out in California. Portugal is warming for the Giants.

"When's Jack get back?"

"He duthint, Dick."

I feel my windpipe tighten. He don't sound upset enough for what I'm picturing.

"What do you mean? It's been three days."

"His mother called."

"You mean his sister?"

"Geth tho. They're gonna try a mental ward. I cleaned the room out already."

"Jesus Christ."

First inning's scoreless. Schill gives up two runs in the second. We get one back the next inning. Entire fourth, Marvin complains about one of the other nurses, Keisha, only one on second shift who owns a car. He knows for a fact she gives Dee a ride each night. Dee only lives a couple blocks from him in Aston. Yet when he asked Keisha for a ride last week, she pretended he lived way out of her way.

Quarter to midnight, he starts going through his checklist. Nurse's closet's locked. Cabinets locked. Fridge is locked. Burners: off, off, off, off. He waves in at me before he goes.

"Good night, Dick."

"Night."

Poor guy's got an hour walk ahead of him. It's past my bedtime by this point. Game is tied though. I stay put for two more innings. Middle of the eighth, Swab wanders in.

"Still tied," I tell him, "2-2."

He nods. We watch Schill hold them through the eighth. Top of the ninth, Stocker reaches on an error. Ready bunts him over, but then Morandini strikes out swinging, and Jeffries grounds out next to end the inning. In the bottom half, Fregosi sticks this kid named Harris in to pitch. He strikes out the first batter then gives up a walk-off bomb to left. Swab chuckles. I'm already standing by the time Scarsone's rounding third. Swab sets his legs where I was sitting, shuts his eyes.

■□■

As I'm bending at my door, aiming my key into the lock, I hear this single shriek from inside Zorro's room which could've come from Rainy. I unvelcro my shoes, lie back in bed. I stare at the corkboard overhead. Mind keeps alternating between Gums and Rainy. Neither one's improving.

This is no place to get your act together.

That's Rainy down the hall alright. She's screaming obscenities at Zorro now. He slams his door. Next thing, I hear these sluggish footsteps. They slow down to a halt. Three knocks.

"Open up, Popsicle!"

Her words are slurred, but there's this tremor in her voice as well as if she's equal parts upset and plastered. She knocks one more time.

"Poppppppsicle. Open up."

"It's unlocked."

"What'd you say?"

"Come in."

Light's off. Hallway's dark as well, so I don't realize right away that she's completely nude. She shuts the door behind her and bumps back against it harder than intended. Jeans are balled up in her hand. Bra's knotted around her wrist. Because I'm lying down, her pelvis is at eye level with me. Hip bones stick out sharply. Pubic area reminds me of a steer head after all the skin's been boiled off. No hair.

"How come you're naked, Rainy?"

Her head turns towards the dresser. That's when I notice how swollen her lip is on one side.

"Donald kicked me out, that asshole. You'd think if you suck somebody's cock they'd let you stick around long enough to dress."

"You would."

"We got in an argument."

"Over Paul?"

She slides her right foot up the door and glances at her chest. "My tits shrank since I moved here." She drops her clothes and squeezes them. "What do you think?"

"Could be the cooking. Marv boils all the vitamins out of everything."

She laughs somehow. "Popsicle, I'm thirsty," she says, "You got any alcohol?"

"Nope."

"C'mon! Let's have a little drinkie-poo together."

"Nothing but cloudy apple juice in here." I point at my pisscup on the nightstand.

"C'mon! Break out the booze. I know you're hiding some."

"I haven't had a drop in...fourteen years, eight months, matter of fact."

"Matter of fact," she repeats, "Matter of fact, I don't believe you. Matter of fact, I'm gonna find your stash."

Tipsily she checks around my room: nightstand, all five dresser drawers, four of which I've never opened, far side of the bed. Harder she searches, the sorrier I feel for her. She squats down on the floor to feel under the mattress last. Convinced there's nothing in here finally, she rocks back on her ass, gripping my shin for balance. Now she starts rubbing it. Wonder what the going rate is nowadays. A pack? Couple dollars? Way everybody's benefits keep going down, I bet I could be stingier than that. She trusts me. Bet she'd take an IOU.

"Know who you remind me of?" I ask to snap her out of it, "My second wife."

"How many were there?" Voice is muffled, way her face is smushed into her forearm.

"We had to separate. I was determined to lay off the sauce. She was not. Plain as that. I couldn't risk being around her anymore. We had a little girl."

"Now you sound like Tom."

"Is Tom your husband?"

"Everybody sounds like Tom."

"What's your daughter's name?"

"Amy."

"How old?"

"Nineteen."

"I got two daughters. Four boys that I know of. First go-around, I wasn't ready to be married. All I wanted back then was to have a ball."

She rubs me on the shin again. She don't want to listen either. Since I clearly have no drinkie-poo, she leaves.

I don't realize until morning she forgot her clothes.

■□■

Following day, she ain't around.

Early Sunday, I'm walking the sidewalks at 6:30 in the morning when I spot her sitting by herself on my bench. In front of her, two members of the Dawn Patrol are working their respective sectors of the yard. Air's thick with fog. Rainy's so focused on the driveway, she don't notice me until I'm pulling up beside her.

"Hiya, Popsicle," she mumbles like she hasn't slept all night.

"Morning. Whatchoo doing up at this fine hour?"

"Friend of mine went to get thirty dollars from a drawer. He had to walk all the way to Eddystone though to get it."

"Is it his drawer?"

She checks the parking lot again. "Nobody gets busted in Eddystone. Not sure what takes all fucking night though."

Two days has turned the bruise on her left cheek a nasty purple. Lip's gone down a little.

"Got a spare ciggie, Popsicle?"

"You know I don't smoke. Better frisk me to make sure though."

That gets her good. She snorts so loudly all four members of the Dawn Patrol glance over at us. She even looks my filthy sweatpants up and down, pretending to consider it, then digs into a pocket for her emergency cigarette which she slides in the main gap in her front teeth, letting it seesaw there a second while her fingers fish the lighter from her other pocket.

"Makes me smoke my last one," she sighs, tisking at me once she gets it lit, "Some gentleman."

Her bottom lip has shrimp lines on it.

For five minutes, we're observing these four scavengers in front of us. New guy's system seems more sanitary than the others. What he's doing, rather than smoking the winners on his knees, is pinching any leftover tobacco from each butt into this long-necked pipe for later. Think I'll call him Sherlock. Rest are biting all the filters off the butts and spitting them away in order to receive a stronger kick.

Rainy squeezes my right leg above the knee.

"Can you believe these pigs?"

"Nope."

"How long you lived here, Popsicle?"

"Almost two years."

"Wow."

"Feels like ten already."

"Uhuh. You probably don't know John?" She points over at D.

"How's he look?"

"I don't know. He's okay looking."

"Never met the man."

She runs two figure-eights along my thigh with her ring finger, mulling something. Now she stands up and says, "Tell John I'm in Mark's room, okay? No, Matt's room. If he comes."

"Okay."

I watch her walk back to her old building. As she yanks on the front door, a phonebook that was wedged in there flops down onto the stoop. She picks it up and sets it back real carefully for the next person.

■□■

Yard's been meaner lately. Crutch agrees with me on this. The frequency of bumming remains constant, sixty to seventy requests per day. What's changed is this new nasty edge in people's voices after we refuse them. I attribute it to that tobacco tax which Congress passed last month. You should've seen them Friday after. We had a full palace revolt on our hands the second word got round Warden went and upped the price of packs by forty cents. That started the weekly chain in motion even faster. Now these lintheads are all broke by Monday instead of Tuesday. Ends of each week, there are too many fights to count.

Yesterday we watched this veiny hag in a pink nightgown rub her ciggie out on some guy's forearm. He gave her a bloody lip in turn. Both marched straight up to the nearest nurse. They tried to turn each other in at the same time, which sort of cancelled both infractions, like in football.

Earlier today, we saw some guy in a Miami Dolphins jacket with no shirt on underneath sneak up to Popeye and cold-cock him in the jaw so hard he rolled right off his bench.

"I told you I'd get even," Dolphin said, still looming over him.

Popeye's back on that bench, keeping his jaw limber by recounting to his two companions, Dollar Bill and Penguin, all the details of this altercation. Recently Bill took Cy's place in the Trio after Cy departed for jail. These three roam in and out of all four buildings all day long, testing doorknobs, snatching anything that ain't nailed down.

Today's their Auction Day. Any items either found, stolen, or gifted to them by their relatives get resold for cash or bartered for one of our other forms of currency. So far this summer, I have seen them hock the following: one dead father's watch, a stack of magazines addressed to a local dentist, two leather belts, one wide paisley tie, one Tupperware container's worth of homemade brownies, some religious trinket Dollar Bill discovered lurking by the schoolyard up the road. I bought a popcorn tin off them myself to use as my spittoon at night.

Cunningly they hold their auctions on Saturdays because the trial isn't on, and people still have some of their allowance left. In a normal auction, the auctioneer presents some item, and the bidders will outbid each other until all but one get bored. Process here works in reverse. Popeye and Penguin stand right in the middle of the Island, turning in a circle with whatever is for sale. Dollar Bill bids downward with himself until somebody buys the item, or he reaches zero.

Chief prize this week is a maroon leather jacket they found sticking out the overnight donations box at the Salvation Army. It's three-quarter length and belted with the same maroon material.

Thin Man shakes his head at them.

Zorro gives them the finger.

Creep too.

Sal and Swab ignore them altogether.

When they hold the jacket up to Crutch, he asks how much.

"Twenty dollars."

"Twenty dollars!"

"It's leather."

Crutch shakes his head.

"Fifteen?"

"Too steep for my blood."

"Ten?"

"Fuck I need a leather jacket for? Gonna be ninety out here soon."

"How about five? Think ahead, Dwayne."

"Go away."

"A pack?"

"Get lost, peckerwood."

They leave. I watch them gesticulate their way across the parking lot, concocting some new scam before they disappear into the shortcut up to town.

I say to Crutch, "This place is ruled by cigarettes, coffee, and soda."

"That's a fact."

"You ever wonder what would happen if they closed down all these places all at once? Guess I'd end up at some old folks home. Where would they stick the rest of these cake eaters?"

"I heard there's a couple thousand of these places."

"Where?"

"Cross the country."

"I mean where you'd hear that."

"Oh. VA."

"They find this place for you?"

"Sure did."

"Figures."

We've been swapping army stories lately. I found out he did a tour in Vietnam. Crutch always wears this tan weightlifting glove on his right hand. It's taken me two years to get the nerve to ask about his burn marks. Other day, to earn the right, I shared how I got shot over in Korea. Nearly lost the leg. Lifelong limp. I told him how two guys had to drag me through the snow four miles to the nearest aid station. By morning, we were all lined up in rows. Doc informed me I'd have bled to death if it hadn't been so cold that night.

When Crutch didn't reciprocate, I gestured at his glove and asked straight out how he got burnt. It turns out it wasn't combat. Simple grease fire. He was an army cook. He smelled some smoke. Second he opened the door, there was an explosion. Injuries were mostly to the upper portion of his body: face, chest, and back. There was also damage to the nerves in his right hand. He takes Skelaxin, same as me.

Three Bags must be somewhere nearby because I can hear Elvis singing. Thinker must be in his camping chair behind us. Pigeons are bobbing across the grass. I notice several heading for the parking lot. More of them start gliding from the gutters to join them. There's a lone seagull over there. All the pigeons are surrounding him. Every time he takes a step in one direction, they move with him.

"Look at that seagull," I say. "What the hell's he doing here?"

"Lost."

"What's it, a hundred miles to the Shore?"

The seagull tilts his head back and shrieks upwards for a solid minute. I get this sense the pigeons are about to peck him into bloody pieces when this cracking sound startles them. Soon as the sound repeats, the birds all scatter.

"What was that?"

Crutch points over by the dumpster. Rainy's standing there with Franklin, of all people. He's crouched with both hands gripping his hips. Spectacles are off. Eyes are closed. With her left hand, she slaps him right across the face. He nods approvingly. Number four is hard enough to frighten all remaining pigeons off the gutters. He groans more approval at her. She gives him another three, then flaps her hand a bunch of times as if the last one really stung.

Satisfied, Franklin reaches in his vest pocket and hands Rainy four cigarettes, looks like. He immediately rushes down the sidewalk straight into his building, we presume, to flog his dummy.

CHAPTER 8: YOUR CLASSIC BOG LADY

Ordinarily, it don't mean anything when a bathtub overflows. Somebody turns the water on, goes off to do some chore, and just forgets to shut the tap in time. You lay down towels. A tub running over with somebody in it, however, somebody wide awake and singing their own made-up church hymns, is less ordinary. That's what's happening upstairs as we're force-feeding ourselves likely chicken, Tuesday night. Unbeknownst to any of us, water has been gradually pooling in the hallway carpet of the third floor, even seeping through the ceiling panels of the second, while we swallow as much of this grayish mass as we can stomach.

Silently we file out a minute later and split off into the usual two lines, one headed for the stairs, the other for the rec room. I'm opening the binder on my lap, ready to call out medications during *Jeopardy*, when Lolly lets this scream out somewhere, freezing everyone in place. The seven of us glance around at one another. Nobody laughs. Nobody smirks. Not even Creep. We're too afraid somebody died.

Everybody follows Marvin out the door to see what happened. I stay back in case they need to cart a body down the stairs.

For five full minutes, all I hear is stomping feet and lots of shouting overhead. While I'm waiting, I flip to the page for our new inmate, woman I call Rosary Beads, figuring whatever's going on must have to do with her since she was the only person not at dinner. Agnes Pierce, DOB: 8/15/52, Admit:

4/6/95, Rxs: Lithium 100 mgs (3x daily). Contact line lists a Teresa Pierce-Wilson with a New York City area code.

Day prior, we swapped her for Gail in one of those prisoner exchanges which occur every few months. I happened to be on my bench with Crutch and Franklin when the move took place. Rosary stepped out of A, dragging a large black garbage bag behind her. She must've scraped it too hard coming down the stoop because the bag burst open, stringing her belongings in an even trail behind her. She kept right on going. No one said a word. Marvin held the door for her. Once she was in her room, he went and gathered all her braziers and panties plus a ream or two of crumpled papers off the grass.

I've been watching the ceiling listening for nearly ten minutes when Thinker enters. He reports how Marvin pulled some pinkish wrinkled woman from the tub in nothing but a pair of wooden rosary beads, how she kept singing as he marched her down the hall through two parting rows of onlookers, and there's an inch of water everywhere including Peg and Mimi's rooms, therefore all towels are being commandeered, all fans. He unplugs the box fan by the sofa and carries it away.

I need to see this for myself.

Draping my towel over my shoulder, I start climbing the back stairs.

At the landing to the second floor, I notice Thinker squatting in his doorway, aiming the box fan where its breeze will hit the affected part of his ceiling. I hear Creep doing the same in his room.

Dirty streams are trickling past my shoes as I ascend the final flight. Up top, Peg is brooming excess water off the side.

"There's no telling in this place," she says, yanking the broom back when she sees me coming, "There's just no telling!"

"Sure ain't."

Soon as I step around her, I'm glad I made the trip. Every other woman in the Convent's marching in place along the hall on every towel and piece of laundry they could find. Two fans are oscillating back and forth. I push the bathroom door inward with my cane. The plain brown cotton dress which Rosary had on yesterday is balled up on the toilet seat. There's twigs and leaves and muddy footprints on the tile. Tub resembles a bowl of chocolate milk. Marvin steps out of Gail's old room and slams the door behind him. A wet shape's imprinted on his apron. He mutters something I can't hear over the fans.

■□■

Next day feels tense awaiting dinner. It took over four hours last night to dry out the Convent and replace the carpeting. Mimi got the worst of it. Her biographies of Hedy Lamarr and Grace Kelly got ruined along with several of her magazines. Luckily all of her VHS tapes survived.

Every few minutes, Marvin jams his face inside the blurry porthole to make sure Rosary is staying where he ordered her to sit. She's cross-legged on the floor under our one-handed clock in that brown dress lumped by the tub last night, oblivious to all the dirty looks coming from Peg and Lolly.

Rosary's as fidgety as Zorro. She keeps running her nails through her black knotty hair. Eyebrows flinch at random. Upper lip is always quivering. I've seen eight-year-olds with lice sit stiller. One instant, she's grinning at the wall across from her as though her favorite cartoon's playing on it.

Suddenly her head flops back to gaze up at the ceiling. Grin disappears. A look of terror replaces it. She shakes that off and runs her palms in circles on her face, groaning loudly, couple dozen times.

Door finally opens. The herd charges in to see what sad excuse for sustenance there is tonight. Marvin's handing out the drinks.

"Agneth!" he calls when he notices her going for my seat.

"Yes?"

"Plenty of room over there, Agneth."

"Over where?"

"Over *there.*"

He points at three empty chairs beside the windows.

"But I already have a seat," she replies cheerfully.

This means I have to squeeze in next to Thinker on the other side. Some type of soggy green-bean casserole is oozing outwards on all plates. I ingest four quick spoonfuls, then push the plate away to observe Rosary. She seems wholly unaware that there is food in front of her which she's supposed to eat. Elbows are resting on the table. Cleavage is whiter than a roll of butcher paper.

She clasps her hands together, and her lips start moving very fast.

"Hail Mary, Lord is with thee, blessed art thou among women, blessed is the fruit of thy womb, Jesus, Holy Mary, mother of God, pray for us sinners, now and at the time of our death...Hail Mary, full of grace, Lord is with thee, blessed art thou among—"

"Whatcha praying for?" asks Swab.

"Blessed is the fruit of thy—"

"I said whatcha praying for? Can't be Lent again already."

Her eyes dart over to him. Those wooden beads are wrapped so tight, red pressure lines are showing on her wrist.

"I'm praying for Mary to come back."

"Mary who?"

"Mary who? *Marrrrrrrrry.*"

"She means Jesus, Joseph, and Mary, don't she?"

"Sure does."

"She visited me here last night."

"No shit? Where?"

"Here. This room. After all of you had gone to sleep. She waited. Then she was right there. *Therrrrrrrrre!*" She points at the wall above the trashcans. "Her robe was so long and white. She had a blue cardigan over her shoulders with a sash. It wrapped around her twice, the sash. The clouds were floating on the wall behind her. Her hands shone. Gold. They were formed in prayer, like this. Her feet shone too."

"Well, that answers that."

"What a blinding gold!"

Entire canteen's eavesdropping by now. Thinker lowers his book, intrigued. Sal is smiling fondly at her, as one Catholic to another. None of the women can believe they have to share a bathroom with such a bona fide lunatic. It's clear Marvin regrets he ever traded her for Gail.

"What'd she say?" asks Swab.

A plump blue vein is bulging through the middle of her forehead.

"She must've said something. What she say?"

Rosary's breathing heavily. Her voice remains low but vehement when she finally answers. "Mary told me be a generator running on my own electricity. She told me know all my own powers. All cosmic powers. All psychic powers. She told me my womb's a solar system deep inside my body, a bright red sun with ten planets circling around it. She told me I must protect all the planets. That's why they put my womb in a glass case, to protect it."

"That whatcha praying for? Protection?"

"Yes."

Swab has been fighting off a chuckle this whole time. He says, "I'll help you pray for that. Show me how," then balls two fists together. "Like this?"

Her head jerks back and forth as if a fly were buzzing near her eyes.

"Not like that. Like this. *Thissssssssss!*"

She clamps her hands together so the fingertips line up perfectly, elevates her chin a little.

Swab imitates her posture.

Now they go through the "Hail Mary" line by line. Once she's convinced he's got the whole prayer memorized, they utter it again in unison. Even though he's obviously mocking her, and everybody else is grinning at both tables, Rosary seems unoffended. She smiles graciously as though she knows some bigger joke's on us.

■□■

Nearly a month goes by without a major incident. I maintain my routine: laps, bench, in for meals, back outside. Temperature stays up around the nineties all July. Drawback is I have to break my laps up into halves or even quarters. Benefit is I am mostly left in peace.

By 2:00 each day, I need to spin my Eagles cap around to keep my neck from frying. Sun's been burning the whole yard for four weeks straight. Ones on the lawn retreat their chairs ten feet an hour to escape it. Since I lack that luxury, I've started alternating sides. All day, I rotate with the shade until I end up on those empty benches by the parking lot.

One of these afternoons, I feel somebody lurking over my left shoulder, man I've never seen before, standing a few feet inside the shortcut, sort of taking in the yard suspiciously.

To try to flush him out, I wave like some old friendly idiot, and he steps forward far enough to nod politely at me. Total stranger. Doubt he rooms with us officially. Places like ours will draw these transient types sometimes, your full-fledged homeless guys who know how to befriend somebody in order to hole up in their room for a few days or weeks, however long it takes one of the nurses to catch them coming from the showers.

When I glance back again, he's gone. I figure I must've spooked him until he resurfaces a minute later, backpack slung over his shoulder, a funny little guitar made from an old cigar box in his hand. He gestures with his goatee, asking permission to sit down.

"Be my guest," I tell him.

He tucks his backpack underneath the bench and lays that narrow guitar across his lap. Looks like he's pushing fifty. Goatee's pecan-colored. Skin is sunburnt anywhere his tank top doesn't cover and coated in this sweaty grime like he hoofed it some great distance to get here.

Inside of two minutes, I know his full name is Lucas J. Brogden, plus I know his date of birth, social security number, mother's maiden name, and five last permanent addresses, because that's the way he chooses to introduce himself soon as I've finished saying, "Call me Dick."

"If that's my most *personal* information," he reflects in a lightly Southern drawl, "well, I'm already butt-shut and gone then, ain't I, brother?"

"Guess so. What's the J stand for?"

"Jefferson. After Davis, not Thomas. My mother's from Kentucky."

Brog's many permanent abodes have been scattered all across the country: Laredo, Texas; Mobile, Alabama; Phillipsburg, Montana; Berkeley, California. First town he mentioned was in West Virginia, so I figure he must hail from there. I want to ask if he's been sleeping in the trees behind us, but I'm worried that might count as personal information.

Brog lifts his guitar and begins plucking the four strings, a little aimlessly at first. Gradually his fingers slip into a melody I recognize. Man has a pleasant voice. I stay with him another half an hour while he plays through every worship song he knows. Wherever one's supposed to mention Jesus, he keeps substituting Nixon.

■□■

All of August, I continue alternating sides like that. Between my laps, I rest with Crutch and Franklin on the Island. Soon as the sun is in our eyes, I flee over to the parking lot and stay put until the yard empties for dinner. Within a few minutes, Brog always emerges from the trees like he was waiting for me. Together we observe the usual goings-on: the Trio bumming bench to bench, Roadrunner zipping down the sidewalks, Three Bags struggling to inch his heavy walker through the grass, Rainy rotating on her towel at even intervals like some pig on a spit.

Thursday near 3:00, the two of us hear glass breaking to our left. Second floor of A, somebody's fist bursts through their window screen. Several objects follow. First a pillow sails down to the hedges. Next some clothing. Box of crackers. Big shampoo bottle. Other personal effects. Last thing the culprit does is try to jam their mattress through the window.

Whoever it is up there keeps yelling, "Born to die!"

Everyone outside is laughing at this circus act. Brog snickers too, as though this confirms some thought he'd just been having.

"What?"

"Man, you already know. Look at this here. There are people dwelling in insanity inside their homes. They're caught up in not getting along with their folks. Then they venture out in this fucking society," he practically spits, flinging the back of his hand at the whole yard, "and under stress, survivability, and so forth, there's no time for anything else. Tell me you get the picture."

"Oh, I get the picture."

"You're full of shit if you think Russia's the collapsed system. We're the collapsed system. Russia's like a crocodile lying in the water, and you say he won't bite. Touch that motherfucker. He'll rip your fucking hand off. Economy moves so damn fast, people can distort the emotional end to the money end. Then they scapegoat you like you're a little dot on a piece of paper. Their shit and their thing. It's tantamount to murder under how do you survive. Brother, we are headed in a direction."

"We certainly are."

I can hear Tamika hollering at someone while the mattress gets dragged back inside.

"Trading post in Mobile, where my boss went and accused me of stealing fifty dollars from the till, back when I was penny honest. Couldn't give a shit about his money. Or Excel, a farmer's place, and here a black shows up. You know what used to happen on them farms, don't you? Those blacks don't want to work. They leave. The patrols bring them back. Call it vagrancy. No visible means of support. Connect those to Albuquerque. Here I am dishwashing in a Greek restaurant with all these headshots on the walls. Some empty suit up at the counter keeps on saying, hard to tell! Hard to tell! He was referring to the stock market. What's hard to tell about it? Read any *Forbes Magazine*. I may be damned, doomed, and dumb, but my zero is a zero. I'm just fact by fact relating things as they happen. And if I'm lying, I'm dying."

Some thought grabs hold enough to silence him. His eyes drift from that window where Tamika was just shouting to the rectangle of sky in front of us. Today's one of them grayish days where it's not possible to make out single clouds because the cloudiness is evenly dispersed. I let my head flop back against the bench and stare along with him until the cops arrive. 3-0-2. Tamika's waiting on the stoop. She escorts them inside the building. Ambulance pulls up. Few minutes later, the two cops escort that guy who always wears the Miami Dolphins jacket down the sidewalk. One of the orderlies opens the back doors of the ambulance.

All of a sudden, Dolphin makes his move. He shakes free of the cops and sprints full blast across the parking lot right down our driveway. A sarcastic cheer erupts around the yard. I watch Dolphin turn up the street down there. Arms are pumping like he thinks he's some Olympian.

■□■

Next day, Franklin's informing me and Crutch what went down with Dolphin following his run to freedom. Apparently he hid in town for several hours, then grew bored and snuck back in his room at night. When he came down to buy a soda, their night nurse acted as though nothing happened. Dolphin figured he was off the hook, but soon as he went back upstairs, she phoned the Crisis Center. Cops had the good sense to cuff him second time, before they carted him away.

"He'll be back Monday morning. Typical. They haven't even cleared his junk out of the hedges yet. You see him run though? Perfect form. His dad's some famous track coach down in Florida. That's what he claims anyway."

"It shows."

"That honky fast alright."

"How's the mermaid settling in?" Franklin gestures discreetly with a finger at the patch of grass where Rosary is roaming barefoot. "Richard?"

"What?"

"Updates on Agnes?"

"Nothing since the tub caper."

"What's with her and water? She used to wander out all night. Show up at breakfast looking like she walked through a carwash or something. I'm talking sopping wet..."

His voice keeps lowering the closer that she gets to us. As Rosary passes by the Island, he stops talking momentarily and checks over his shoulder three times, four. Even with her out of earshot, he still covers his mouth and whispers something I don't catch.

"Speak up, Jeff, I got hair in my ears."

Crutch peers around me. "You say she hit Dave?"

"Not hit. Bit. I'm telling you guys. Stay the hell away from that one. Why do you think we traded her?"

Breadline's been forming this whole time. People are pouring down the stoops. Line's over thirty. Bad leg's informing me it needs a stretch. I spin my cane around.

"Due for a lap," I tell them.

Crutch helps me stand. I head towards A at first then veer towards D instead, second I notice the Trio pestering all passersby down thataway. Rosary is plucking clover for no reason next to Thinker's tree. Normally he minds having his reading interrupted, but he's nodding warmly in agreement at whatever nonsense she is spouting at him.

Sidewalk by the office is too crowded, so I step onto the grass and march beside this row of anxious idiots. Warden upped the price of packs another twenty cents. No one looks happy. Withdrawal lines are an inch longer on their faces. Brows are furrowed. They're calculating how much twenty extra cents affects their bottom line.

"Time for the firing squad?" I ask no one in particular.

"Go blow it out your giggy!" someone yells.

"Prosperity is right around the corner!"

"Shut the fuck up!"

Three Bags is staring at some kind of Christmas catalogue nestled in his basket. I see children splashing in one of those molded swimming pools there on the page. Otis Redding's singing faintly from his radio. Gail and Lolly are in line behind him, murmuring to one another.

As I pass Zorro, he brushes my arm and says, "Virginia plates," then points towards the parking lot where I'm headed, tapping an index finger to his crusty lips.

I nod conspiratorially.

■□■

Twenty minutes later, I'm watching the line pass single file through the office from my other bench with Brog. Process takes over an hour. Near the end, I know I'm way too tired to walk over for my turn. It's fine. I'll get two shares of bread next week.

At 4:00, the daynurses file past us. Some black guy in starched hospital whites strides by them up the driveway swinging a red plastic toolkit in one hand, white and yellow requisition form rolled in the other. Hospital sends these technicians down the hill sometimes to draw our blood or urine, or to help us fill out paperwork.

"Hey man," he says, rechecking the requisition form, "You know an Al...Moonsicky?"

"Unfortunately."

"Well, where he at?"

"He ain't around. What do you want him for?"

"Test." He wiggles the toolkit in his hand.

"You're better off trying the WaWa. One past the cemetery."

Technician twists around and scans the couple dozen people scattered in the yard, then every window on the walls. Clearly he's debating with himself whether it's worth the trouble to search around this dump for Creep or not. This happens every time. No one here can be expected to remember their appointments.

"None of them is him?"

"Nope."

Now he starts eyeing me and Brog, probably convinced that one of us is Creep, the other in cahoots with him. Finally he shakes his head and leaves. Brog hesitates a moment.

"Remember," he says, watching the technician stride back the way he came, "Remember how Yellow Cab was gonna make a national fleet? Look a minute at all this shit, how it floods together. There you got Yellow Cab. You got the Japanese are gonna take over real estate. That's all you gotta have's the land. If you got time, space, energy, you got the people."

"Might be on to something there."

"Flagstaff, Arizona. This taxicab driver was muscle-bound. Without any of that Charles Atlas shit. Just a solid motherfucker. Born solid. Type you'd picture in a mineshaft. Well, he tells me the government's been in the junkyard, checking all the cab meters. You know what a meter spells, don't you?"

"No, what's a meter spell?"

He arches a disappointed eyebrow at me. "It's obvious sense what it spells. Don't you get how these cabs can be the actual spy system? On where you're going. On who with. Man, these fucking beauticians too. Never set foot in a beauty parlor."

"Alright."

"They are the nosiest motherfuckers. They'll ask you question after question after question til you say, lady, if you ask me one more fucking question, it's gonna be your hair on the floor, not mine. Right there you got your spy network set up. Cab drivers. Beauticians. Prostitutes."

"Male nurses."

His eyes tighten like he's trying to gauge how serious I'm taking him. A faint smile flickers on one corner of his mouth.

"There. There! You see it. I know you see it. Don't that add up to a beautiful piece of pie?"

"Beautiful piece of something."

"Look, all I'm trying to do is plow back into the history of this country and put some reasonable connections together."

I grunt. Sal's passing by us on the sidewalk.

"Yo Dick, guess what?"

"You need a quarter?"

"That's right."

"I gave at the office."

"This fucking guy," he says, "Always says that. Hey, what that other guy want?"

"Who?"

"That black guy."

"Oh, he was looking for Al."

"What he want Al for?"

"Good question. Check his blood pressure. Check for a pulse. Who knows?"

Sal nods and goes inside.

■□■

Little later, I spot Marvin rushing up the driveway in a hurry, thirty-forty minutes late. He must've missed his bus. Yard's slowly emptying. It's almost dinner time when Creep ducks through the shortcut with his bag of pretzels and his coffee.

"Yo Al!" I call as he goes by. He ignores me, probably thinks I want a pretzel. "Al, some guy was looking for you earlier."

That halts him.

"Nobody was looking for me. Who?"

"Relax, just some guy from the hospital. He wanted to check if you had a pulse. Don't worry. I told him you didn't."

"Oh, not those assholes again. He'll come back tomorrow. I don't like it anyway. Those people ask too many questions."

I flip my cane around and pull down on the handle.

"You hungry?" I ask Brog once I'm finally standing, "I could sneak you out an ice cream sandwich, long as you don't mind it being in my pocket."

"No, thank you." He lifts his guitar.

"You sure? They're wrapped. It won't melt too much."

"That's awful kind, but I'm alright."

Brog keeps plucking his guitar the whole time it takes me to cross the yard. As I'm tugging on the door, he strums this old bar tune I recognize.

"Mabel, Mabel, sweet and able," I start humming on my way inside.

■□■

Phils are out West again, so after *Jeopardy*, same night, I hike up to the Convent to watch *Stalag 17* with Mimi.

Leaving her room around 11:30, I hear heavy footsteps thumping down the hall. Rosary barges past me clutching toiletries, her gray towel draped over her shoulder. I hate these close calls. Another step and she'd've knocked me on my ass. Same brown dress is clinging to her hips. Dried chunks of mud are dropping from her calves with every step. I'm standing there admiring her figure when this devious thought occurs to me. I probably have an hour if I want it. Rosary don't lock her door. Other nuns up here are fast asleep.

Soon as I hear the tub running, I turn and hurry down the hall. Act confused if someone spots you, I tell myself along the way. My doorknob's always turning in the middle of the night. Just ask which floor you're on and mumble something random if you're caught.

I place my ear against her door a moment. Nothing. What becomes evident soon as I open it is that she doesn't use her bed for sleep. Blanket and pillow are arranged into a simple pallet on the floor. Trash bag she carried her belongings in is balled up in the corner. Three more identical brown dresses are drying on hooks tucked in her blinds. A hundred pens and colored markers are lined up along the dresser with some scrap paper.

Main attraction though are all these portraits of the Virgin Mary which she drew herself and thumbtacked to the wall above her bed. Most are your standard halo stuff—white gown, blue shawl, couple poor kids around her—but there's one where Mary is in street clothes with a black eye, another with a topless dark-skinned Mary who's bleeding profusely from both nipples.

I assume she prays to them because there's knee spots on the blanket, two thick candles standing on the mattress with these stacks of scribblings from ancient times arranged around them. Each page is crinkled up as though they all got wet one time and dried back out. Handwriting looks frantic. Words are slanted at all different angles. Often she will write right over whatever she wrote before, filling the empty spots with doodled crucifixes or those p's with x's through the middle. I pick a page at random and read every phrase that's legible under my breath.

All women captains of starships! All women crewmembers! All women on all planets must wear thick steel shoulders down to feet. Work with atoms all materials all cells all genes all pores all fetuses all plants all solar centers in our bodies. Atomic or molecular or cosmic or creative powers. All convalescent homes in all of USA must have sufficient splendid flowers many colored fruit trees many water fountains many lakes with paths to walk on many games for patients every form of animal on four legs for them to ride many training classes watercolors gardening telepathy astrology music. None must have sex in there. Man only wants dirty rape for man in sex. Every woman must abstain in order to attain her own assumption. Every woman must be pure and cognizant of all her powers. Let us guard our radiant wombs in their glass cases. Let us be generators running on our own electricity. Let the processions come hither.

I set the page down where I found it. I read another, then another. There are hundreds of these crinkly parchments, some too waterlogged to read, but every one that's legible is full of similar gibberish.

Better go. I don't want to have to fend her off with my quad cane. Prospect of being bit by her does not excite me either. As I'm listening from the inside of her door, I feel something little crunch beneath my shoe. Lifting it, I find one of her pink capsules flattened on the carpet.

■□■

Mornings and evenings are becoming chillier again. First and last laps most days have been forced inside. By mid-September, I feel fall arriving through the extra rigor mortis in my arm. Afternoons stay warm enough, provided I reverse my motions and move with the sunlight, rather than the shade. This means I pass my mornings beside Brog. We watch the delivery trucks pull in and out.

At noon, I keep offering to sneak him out a sandwich. He always refuses.

After lunch, I usually have the Island to myself. Everyone's inside again. O.J. trial's almost finished. Prosecution just rested its case. Closing arguments are underway.

■□■

Last week of September's oddly windy, therefore even chillier. Aware what I'm in for over winter, I pull on my Eagles sweatshirt and my ski cap and spend every second storing sunlight up outside. Thinker does the same. While he is putting all his thoughts down in his notebook, grass around him's slowly filling in with maple leaves.

■□■

Friday, my mind's been wandering a solid hour when I hear the Warden's Buick pull into the parking lot. First thing she always does upon arrival's change her shoes. That silver door swings open. Under it, I see her hand place beat-up sneakers on the tar. Her stockinged feet slide into them. Marvin told me once she owns two other places down in

Delaware. One's much like this. Other is much nicer. He's picked up a couple shifts at both of them.

Once Warden's shoes are tied, she walks back to the trunk and empties all our cartons for the week into a single cardboard box. I watch her lug her loot along the sidewalk, calculating in my head. Thirty times twenty times fifty-two...I start over. Thirty cartons times ten packs times twenty per pack times fifty-two weeks in a year...three hundred, six thousand, fifty-two, three thousand, add two zeroes, carry the twelve: 312,000 butts a year. And that don't count what people buy in town.

She's fishing her keys out of her purse now. Box is braced against one of her stomach folds while she unlocks the office door.

Mind goes back to wandering. I wonder how Gums is doing. I wonder whether my ex-wives are still alive. What about my older sister? Last time I heard from Shirley, I found out I had four grandkids. There must be more by now. I let the squirrels distract me. It don't do me any good to think about them here.

A long while passes, maybe an hour.

I'm staring straight into the shortcut, curious what Brog's up to back there, when I hear children giggling to my right. Two black kids are hiding behind a three-foot leaf pile between A and D. Those half-houses go on for blocks and blocks in that direction. Boy on the left pokes his head up then ducks down soon as he knows I've spotted him. One on the right pokes up and down much faster. They're giggling again. I'm ready when they pop back up. I've got my good hand fashioned into a rod. I fire three shots. They duck then return fire. I let my head flop back and stick my tongue out like they got me.

■□■

Later that night coming from Mimi's room, I'm forced to detour through the second floor because Zorro's arguing with Rainy on the stairs again. Thinker's door's ajar. That's not unusual this late. I only stop because I hear him reading to somebody.

"Now there is at Jerusalem by the sheep market a pool, which is called in the Hebrew tongue Bethesda, having five porches. In these lay a great multitude of impotent folk, of blind, halt, withered, waiting for the moving of the water. For an Angel went down at a certain season into the pool, and troubled the water—"

"That's in Bethesda?" Rosary asks him.

"Different Bethesda. They mean near Jerusalem, not Maryland. You can't walk there, Agnes. Whosoever then first after the troubling of the water stepped in was made whole of whatsoever disease he had. And a certain man was there who had an infirmity thirty—"

"But that could be here. Another pool that works the same. She told me I need to find it. That's what she said. I need to dig the water out and rub it on my scar."

"Then what? Your scar's supposed to disappear? Your insides be made whole?"

"That's all she said."

"Any mention of ascension afterwards? Thou shalt rise, body with soul to Heaven, or even better, thou shalt drift into dormition. Wake up next to Mary in the morning."

"That's all she said. I need to find it."

"Well, where have you tried so far?"

"I've tried Crum Creek and Ridley Creek. I've tried Darby Creek. Oh, and that other little creek next to Bryn Mawr."

"What about the ornithological refuge?"

"Where's that?"

"Down by the airport. It's full of little pools. You better bring a shovel."

Thinker continues humoring her like that for several minutes. I eavesdrop long as I can stand, then head downstairs to bed.

■□■

Following morning's warm enough to do my laps outside. It's still so dark when I set out that I pass Rosary two times without realizing that the lumpy shape stretched on the grass is her. I step up cautiously to check if she's still breathing. She's on her side, all soaking wet, with leaves stuck to her dress, mud in her hair. Bottoms of her feet are black.

I'm right about to poke her with my cane when this rough snore shoots out of her so suddenly I almost jump. I back away. She's fine.

Shortcut is staring at me when I reach the sidewalk. Over and back isn't that far. Objectively it's half a lap at most. I've been curious what's over there for years now, yet that walk has always seemed a little ill-advised. I step down off the curb and hobble over to the trees. Looks like a footpath winds for thirty feet or so up to an iron gate. I bat a branch out of my way and duck inside. There's many pinecones to avoid. I need to twist my cane into the dirt in order to maintain my footing.

Halfway down the path, I note how several branches have been bent into a cave-like shelter in which Brog is sleeping on a flimsy mattress. That maroon leather jacket which the Trio tried to sell us several months ago is draped over the branches like a tarp. A gallon jug of iced tea rests beside a hubcap full of kindling. Brog's only change of clothes is spread out drying on a branch.

I step by him.

At the gate, I gaze into the cemetery. Everything's immaculate. No butts. No trash. No bald spots in the lawn. There's a giant willow in the middle. Their yard's so much nicer than our yard. Suppose it should be. All the headstones on this side have slopes to them like pillows. According to the nearest one, some guy named Samuel died in 1863.

CHAPTER 9: MISCHIEF NIGHT

Yesterday was my birthday. Tomorrow's Halloween. Tonight we're supposed to hold our second annual costume party during cookie hour. Marvin's idea. I've reached Lap 38 when I run into him tiptoeing secretively down the stairwell with two bulky trash bags on him.

"What's all that?"

"My cothtume. Don't forget, you're judge thith year," he reminds me before locking himself inside the canteen to start decorating.

I return to my room. Rather than resting by my window for the eighth time in a row, I decide to lie down in bed, permit myself a short nap, twenty minutes, half an hour tops, but I remain asleep much longer.

In this dream I have, there's a vast wilderness behind our buildings. Entrance to it is a narrow chain link gate set between A and D. The gate has a minor design flaw. There's no fence to either side of it. You could just walk around, but for some reason that feels disrespectful, so I unlatch it properly and step onto this long leafy trail. I'm dressed in normal clothes. Hand works fine. I have been walking for what feels like an entire day, minus my limp, minus my quad cane, when somebody's door slams down the hall, waking me up.

Ten to six.

I rock off my bed. I lock my door. Half-groggy when I turn the corner, I find everyone already crowded in the hallway, grumbling about their hunger. Sal and Swab scoot over for me on the pew. To pass the time, I reread the entire list of regulations posted on the noticeboard:

1. *Refrain from spitting on the carpet.*
2. *Refrain from placing large items in the toilet bowl.*
3. *It is never acceptable to urinate in corridors.*
4. *Storing perishables inside your room is not permitted.*
5. *Smoking in bed is absolutely forbidden.*
6. *Verbal abuse of staff will not be tolerated.*
7. *Stop sticking gum on windowsills.*
8. *Do not enter each other's rooms without permission.*
9. *No overnight guests allowed.*
10. *No propping open exit doors after hours with phonebooks, rocks, etc.*

List keeps getting longer every year.

A gray cloud of exhaled smoke is hovering around the faces on the stairwell. Zorro appoints himself the one to bang six times on the door.

"Time to fucking eat!" He twists around to look at us. "He blacked out the porthole."

"What?"

"This fucking window. It's covered with construction paper."

At the sound of the bolt sliding open, everyone crowds up behind him. Door swings inward, and a sudden high-pitched howl comes from the canteen, causing half of them to drop their cigarettes and clutch their chests from fright. Marvin comes rushing out in a brown werewolf mask and gloves with some mismatched gorilla suit. Claws poised, he growls at everybody bunched around the door.

"You crazy motherfucker!"

"I have a heart condition, asshole."

Marvin peels his mask up past his forehead so he can cackle straight in their faces while they're shoving their way by him. I don't begrudge him any of these little moments of revenge. The few good-humored ones like Creep and Rainy laugh. Rest are cursing him for scaring them half to death. I go in last.

Canteen's been decorated for our costume party later. Cutouts of skeletons and bats are taped onto the walls. Each table has a glowing jack-o-lantern in the center with fake cobwebs made from pillow wadding spread around it. Dinner's scrambled beef with creamed corn and a roll.

"Happy Halloween!" Marvin wishes the room, his voice muffled by the mask he's tugged over his face again.

"Happy Halloween."

"Happy Halloween."

Swab says, "I thought it was tomorrow?"

"I took off tomorrow."

"Aren't you past the cutoff age for trick-or-treating yet?"

Marvin ignores this. Mask stays on while he's finishing the dishes. Everyone's so hungry that we eat in total silence.

As we're filing back out, the werewolf holds two giant bags of chocolate up, shaking them at us, a blatant bribe to make sure we'll return at 8:00 to hold this party.

"No cothtume, no candy. Dick will be thelecting the winner thith year!"

This clearly means much more to him than us.

Last one out, I find Thinker lighting his after-dinner cigarette while he's waiting for the stairs to clear. It looks like Peg is holding up the line again. Climbing forty steps has gotten challenging for her. She's put on so much weight the past six months, she nearly fills the narrow stairwell. There's no room for anyone to squeeze around her.

"Clear a path!" yells Dot.

"Hold your horses," Peg groans, tugging on both railings with her hands, "I'm going as fast as I can."

"Follow me," says Thinker, pointing with his cigarette, "Let's take the steep and thorny way instead."

We proceed down my hall. This first section of the carpet is so crusted-over with varieties of scum, my shoes keep sticking to it. Only light in this direction extends out of Zorro's room. A door slams down the end. We hear the rapid pitter-patter of my neighbor, Jiggles, charging towards us for his seventh or eighth shower of the day. I close my eyes too late. For a second, I make out his torso as he passes through the bar of light. He's built like an ox. No flab on him at all. Stomach and thighs are covered with tight spools of coarse black hair. Pecker's flicking up and down. I lean against the wall so he won't knock me over. Thinker does as well. Our noses wrinkle at the smell of sour sweat as he stomps by.

"That man could barge through an open field," says Thinker.

"Spare a smoke?" asks Zorro, leaning out into the hall. He scratches his bare belly, eyes trained on the cigarette in Thinker's hand. Tattoos of two faces—one male, the other female—fill his flabby pecs. "C'mon, gimme a smoke. Gimme a smoke, and I'll keep quiet. I won't go to the State Police, I promise." He turns his eyes on me. "See how I blackmail these fuckers all the time."

"What did you do to your head?"

In the dark, I didn't notice it at first, but Zorro's scalp looks like he raked a butterknife across it until he'd managed to remove the majority of hair. Missed bits of stubble poke through six or seven rows of drying blood.

"That's classified. I'm supposed to put this stuff on it."

He beckons us inside, backing around the shadeless lamp that's resting on a stack of fuckbooks in the middle of the floor. I go in first. Thinker only steps a foot inside the door.

Off his dresser, Zorro grabs a bottle of mercurochrome and some old sock. He slides the sock onto his arm just like a puppet, tips the bottle onto it, and dabs his head while we take in everything he's done to the inside of his cave.

All four walls and ceiling are covered with colored drawings of elaborate disasters. There are two separate shipwrecks where scores of sailors are drowning amidst the wreckage. Some are clutching jagged pieces of the hull. On the ceiling, a giant brown volcano has erupted and is burying a building with a strong resemblance to ours in piles of black ash. Across the longer wall, he's staged a full-scale battle with artillery plus tanks and air support. There must be a thousand soldiers firing at each other from positions on both sides. It must've taken months to draw. Above his pillow, there's this yellow dump truck with its back raised, spilling shriveled bodies out into an actual hole which I assume he bored into the wall himself. Crayon flames are shooting from the hole.

"Nine years," he declares boastfully, "Next year, I'll be fifty, and a ten-year dealer."

Over by the window there's another drawing of a cell block with its prisoners pressed against their bars. Their names are etched above their heads: *Einhorn, Heidnik, Savitz, Seegrist, Kallinger, Scarfo, Dwyer, Graham.*

"What's that supposed to be?"

"Oh, I used to be what's called a Sick Crimes Investigator at the FBI. It was my job to interview all major schizoid defectives in the Tri-State area."

He proceeds to share a series of stories about every local sicko he personally caught, referring to them only by their first names. Time he slapped the cuffs on Ira, Ira told him if he wasn't collecting welfare in at least five states, he was a no-good lazy bum. Gary was chopping celery and carrots for his dark meat stew as they busted the front door down.

I'm facing him as he recounts all this. Scalp's completely orange now. A fresh cold sore's shining on his upper lip. Each time the sock makes contact with his head, he bites down on his tongue. Cuts are too fresh. An orange line starts dripping down his nose.

"Stench at Eddie's place was worse though. You know how he answered the door?"

"How?"

"With a kid's potty on his head," he says, fighting off a giggle, "He held the lid up to talk to us. Like this. Know what he said?"

"What did he say?"

"Now's not a good time."

That makes us both giggle.

"You fucking lunatic."

"It's always the smell that catches them."

Thinker mutters something in a foreign language in my ear while tugging lightly on my arm. As I follow him out, I notice all the swastikas carved on the inside of the door.

Before I can ask Thinker what he said to me, a screaming match begins down by the canteen. Swab is threatening to kill somebody if they don't stay out of our building.

"Go fuck yourself!" some guy yells back at him.

"Man, I will rip out your fucking trachea!"

"Fuck you! You don't have the authority."

Zorro pokes his orange head into the hall. "Everybody always wants to scrap down here. Yesterday this guy from C was really insulting Rainy, right, and nobody was doing anything, so I told him, come on, motherfucker. I didn't think he'd wanna go, but then *boom boom boom*, he dropped me. Prick used pressure points. Before I knew it, my whole forehead's caked in blood. Look what he did to me."

I don't bother looking back. Thinker's rushing in that shuffley way he walks whenever his bladder feels too full. He turns the doorknob frantically. Luckily nobody's in there. On his way inside, he repeats that same foreign phrase.

From the doorway, I watch him fumble with his zipper.

"What do you keep saying?"

"*Fiat mihi mingit.*"

"Fuck's that mean?"

"It means let me micturate."

A short burst of piss hits the bowl. He groans. A longer burst follows, another.

I decide to get a head start up the stairs. As I pass under the FIRE sign, I notice Brog is stretched out sideways on his sleeping bag, smoking, four steps up. He inhales forcefully and stares at me a couple seconds before two wide plumes of smoke begin to funnel out his nostrils.

"Ask me what year I told my father the Bible's a bunch of shit."

"What year?"

"What year what?"

"What year'd you tell your old man the Bible's bullshit?"

"1974. That's when I finally told him. All this poverty, all this insanity, all of this prison shit. But what I need on my day off's to listen to some kiddie fiddler jawing about the blood of the lamb? Horseshit! I'm in that pew hearing all this static about man's purpose, about what's he seeking, why's he speaking. I stood up, mid-homily. I spun around and told that congregation, he's the one took our purpose from us. Him there! Man on the Cross. People already know who they are, why they're here. Evangelism. Mohammedism. Judaism. They all got their own little bedtime rules. It's just one argument over another on which charm bag'll get you there the fastest. Tell you what. That Jew from Tucson was right when he told me he could prove we had the same God."

Brog's back is pressed against the right side of the stairwell. When I gesture that I need the railing, he swings his feet around and palms himself over to the side to let me pass. I begin climbing.

"Listen to this now," he continues, "Because if I'm lying, I'm dying. El Paso. This is back when Children of God was running. You ever met any of them folks?"

"Can't say I have."

"Better off. I was living on the border, Texas side, and I seen them all in the fields. Kohoutek was coming. They were charging like buffalo to get away from this fucking comet. Hundreds of them. There's this bishop set up aways, just there to observe. Tells me the Dallas Diocese sent him. You know what else he tells me?"

"No clue."

"This bishop tells me he was in Rome in '63. He sat three seats away from the Pope after Kennedy was shot, swears to me they drank two-hundred-year-old kegs of wine to celebrate. Don't that make a picture? Well, let me make it even clearer for you. There's this Jap with the bishop, Tira-something Yanagi, who invites me to his temple to worship Buddha. He's from their world study, and he's going on about Hiroshima and hunger, snapping pictures of all the food. When he held my hands in his, mine perspired like they never had before. There you got the Jew from Tucson. You got Yanagi. Watch all these connections now. How it floods together. This is Jewish. It's Catholics. It's Italians, and it's Japanese. All of them asking me to have supper. Hold up, man!"

Brog keeps turning, farther I keep climbing.

"Say I say Krishna to you. That means one thing, right? But if I say Zoroaster, that means something else to you entirely. And people will war, man, will war like fucking mad dogs over that. Same God. Same fucking God!"

Five steps up, Kneeslapper's in my way, batting herself in the forehead every couple seconds. I switch sides to veer around her. There's a pack of cigarettes and lighter tucked between her feet. Right thigh is redder than I've ever seen it. She pauses while I'm going by. I hear her hit herself again soon as I've passed.

I'm on the landing, inhaling, exhaling, when Thinker catches up to me. He takes my cane and gestures below us with it.

"Here feel we not the penalty of Adam," he says.

"Certainly do."

We continue up the second flight together.

This always goes better when I place my weight onto my good leg first, then swing the bad leg upwards after. We avoid this brownish stain which could be coffee, shit, or blood, no way to tell. I keep laboring upwards, right leg first, then left.

After a few more steps, he says, "Bet I know what you're thinking. You're thinking that'll be me in ten years, aren't you?"

"What, talking gibberish in a stairwell?"

He nods a little grimly like the prospect actually frightens him for once.

I shake my head and reply, "Eight."

"Why eight?"

"Cause you've already lived here two."

"Funny."

"Have I ever mentioned—"

"That I don't belong here? Only a thousand times."

There's six steps left until we reach the second floor. Light alters above us. Looking up, we find our blind man Simon, tilting forward in the stairwell in his baggy trousers and favorite lime green polo shirt. Two greasy clumps of hair hang down his chest. Head is cocked. He's listening intently to make sure nobody's sneaking by him. His cane swipes back and forth across the floor to check.

"Who's there?" he asks.

"It's only us, Simon."

"Us who?"

"Dick and Harry."

"Yeah, we can't find Tom."

"Tom who?"

"Never mind."

"Nobody, Simon. We're just going to my room."

"Go then."

With his cane, he sizes up the area in front of him. Once he's located the edge of the top step, he leaves the cane there so he'll know precisely where the edge is while he backs up just enough to let us pass. I hobble out into the hall. It's slightly brighter than downstairs because the bulb at this end works.

Bathroom door is partway open on our left. I notice Creep is seated on the toilet, linty trousers bunched around his ankles, wads of toilet paper lined up in the crotch for later. Giant coffee's on the tile by his feet. His hands are wrapped around one of his pretzels. With my cane, I push the door open a little wider. Startled, he yanks the pretzel he was nibbling down just like a squirrel.

"I'm on the fricken toilet!" he says, squirming sideways on the seat.

Words came out all garbled from the dough. He lets go of the pretzel, and he slams the door right in my face.

"Well, that was the height of something."

Simon has caught up to us. His cane bumps into Thinker's moccasin, causing him to reach out with his free hand to identify what's in his way. His fingers land on Thinker's neck.

"You said you were going to your room."

"We are."

"So go."

We hurry onward.

Safe in Thinker's room, I'm resting on the banker's chair, watching him don his hippie costume for the party: tie-dye shirt and satin vest, round sunglasses, red bandana.

"Notice any change in here?" he asks.

I check everywhere. That German clock is on the dresser. Mannequin is in the bushel, staring at the ceiling. There's a few terms I don't remember ever reading on its skull before: *Anhedonia, Glossopyrosis, Pyorrhea, Ague*. He's filled up two or three more notebooks since the last time I was here. Books on his desk are *The Anatomy of Melancholy, Bouvard et Pécuchet*, and *De Vulgari Eloquentia*. I don't spot a single change worth noting.

"Got me."

"You're relying on the wrong faculty."

"What's that mean?"

"The eyes deceive. Listen."

From where his room's positioned in the middle of the middle floor, I can hear voices coming at me from all three-hundred-sixty degrees. Peg is giving Mimi some instructions through the ceiling. Zorro's giggling away below our feet. I hear coughing. Rainy's radio is blaring somewhere. Every evening, all this noise accumulates into one single sourceless shout.

"Give me a hint."

"Fine. What *don't* you hear? I'll give you ten more seconds. Actually, that's two hints."

Now I get it. Only sound I don't hear is the ticking of his fancy clock.

"Your clock stopped."

"Correct!" he says a little too excitedly, "We have officially burned through another four hundred days."

"When did it stop?"

"Your guess is as good as mine. A month ago? This morning? I was starting to hear it in my head."

"Well, when did you notice?"

"This morning when I went to dust it."

Carefully he turns the clock around then slips the lanyard with his room key and the iron clock key off his head. He makes sure I'm ready first, then winds the iron key counterclockwise, four times in a row. *Tick, tick, tick, tick, tick,*

tick, tick, tick... As he's sliding the glass dome in place, Creep hops into the room dressed like the Riddler in an eye mask and green t-shirt with a black question mark drawn on the front. Pretzel's gone.

"I'm winning the prize this year. Bank it."

"Marv made me the judge. Have I really sunk this low?"

"It's already over." He takes a gargly swig of coffee, swishing it around his teeth before he gulps. When Simon passes in the hall again, Creep calls out to him. "You gonna be a blind man again this year?"

"Your sister."

"Yeah, how much?"

Creep backs into the hall. I follow him. First couple steps, my bad foot feels numb when I put weight on it. Creep is kind of kicking his way down the hall ahead of us, humming the Batman theme. Swabbie's squeezed into his Navy whites against the wall, rubbing his belly with both hands.

"Admiral."

He smacks his lips a couple times. "Hey, you feel sick at all? Guys? I mean to your stomach. I think that beef we ate was off. I've got that acid taste like I'm about to puke."

We shrug. He falls in line behind us.

At Sal's open door, Creep stops abruptly and points downward in the room.

"How come you're sitting like that?"

"*Va fangool.* I'm waiting for your mother."

"Get a load of this idiot!"

Creep makes room for all of us to look inside. For some reason, Sal's positioned on his bed with both legs aimed straight up the wall, arms out, head hanging a few inches from the floor. Face is a bluish purple. Clearly he's been upside-down awhile.

"Helps my sinuses," he tells us, rolling to one side and slowly standing up. "Is it time for that party yet?" He ties a black cape over his white dress shirt and slips a set of plastic fangs over his real teeth. "Let's go. I want my chocolate."

At the stairwell, I let all of them pass by me. I turn upstairs while they head downstairs to the canteen. I hear their voices echoing below.

Glancing up to check my path is clear, I spot a pair of bare legs at the top. They're spread two feet apart. About halfway, I recognize the hem of Rosary's brown dress around her thighs. With four steps left, I catch a glimpse of her gold satin panties. She's in such a daze, mouthing her prayers, she don't even see me.

"Hail Mary, full of Grace, Lord is with thee, blessed thou among women, blessed fruit of thy womb—"

"Coming through, Agnes."

Her knees knock into one another, hands shoot up to guard herself, until she realizes it's only me. I set my cane up there beside her, and I groan my way up the last three steps.

"Sorry," I tell her.

I need to take another breather on the wall. She stands and watches me intently. Feet are clean. She must've just taken her bath. Soon as I grip my cane, she skips ahead and then steps backwards down the hall.

"Oh while we walk," she says in a girlish voice, "I want to tell you something that happened. I saw her again."

"When?"

"Yesterday. She had a long white dress on, *lonnnnnnnng*, and she was standing between two trees with the most perfect grove of roses all around her—blue, yellow, pink, white—and also the ground was soaked from all that rain over the weekend, but no dirt got on her dress at all."

"Where this happen?"

"There was an altar behind her, a marble altar, marble, marble, with a white cloth right down the middle and two tall candles, one on each side, and above the altar a wooden crucifix was floating, right above the altar, about twenty feet above the altar, and it had these suns around it, five glowing suns, they *glooooooooowed*, and ten planets were circling them very fast, five suns, fifty planets. Mary was praying for all of them. One was ours."

She shoves her hair out of her face.

"Did she speak?"

"Let the processions come hither. She said here is my true church, let the processions come hither."

When her hand touches the molding of her open door, she pivots halfway in the room and hugs the doorframe. Eyes snap shut. She rolls her forehead roughly on the molding several times, then presses both lips against the wood and sputters wetly.

Door behind me opens. Lolly steps out wearing a bedsheet with three holes cut out of it for eyes and mouth.

"They're egging us again," she tells me wearily.

"What?"

"Are you deaf? I said they're egging us."

"Who is?"

"Them little high school bastards." She moves out of the way for me to see the yellow slime clumped on her window screen.

"That'll stink if you don't rinse it off."

"They're also chucking toilet paper in our trees."

Dot passes between us in some leopard leotard with furry ears atop her head and six white whiskers drawn on her plump cheeks. Lolly follows her downstairs.

Next room I reach is Mimi's room. Door's cracked an inch. I hear her talking to her mother.

"Try again," she says.

"I have no idea. Bob Hope."

"Close. Jack Benny. How about Laszlo Lowenstein?"

"I don't know. How come they all sound Jewish?"

"That one's Peter Lorre. How about Lucile Langhanke?"

"Langhanke? What the hell kind of name is Langhanke?"

"Guess."

"Lucille Ball."

"Wrong, Mary Astor. How about Constance Ockelman?"

"No idea."

"William Claude Dukenfield?"

"I have no idea."

"Archibald Leach?"

"Nope."

"Margarita Cansino?"

"No idea!"

"Next one's easy, Ma. Norma Jean Mortenson?"

I tap on the door. "You two decent?"

"No, but come in anyway," says Peg.

I push the door open and find Mimi in a white pleated dress with a blonde wig, one mole painted on her left cheek. Peg's seated beside her in a black dress and black pointy hat. Her face is painted emerald green. Mimi's been adding warts around her mother's chin and nose.

"Guess what I am," says Peg, "Dick, where's your costume?"

"I don't need one. I'm the judge."

"Finish my makeup, Mi. The chocolate will run out."

"I'll see you two down there."

"Dick, you still need a costume."

I head for the stairwell. Bathroom door is open to my right. Rainy's standing at the mirror, naked from the waist up. She's doing something to her chest that makes her flinch with pain. When she catches my reflection in the mirror, she turns around and smiles serenely at me. Little trails of blood are running down her chest.

"What are you doing?"

"Popsicle, you shouldn't be up here."

"Why are you bleeding?"

"This is the ladies floor," she reminds me, "You don't belong up here."

There's a straight razor in her hand. All the moles she's managed to cut off so far sit in a row along the sink.

CHAPTER 10: A DISAPPEARING ACT

Nothing seems noteworthy next couple weeks. We hibernate. I don't know. Maybe I have finally grown tired of describing the same dozen people, but I'm finding it much harder to see any humor my third winter trapped inside this building. Half my roommates never leave their cells. Rest watch *Columbo* reruns in the rec room until cattle call goes off for lunch, then dinner. Only verbal effort anyone puts forth is to squeeze ciggies out of one another.

Main fear's no longer being stuck in here forever. It's that I'll turn into one of them, meaning dead already, simply waiting for it to be made official. That's why my routines are so important. I can feel their sorry habits creeping up on me. Earlier, I caught myself staring at the rec room wall. I wasn't thinking anything. I had been rotating my wrist, but I just stopped. Laps are down as well. I've done thirty-four today. Normal's more like seventy or eighty. Leg ain't why. Real reason is I'm sick of the same scenery all the time. With three months left to go until spring, I better find another case or something before I turn into one of these sofa statues seated here around me.

■□■

It's Thanksgiving. Marvin tacked those glossy cut-outs of the grinning Indian and Pilgrim to the wall again. Each table has a wicker basket full of artificial gourds. Our plates have turkey slices and boxed stuffing on them, plus some succotash.

"Happy Thanksgiving," someone bothers saying.

Under half of us repeat it. We're all waiting on the gravy Marvin's stirring at the stove.

"Yo Marv!" yells Swab.

"Hang on."

"Yo, where's Agnes been? She get moved again?"

"No chanth."

"Well, she ain't had dinner for about a week."

Marvin stops stirring and peers up at the exhaust fan. "You're right," he admits, "I haven't theen her either."

After he's worked his way around both tables, ladling the gravy, he heads upstairs to make sure she hasn't reflooded the Convent. Ten minutes later, he returns and tells us Rosary is nowhere to be found, not in the tub, not in her room either, though most of her belongings seemed to be. Couple of us shrug. This ain't unusual. It's not like anyone keeps tabs on who skips meals. He thinks it over for a minute, then unlocks the cabinet phone and dials 9-1-1 while we await our pumpkin pie.

■□■

Following afternoon, two officers arrive to take our statements. Older one's in plain clothes. Younger cop's in uniform. I'm staring at the Breadline out the windows when I spot them coming up the stoop. Rainy is playing solitaire beside me. Swab and Sal are flipping through two halves of Wednesday's paper. Thinker and Creep are at the corner of the ping-pong table, playing chess as always.

To save on time, they interview all six of us together. Neither cop looks overly concerned until they inquire when we saw her last and get six different answers, ranging from a few days to a month.

"How would you describe her personality?"

Swab chuckles loudest out of all of us. "Her personality?"

"Yes, was Miss Pierce generally happy or depressed? Did she have any particular reason to leave?"

Swab levels with them on behalf of everybody. "Look fellas, I love her and all, but Agnes is a total nut."

"Nut how?" the older cop asks pointedly.

"I mean she wasn't smearing feces on her face. Nothing like that. She's more the kind to hold a conversation with the Virgin Mary. You know, see her on the walls like it's TV."

Both cops are taking all this down on spiral pads. Younger one's having a harder time holding back that goofy grin first-timers always get in here. Whenever the pen moves in his hand, his leather jacket creaks.

"Tell them about the walks," I say, which makes the older cop glance up at me.

"The walks?"

I meant that comment more for Thinker, but Swab answers first.

"Oh yeah," he says, "Agnes goes out walking half the night. Lot of people here do that. Don't ask me where they go. I'm out cold."

"I saw her come back in the morning, couple times," I add, "She was all covered in mud, her feet. Also her dress was soaking wet."

"Any idea where she went?"

I shrug.

Thinker clears his throat and holds a finger up. "Do you gentlemen know that ornithological refuge, down by the airport?"

"You talking about Tinicum?"

"I am."

"They call it Heinz now, sir."

"I know. You saying she goes there? That's awful far."

"Goes and sleeps over."

"What do you mean sleeps over, sleeps where?"

"The impression I got was along the riverbank."

"She told you that?"

He nods uncomfortably. "Agnes is prone to odd interpretations of the Bible. She's convinced herself that place is holy. I would check there first if I were you."

Last thing they do is take down all our names. After that, Swab escorts them to the rec room to find Ocky so they can search her room for clues. Thinker and Creep resume their game. Latter's white today. Kings are opposed in the center of the board, two pawns apiece along the flanks. I go back to staring out the windows.

Not a single word's exchanged for ten full minutes though I'd wager every one of us is wondering the same thing. What temperature's it gotta be to freeze to death? All week's been in the forties. I have no idea how cold it's been getting late at night, but Swab just put his coat on to wait in the Breadline in the middle of the day. He's behind Dolphin, far too focused on the office door to notice the two cops as they pass by him on the sidewalk. Younger one has Rosary's papers in his hands.

"They're leaving," I say.

"What? Oh."

"Bet she got attacked," says Creep, pushing a pawn, "She's curled up dead somewhere. Bank it."

"God, you are one polished asshole," Rainy snaps at him.

"These things only end one way."

"How come nobody kicks her out?" I ask the room.

I'm picturing the route she'd have to take to reach that bird refuge. It must be six or seven miles from here. Assuming she took Upland Avenue, she'd reach that cinderblock yard along the overpass eventually. If she kept going, she would end up by the marina. Area is mostly warehouses. You'd need a car, rest of the way, less you're prepared to hop a fence or two and trudge along the reeds. Easier option is to walk straight down a boat launch, slip into the water, swim across, I guess, sandbar to sandbar.

"What do you mean?" Sal asks me, "Kick her out of here?"

"No, I mean the park. How come they don't kick her out?"

I swing back around, annoyed. Creep is calculating some maneuver with his thumb pressed to his lips. Thinker's sliding his four fingers back and forth along the dulled edge of the table. I call over to him.

"What did you mean, Harry?" Don't think he heard me. I repeat myself much louder. "Harry, what'd you mean she thinks that place is holy?"

"Who are you imagining would kick her out exactly?" he asks dismissively, "Some park ranger? They'd have to spot her first. It's not a little place."

"Nobody else reports her?"

"What for?"

"What do you mean, what for? To stop a grown woman from swimming in a swamp."

"It's not a crime to wade."

"Jesus Christ. This place needs a fucking curfew."

Sal shakes his head. "This happened with a girl over at Elwyn. That's where—"

"You told me."

"I did?"

"Yeah."

"Climbed right out the window. Second floor." He tugs some change out of his pocket, counts it twice. "Say, you got forty cents?"

"I gave at the office."

"Yeah, yeah, c'mon, I really only need twenty cents."

I ignore him.

"Agnes is definitely dead somewhere," says Creep, retreating his king another square. "One of them weekend boaters'll find her face-down in the water. Watch."

■□■

Monday, this place finally makes the paper. Ocky brought a copy in for us to read. It's getting passed around my table during lunch while she is wiping out the sink.

> *Chester Police request your assistance in locating of a missing person: Agnes Pierce, Caucasian, 44-years-old, last seen approximately 10 days ago, 5'5", 130 pounds, black hair, blue eyes, light complexion.*

There's a younger photo of her fitted above ads for Christmas sales at MacDade Mall. She's decked out in some kind of bridesmaid gown with busy sleeves and beading on the neckline. Eyes seem far less riled than they ever did in here, which makes me wonder whether Agnes once was sane, whether those visions snuck up on her suddenly.

Everyone around me's nibbling on their sandwiches. I'm reading the headlines on the paper Rainy's holding. *No Shift in Bosnia Accord. Gimmicks Imperil Deficit Cuts. Adults Find Attention Problem Has a Name.* There's a large photo of Ricky Watters shedding a defender. Yesterday we beat the Redskins, 14-7.

"What a sin," Rainy mutters, mostly to herself. "Miss Pierce is a graduate of Bryn Mawr College, Detective Roberts noted. I didn't know that. You guys know Agnes went to college?"

Sal starts laughing over her right shoulder.

"What?"

He gestures at the paper with his chin. "They called this place an apartment house. Where are the apartments?"

■□■

Later, I'm upstairs in Thinker's room. Night School recently reopened. Same drill as before. He recites passages to me and comments on them. I pose simple questions from the banker's chair. Book he's telling me about tonight is called *Degeneration*. Some Hungarian doctor name of Nordau wrote it in the 1890s. His whole theory was that countries can get sick, the same as people.

"Europe was one giant hospital to him," Thinker's explaining from his bed, "It's how his mind was trained. He saw everything in terms of diagnosis and prognosis. Every opera he attended, every gallery, he'd meet the same type of twitchy dilettante. None able to focus. They were overly excitable, according to him, because their peripheral nervous systems had been worn down by the Industrial Revolution."

"So it wasn't their fault?"

"Technically not. He still found ways to judge them. Nordau was quite the crank. He hated everything."

"What do you think he would say about here?"

"He writes about America too."

"No, I mean this place."

"Oh, God." Thinker ruminates on this awhile. Book's rising and falling on his stomach. "Well, nerve exhaustion, morbid temperament, vagaries of mind...we definitely fit the typology. Classic degenerates!"

"No argument here."

"To be consistent, he would have to see us as the symptom of some larger force."

"The Warden?"

"Who, Robin? No, no, she's a medium-sized cog at most. Nordau wasn't Marx. He'd seek something subtler than her crass profit motive. Something in us. Something that could only be revealed by studying our day-to-day existence. Listen to this coda."

While Thinker's flipping to the final page, I'm thinking I agree with Nordau. I used to blame the Warden for all the problems here, least the ones involving soda, cigarettes, etc. Three years has taught me better. Real problem's the habits they brought with them. I can't blame her for those. Truth is you could stick the lot of them in a much nicer place—healthier food, cheerful rooms, capable nurses—end result would be the same.

At the sound of the book shutting, I realize I've been so lost in thought I missed half the passage he was reading.

Thinker sets the book beside him. He gazes upwards at the water stain across his ceiling. That fancy handless clock of his ticks for awhile.

"I went to look for Agnes," he blurts out.

"What? When?"

"Saturday."

"Where?"

"The ornithological refuge."

I'm too stunned at first to respond. He acted so glib about the situation Friday after those detectives left, I figured he didn't care what happened to Rosary. On the contrary. He says he borrowed Swab's pea coat, pair of gloves off Sal, and hoofed it seven miles to go search around that swamp for her.

Walk took him two hours. Near the end, he had to climb the shoulder of an on-ramp, hop a cement divider and a four-foot fence to get onto some jogger's path inside the park which led him through a narrow section where the river runs right next to 95. There's this long row of rotting benches every twenty yards along the river. When he found one of her candles resting on a bench, he started calling out her name and didn't stop until he reached the observation deck. There was an older couple there, well-dressed retirees engrossed in slowly scanning the whole estuary through their binoculars. Birders. Under any other circumstances, Thinker says, he might've interrupted to ask what there was to see this time of year. Weren't all the birds worth counting on their way to Florida by now?

He also could not bring himself to ask the couple if they'd spotted any crazy women praying in the reeds.

■□■

Week before Christmas, a new inmate joins us, triggering one of those double room transfers. Marvin sticks him in Rainy's former room same time he's relocating her to Rosary's. Hospital sent this one over. Name's Bernard. Binder claims he's ninety-five years old. I happen to believe it. DOB: 1/6/00. Admit: 12/20/95. Rxs: none. Allergies: none. Emergency contact line says "Son" with some upstate PA phone number.

Bernard's face is so withered it resembles lacquered bone. One eye's messed up. Spine's shaped like a letter S. It curls so far forward that his nose sits lower than his neck. I've dubbed him Old Hat, owing to the reeking orange ski cap he insists on wearing constantly.

Old Hat grew up not far from here, over in Leedom, however he moved north to Allentown for work when he was in his twenties and remained there until his wife passed, almost thirty years ago. Son's a former probate lawyer who's retired too. Another son who'd've been my age died in Korea.

He is sharing all of this with us at Christmas dinner, Monday night. We've got a decent slice of ham this year, plus garlic mashed potatoes, plus some carrots cooked with too much dill. Three custard pies are thawing in the oven.

His whole career, Old Hat continues telling us, he worked for some cement company upstate. He was what's known as the gauger, meaning he was in charge of checking all the levels on the sintering oven. Pay kept getting lower through the 1930s, year by year, the hours shorter, but he never lost his job outright like my old man did. Temperature is too important to cement. The Old Hats were still forced to take in boarders though, this Swedish family named the Larsens who quietly occupied the two front rooms of Old Hat's house for five full years.

Before things turned truly bad, all the country people used to come and do their monthly shopping there in Allentown. The city fathers decided to construct two lavish comfort stations underground, mens and ladies, with grand cement entrances, tiled waiting rooms, Ragtime music playing from a phonograph.

Old Hat sets his fork down and snaps his fingers to help jog his memory. Everybody at our table has been grinning at him off and on, marveling how anyone so old could speak so energetically.

"Dwell here and prosper. That's what it said!" He makes a fist and bops the table lightly before picking up his fork again.

"What what said?" asks Sal.

"They put the town slogan over both the entrances."

"Entrances to what?"

"To toilets! Dwell here and prosper. Right over the entrances. Dwell here and suffocate's more like it. That's what we used to say. Soon as all the shops closed, Hamilton Street went dead. But if you went down in those stations, they'd be full of people. You'd see whites and coloreds on the same benches, keeping warm. You could even take a shower for a nickel down there if you needed."

■□■

Later in the week I'm up in Mimi's room, rewatching *The Lost Weekend* for the second or third time. We ran out of movies months ago. We're at that point where Ray Milland uses a rope to hide his scotch out on the fire escape. All drunks devise their tricks like that. Mine was the inside of our children's toy chest. Backup was the bottom of my toolbox underneath some oily rags.

Tonight there's no fear of being interrupted because Peg is over in the hospital. Two days ago, she slipped and broke her foot. She'll be away rehabbing it next couple weeks. Her medication's been an issue too. Doctors keep experimenting with the dosage. Whenever they raise it, she goes catatonic, barely blinking at whoever sits across from her, entire meals. Lower it too much, her temper reemerges.

Monday night, she snapped at Mimi for not hurrying to lift her from a chair. "Help me, bitch!" she shouted. Every one of us looked down, embarrassed for the both of them.

Poor Mimi. She oughta be giddy at this two-week vacation from her mother, but she seems too racked with worry to relax. Earlier, she told me Peg might need to move to Redbeard's former room upon return. That's when I suggested Mimi hold onto this room upstairs. She don't think Peg'll allow it.

Ray Milland is lying on a gurney now. They locked him up. His face is drenched with sweat. Two nurses have to hold him down while he burns through the shakes.

I glance back at Mimi. What will her purpose in life be without her mother to wait on hand and foot the way she does?

■□■

On Thursday nights, the canteen turns into a temporary barbershop right after dinner. Four or five of us stay put to get our haircut and our shave. Rainy provides these humble services for a mere buck. She'll still trim you up if you are broke. You can either owe her the eight bits or trade a can of beer, fistful of cigarettes, a candy bar.

From the number of extras who stick around to watch, you'd think she was performing surgery. I count seven in the peanut gallery when my turn comes. Chair's positioned by the sink. Rainy whips Creep's hair out of the only bath towel and wraps it around my neck, tucking the corners in my collar. She dunks our communal comb into a mug and runs it through my waxy hair a couple times. I feel her pull a fingerful and snip most of it off. Eight pairs of eyes are staring at my head.

"What's your alma mater, Dick?" inquires Old Hat, "Go to Eddystone?"

"Nope."

"Not Ridley?"

"Yep."

"A Ridley boy, huh. Play football?"

"Til my undercarriage dropped."

"What's that mean, a hernia?"

I nod, to which he groans and taps his cheekbone.

"They made me quit too. Been blind in this one eye, account of all the hits I took back in the leather-helmet days. Retina shattered. It stopped me going in the war with my big brother."

Creep turns and gawks straight at his busted eye which don't seem to bother Old Hat none. He faces Creep and lets his jaw drop open to give him a better gander at it. Orb's completely whitened over. No iris. If you stare at it too closely, it looks like a moistened gumball, swishing round and round in someone else's mouth.

"World War Two?"

"No, sir. I meant the Great War."

"Which one was great?"

"World War One. I'm ninety-five-years old. Turn ninety-six in January. Couldn't go on account of this eye. I been through it. Get a load of my shinbone."

He slides his pantleg up for everyone to see this healing scab, six inches long. Skin's a disturbing shade of blue around it. Mimi hisses. Creep makes one of his sickened faces.

"That was on my seventh stroke. I went down the cellar to grab a soup can off the girder. Fell."

"Seven strokes!"

"Nine now. I lost count. Mine are minor. They still stick me somewhere every time. After a month or two, they send me home again. What's the point? I always tell the nurses, like MacArthur, I shall return! They screwed a plate in there after this shin ordeal. Heck. Half-blind. Hair in my ears. Hemorrhoids the size of turnips. My son's too old to take care of me now. Know where he is? A nursing home. Tell you, I been through it, sir."

His mind drifts off. A minute passes to the snipping sound of scissors. Marvin's waiting at the other table with the broom tilted against his thigh.

After Rainy finishes my neckline, she pauses to check both sides are even. She used to be a hairdresser in Sharon Hill, so this always brings out the perfectionist in her.

"Close enough for government work?"

She keeps leaning side to side. Finally she nods, then rubs her finger up against the stubble on my chin. Flakes of dead skin are constantly accumulating there. One ends up on her fingertip. She examines it before flicking it away, reaches past me for the can of shaving cream, sprays a big snowball in her palm, and smears the stuff around my jaw and throat, across my upper lip.

"A-positive," I tell her while she's fishing a new razor from the pack.

"What's that?"

"My blood type."

"Hilarious. You need to moisturize this skin more, Popsicle."

Now she starts scraping away, rapid little strokes as if she's chipping paint. She does the good side first, repositioning my head as needed with her other hand. The hairier the area, the slower that she has to go.

"Township was split in two back then," says Old Hat. He's been recollecting this whole time. "Half the kids went to Ridley. Half went to Eddystone. The blacks went to Chester. We beat you in 1916."

I can't risk talking at the moment, so I double-pump my arm at him.

"Quarterback? No sir, I played halfback and safety. Punted too. I could do anything on a field. That was the year my brother went over. They had the blue laws in those days. Know about them? You couldn't play football on a Sunday. Couldn't show movies. Couldn't fish. Couldn't buy a malted. It wasn't so easy to get into trouble."

Sal looks up from Tuesday's paper. "Who you like this weekend, Dick?"

"I like us," I say real quick between two dunks of the razor in the cruddy water, knowing it'll make Sal smirk and shake his head.

He does. "Never loses faith. I ain't too sold on this Mamula kid. Five sacks, all season."

"This is the year."

"You said that last year too."

"Yep. I'll say it next year too, assuming I'm alive."

"Quiet, you!" Rainy orders, switching to my bad side. Skin over there's as droopy as a popped balloon, due to the stroke. She has to stretch it outwards with her fingers to get any of the stubble off. I swallow some drool. Last step's to tilt my head way back so she can do my gizzard.

■□■

Today is Friday. Past hour, I've been hiding in my room from the same priest who pays us house calls every year. St. Francis Parish sends him over close to Christmas. Father Scanlon. I call it Confession Day. Father travels door to door with more equipment on him than our janitor, more envelopes stuffed in his pockets than the mailman. If you answer when he knocks, Father enters your room and turns this little folding chair ninety degrees beside your bed, then lets you pour out all your troubles or your sins for fifteen minutes. He don't say too much. Eyes stay level. Man's an expert at ignoring your appearance. That way, you'll never feel ashamed to have a visitor whose clothes are cleaned and pressed by someone else. Afterwards, he'll pray with you if you are so inclined.

I know all of this because last year, he caught me on my laps out in the hallway. That's why I was forced to let him in my room. I kept the topic to my parents. I stressed they were Methodists, hoping that would hurry up the conversation. At some point, I slipped and mentioned how it dawned on me I am now older than my parents ever got. Dad died at fifty-eight, cirrhosis, mom at sixty-two, lung cancer. I told him that sort of flips a switch inside your head. All time feels borrowed suddenly. Your number's next, you realize, which leaves you no choice but to resign yourself to certain things.

That was his in.

When he inquired what I meant by that, I gestured with my good arm at the bad one. That got him sermonizing about how there can be good in resignation too, so long as your resigning means aligning yourself with God's plan for you. That didn't sit too well with me. I had to remind him how that might be slightly harder to see from my position. He nodded, and we left it there.

He's talking to Jiggles now, next door. Their voices sound a little garbled coming through the wall, but I can hear enough to know that Jiggles is repeating the same diatribe as last year, verbatim. None of his children visit, eldest is in jail for manslaughter, youngest has four kids by three different men. Father keeps on gently urging him to forgive so he can be forgiven.

Overhearing all of this reminds me of AA. My sponsor asked me about this stuff when I did my inventory: all my anger, why I used to get into so many brawls, why I would drop whatever I was doing to cheat on my wife at every opportunity. Rock bottom was that fight I started at my father-in-law's funeral. Next day, my wife lined our four kids up for the ultimatum. Us or beer, she told me. I chose beer. I actually said it.

Visit's almost over. They're reciting the Our Father. Minute later, they are making small talk in the hallway. Jiggles shuts his door. This means I'm next. I hear footsteps coming towards me. Father knocks four times. I'm seated over by my window. For a second, I consider answering, consider letting it all out, listing each and every reason to this stranger why I cannot bring myself to call my son.

He knocks four more times.

I look myself over, these filthy rags I'm wearing, my bare feet. There's a bad sore on my left heel. Last shower was on Christmas Eve. Doubt I smell too good. Besides, what's the use of going into all of that with him? I stay very still to make sure my chair don't creak. He'll go away eventually.

"Pardon me," some voice calls down the hallway. Sounds like Zorro. "Pardon me. Hey Father, hey sorry, think I missed my turn. I was sleeping. Did you bring the communion?"

"Are you Catholic?" Father Scanlon replies skeptically.

"Yeah. Not your parish though."

"No matter, but I will need to absolve you first."

"Good idea," Zorro giggles, "Holy water tends to boil when I touch it. Hey, what's that thing you keep them in called? The hosts, I mean. It got a name?"

"It certainly does. This is called a pyx."

"A what?"

"A pyx," he repeats crisply, "P-Y-X."

"They got names for everything, don't they?"

"Pyx just means box."

"Come on in here, Father. I worked in a church once. You'll find this interesting. Know what I was? The window restorer."

Zorro's door shuts. I go back to staring out my window like some bored canine. This corrugated well in front of me is two-thirds full with soggy beech and maple leaves. Sidewalk's about thirty feet away. Part I can see is where the nurses catch their buses. Further to my right, there's that long road which runs up to the hospital. Cars come and go over that hill all day. Sometimes an ambulance zips by, its floodlights whirling, sirens off.

CHAPTER 11: THE YEAR IN REVIEW

New Year's morning, I sit on the sofa next to Swab who's snoring loudly, one hand cupped around his nuts, the other gripping his half-empty bottle from last night's festivities. Mummers Parade is on TV. Some string band wearing pink-and-yellow sequined costumes marches towards the camera in a peppy rendition of "When You're Smiling."

Hip's aching, so I shift my weight, which causes Swab to wake up with a start.

"Shit," he grumbles, checking his surroundings, back and forth, "Did I sleep here?"

I shrug in a *where else* kind of way.

As he lifts the bottle to his lips, I can smell my preferred whiskey of yore, Ballantine. Label hasn't changed. Swab takes a short swig, another, then that third one alcoholics always take mechanically. Bottle gets wedged between his hairy thighs.

Three men are playing clarinets in front of us, six feet apart due to the giant feather wheels hitched to their backs.

"How much them feather getups cost?" I wonder.

"Fuck if I know. I don't own one."

"Why wheels?"

"Ask Sal."

"Ask me what?" Sal groans behind us.

"You in here too?"

Swab twists his head around to locate Sal back on the love seat where he clearly spent the night as well. Cone hat's still strapped under his chin. *1996* is printed on it in gold letters. Why does Marvin insist on going overboard with every holiday? String lights and tinsel, glossy cut-outs of old Father Time bent over his walking stick with little Baby Time beside him in a clothespinned diaper, twenty pairs of novelty glasses, corny hats, every imaginable kind of party favor. Rainy brought her boombox down. I lasted until 1:15. Marvin hadn't left yet. All of them drank far too much. Every thirty seconds, someone blew through their kazoo.

Swab calls over his left shoulder, "Ain't your cousin one of these Mummer homos?"

"Uncle."

"Skin flute?"

"Tuba."

Swab grunts. Within a minute, he has drifted back asleep.

Next act isn't holding any instruments. There's ten of them, all dressed like grade-school hoodlums with band-aids and black eyes painted on their faces, missing teeth, patched pants. Other two are wearing milkman uniforms, crisp white with those black-brimmed caps they used to wear. They're waving to the crowd alongside an original Good Humor truck. Soon as the music starts, the hoodlums crowd around them, turning out their pockets, pleading for some free ice cream. In response, the milkmen jab a finger in their palms, demanding money first, at which point the hoodlums beat them to the ground then help themselves to ice cream from the truck.

■□■

During my morning laps, hearing all these partygoers puking in their rooms, I keep having the same thought. Nobody's getting any better in this place. I know that's obvious by now. Thought still strikes me as profound, due solely to the date, I guess. 1/1/96. It's hard to believe I've served nearly three years in this toilet. Bunyan's dead. Redbeard's dead. Cy's in jail. Gums is in some madhouse. Brog headed south. Rosary's still missing.

First week after her disappearance, Rosary was the only topic during meals. Was her corpse rotting beside a bunch of mobsters at the bottom of the Delaware? Was she on some pilgrimage to Maryland? Cops had no idea. We checked every paper nervously, expecting another story on the missing woman, but no story ever came.

Night School one night, I brought the situation up to Thinker.

"You two ever?"

He smirked at the ceiling. "No. Well, mostly no. Nothing to preclude her from entering the Pearly Gates if that's what you're insinuating. Let's just say I countenanced her countenance."

"Speak English, Harry."

"I liked her face."

After that, we never brought her up again, neither at Night School, nor at meals, nor in the rec room when the evening news came on.

Agnes is with Mary now was the consensus.

Where's that leave the rest of us? I sure hope Gums is doing better, wherever he ended up. It's not like I haven't tried to help a few of them: Harry first, then Jack, Lorraine, and Mimi too. Others, I never even bothered. Swab reminds me of myself at his age. He's on track to drink himself to death within five years. Sal's lungs are going. He sounds more like Redbeard every day. Creep's packed on thirty pounds of pretzel weight. Army jacket doesn't fit him anymore. Peg's now officially too frail to climb a flight of stairs. Each night, I flip through the entire binder, calling out their names and corresponding pills to Marvin.

Every single one of them's deteriorating.

Guess it stands to reason with all of this greasy food, washed down with ten to twenty cups of sour coffee every day. Add eight or nine sodas. Add two- or three-pack habits. Only change in scenery comes from TV.

More I dwell on it, I keep returning to what Zorro said that day to the repairman. Thirty days. Walk anytime. Notice form is blue. Exit date and reason. Mine stays in my nightstand. Zorro had a point. It does make things worse in a way.

■□■

Sunday afternoon, I'm on the rec room sofa with a few remaining others, watching us get clobbered by the Cowboys. This is not the year. Season finished 10-6. Wildcard. That made three more wins than last year. Main reason for the turnaround was our new owner fired Kotite and replaced him with Ray Rhodes who rounded out the roster with a slew of crazy guys right off the street—former trashmen, grocery baggers—kind who are just dying for a legal chance to maim somebody. Way we beat up on the Lions last week, fifty-something points, I tricked myself into believing we could pull an upset out in Dallas, but the Cowboys are too quick. They knocked Peete out of the game in the first quarter. Shoulder sprain. Randall is rusty. Running game never got going. Boniol is lining up to kick another extra point. It's good. 30-3.

"Ya still like us, Dick?" Sal asks, standing up beside me.

"Fuck you."

"Yeah, same to you, sweet talker."

"Is Mamula even on the field?" asks Swab, next off the sofa.

They're heading for the pew to wait for dinner. Creep rushes after them.

"You guys should really listen to me more," he gloats.

"Go fuck your mother, you fat sack of shit."

That's all Creep was after. He howls and claps two times, following them out the door.

Old Hat taps me on the arm. "Remember Greasy Neale?"

"Sure."

"You ever hear how Greasy kept them limber in the olden days? Before aeroplanes."

"Nope."

"Well, they used to have to ride the buses real long distances to games. How far's Wisconsin? Fourteen hours? Greasy was the coach back then. He won in '48 and '49."

"I remember."

"I heard Bill Campbell call it on the radio."

"I was there in '48. Never missed a game in those days."

"What Greasy'd do is have the bus driver pull over every couple hours. He'd hold drills in empty fields. Don't stretch, your muscles cramp. You'll get yourself killed playing that way, so Neale'd stop off somewhere like Lancaster and line the whole team up for calisthenics."

"Smart."

"Imagine what them Amish people must've thought. You're tilling your field one day, minding your own business. A bus pulls to a halt. Fifty men rush out. They start doing lunges and wind sprints. The oldest guy keeps blowing a whistle at them. You don't know the reason."

"Harry'd get a kick out of this."

"It could be the Russians invading, for all you know about football. You don't understand they're practicing to play the Packers."

Old Hat pauses because we just scored in garbage time. Randall ran it in against their backups. 30-9. Now we're lining up for two.

Zorro and Rainy leave together. She's wearing his flannel shirt.

Old Hat reaches for my cane. He lifts it off the ground a foot to gauge its weight then sets it down. "Were you at Crozer?"

I nod. "Bout eight weeks, six more at the rehab."

"It mess up your words?"

Two point conversion worked. 30-11. Eight plus eight plus three would tie it now, except there's only 2:14 left on the clock.

"Some, at first. I knew what I wanted to say. It just came out all raspy. I had to repeat myself a lot."

"Did your children have to translate for the nurses?"

"Something like that."

He's got me picturing that day. I was out golfing after work at Clayton Park. There's that par-three where everybody leaves their bags up on the hill because the walk down's steep. You take your putter plus a seven- or a nine-iron. I shot a four. I can remember climbing back up the hill. Rest is harder to describe. It was like there was no hill all of a sudden, no golf course. I was staring at my clubs like they were tools from work I didn't recognize. I let them drop and sort of wobbled to the ground. That's when my friend rushed over. Words I got out were so slurred, his first assumption was I'd fallen off the wagon.

"They sure put you through the paces, don't they? Gymnastic bars. Them practice stairs. God. All those silly questions too! Honestly, what do I care who's president at my age? What month is it? What state? I used to say Arkansas sometimes, just to see their faces. Hey! Wish me happy birthday, Dick."

"When was it?"

"Day before yesterday, I think. Anyway, I'm ninety-six years old. I'm gonna catch George Burns."

That makes me chuckle. "Say goodnight, Gracie."

"Goodnight, Gracie."

"Happy birthday, Bernie."

"Thank you."

Everybody else is waiting in the hall for dinner. Aikman's on the sidelines with his hands tucked in the warmer at his waist. Second stringer's taking knees for him. Season's over. Some blizzard warning runs across the bottom of the screen.

Heavy snow is in effect across the Greater Philadelphia area. Complete update will follow the game.

■□■

Thinker's not at dinner. After the dessert course, I go up to check on him. He's been acting goofy lately, all this excess laughter at his obscure jokes.

"Approach and read!" he shouts like he's preoccupied with something when I knock.

I find him crouching by his wall of books, scanning their titles one by one.

"Have a seat. I'm hunting down a quote."

"On what?"

"The downfall of Rome."

"Okay."

From the banker's chair, I watch him run his finger down the fourth column of books, up the fifth, down the sixth. Snow's already drifting past his window. Suddenly his finger freezes. He yanks a bulky green book out and begins flipping through it carefully, even checks its index, before placing it behind him with the forty others scattered on the floor.

"You missed dinner. Bernie told this story you'd—"

"A moment!" he snaps at me. Next book he grabs is leatherbound. He skims several chapters of it, line by line, then slams it shut. "Where is this godforsaken thing?" He rolls off his knees onto his ass. "I give up. I give up! Forgive me, I've been searching for this passage ever since your game. It's too perfect. I was watching all of you scream at the TV set, and I started hearing it inside my head. Something about frequenting circuses. You'll appreciate this more than anyone, actually. It confirms every thing you've ever said about this dingy labyrinth of ours. Come to think of it, I'm pretty sure it even mentions cigarettes."

"Well, what book's it in?"

"I can't remember."

"Who said it?"

"I can't remember that either."

"You check Nordau?"

"Yes, but Nordau doesn't mention sports. He was too cosmopolitan. No, it's too bucolic to be Nordau. Fresh air. Vigor. I went through Muir and Kipling, Stegner, all of Hemingway. It's too modern to be Nicholas Bownde. I thought maybe Solberg, commenting on Bownde. I went through every page. It's not in there."

"What about Hitler?"

"Hitler never mentioned football. Oh, who said it? It really nails the whole grotesquerie of watching sports. I cannot stand it when this happens."

"What's football got to do with Rome?"

"Oh no!" he gasps.

"What?"

"What if it's Gibbon? I'll never find it if it's Gibbon."

"Harry, what's football got to do with Rome?"

He's not listening at all. Teeth are clamped down on his knuckle. I've never seen him quite so agitated. He pries his finger from his mouth, wags it in the air, then points at the stack of notebooks on his desk. I know what he's thinking. He's thinking if he thought this much of it, the quote I mean, however many weeks or months or even years ago, then he certainly copied it down in its entirety. Problem is there must be over fifty of them notebooks.

■□■

By morning, an even line of snow leans a foot high along the canteen windows. It's barely 5 AM. Building's totally silent. TV's even off. I drink some orange juice, then check outside. All the panes are damp with condensation. I wipe enough away from one to watch the snow continue falling. It's as thick as pillow feathers. Yard is buried. So's our stoop past the third step.

■□■

By Wednesday, half the building's come down with some two-end flu. Theory is it must've gotten passed around during the game on Sunday. So far, I feel fine. Little mild diarrhea's all. Others are in far worse shape.

Crossing the second floor that afternoon, I overhear Creep retching into something. There goes four pretzels, I think, unable to stop myself from laughing loud enough for him to hear. Thinker's groaning loudly in the toilet. Sal comes shuffling towards me.

"Occupied," I warn him.

He continues past, clutching both halves of his ass. Moan he lets out from the stairwell minute later indicates he didn't make it.

■□■

Dinner's down to me and Old Hat. The two of us are slurping noodle soup across the ping-pong table from each other. Mimi's helping Marvin lug trays of it with aspirin up to all the rooms. I was surprised our minder even made it here in these conditions. Buses aren't running. Walk took him forty minutes extra. Anywhere the sidewalks weren't cleared, he shifted to the middle of the street. His snowshoes are drying on the counter.

Old Hat's hand is trembling as he aims the spoon into his mouth. He swallows what little didn't spill, then grins at me.

"You still spared?"

"Touch of the screamers. No fever. You?"

"Nary a sniffle. I can't get sick. My son's the same." He tilts over to peruse the paper Marvin left there on the table. "Coast Guard says piles might dam river. Region emerging from historic blizzard. Twelve deaths!"

"What from?"

He squints at the page. "Attributed to cold."

"They mention any names?"

Head shakes. "Just the number. Pity. Homeless shelters bursting at the seams. Four hundred billion pounds of snow dumped on the eastern portion of the state. That's nothing. You should've seen the one in '35. Were you born yet?"

I nod between slurps.

"I had to cut our way out in the morning, that one." He looks back down at the paper. "Expecting more on Friday," he adds, glancing up again when Marvin walks past him in red socks. He watches him arrange four bowls atop his tray, fill them from the pot, then fit packs of crackers all around them.

As he's going by, Old Hat punches the air and calls out, "Into the breach!" Same as the last two passes.

■□■

Friday after lunch, I'm helping Ocky study for some nurse certificate she needs in order to get a raise. Textbook's put away. She's over by the windows watching more snow fill the yard while I read questions off this stack of flash cards to her.

"What does N.P.O. stand for?"

"Nil per something. It means nothin in the mouth."

I flip the card over and nod. "Next question. What are the four main patient identifiers?"

"Ask they name. Ask they date of birth. Check chart..."

"One more."

"Social?"

"Nope. Wrist band. Next. What does B.I.D. stand for?"

She turns her head and shrugs.

"Think pills."

"Oh, right, right, that some Latin too. Twice a day!"

"Correct. How often must patients be turned to prevent bedsores?"

"Daily?"

"Close. Four to six hours."

It's only the two of us in here, though Sal keeps popping in and peering out the windows to make sure the Breadline hasn't started forming yet. Same standoff occurs every winter. You can make out foggy silhouettes of other people staring, same as you, across the yard. Everybody's waiting for somebody else to initiate the line. All it takes is one moron prepared to shiver in the cold outside the office. Sixty people then have to rush outside to stand behind them.

"How often should catheters be changed?"

"Daily?"

"Monthly."

Sal's back at the windows. He has this habit of undoing and redoing the top button on his shirt whenever he gets anxious.

"Witch's tit in here," he says, coughing dryly as he pivots toward us.

"Try not opening the friggin door."

"You're right about that," he admits. "Say, Rich, you don't got fifty cents, do you? It's for a coffee."

"See that office out there?"

"C'mon, Rich. My nuts are falling off. Ain't you cold too?"

"Sal, I'm flat, capeesch?"

"Capeesch! I got yer capeesch, you cheap prick."

He glares at me. I glare right back. Eyes have hollow rings around them, dark as lampblack. He's even skinnier than he looked a month ago. He tilts his head and puts on a large forced smile, hoping it will change my mind.

"Sal, I said I'm flat! Go build a snowman or something."

"C'mon Rich. I'll pay you back in an hour, honest." Thumb points over his shoulder.

"She ain't coming," Ocky informs him.

"Who ain't? What do you mean?"

"Robin. Roads is too bad where she lives. She called a half hour ago."

"Tell me she's sending someone else."

Ocky shakes her head. "She said Monday."

■ □ ■

Word travels around the building fast. During my laps that afternoon, I'm hounded up and down the halls with several dozen near-identical requests. Withdrawal pains are audible in all their voices. Instant my head begins to shake, they curse down at the floor and slam their doors at me.

By evening, everyone I come across has grown so desperate they now try to sell me things. Lolly sticks a scented candle in my face. Zorro offers me a trade: this mismatched pair of socks he's holding for some cigarettes.

"For cigarettes?"

"Yeah, three."

"Cigarettes?"

"Yeah."

"Don, how long have I lived here?" Before he has a chance to shrug, I answer for him. "Three years, Don. Have you ever seen me smoke a fucking cigarette?" He reaches for his door. "Non-smoker, Don," I yell through it. "For chrissake, try planning ahead!"

I continue down the hall. What lap is this? Twenty-six or twenty-seven? I need to get a hold of myself. I can't let them get under my skin like that. Kneeslapper don't seem to register me going up the stairs.

Thinker's door is open. He's at his desk, slowly flipping through one of his notebooks. He don't look up either.

Salvy's waiting for me up ahead.

"I gave at the office!"

He leans out his doorway. "You cheap son of a bitch. Why do you always say that?"

"Coffers are empty, pal."

Now he waves at me to go away as if I'd been asking him for money, instead of the other way around. "I'm not your fucking pal."

Swab cracks up at us from bed. "Give your pal a fucking quarter please. I'm sick of hearing him. Yo, Sal!"

"*Va fangool*, the two of ya!"

"Yo, Sal!"

"What?"

"When are you gonna get this belt you tried to sell me outta my room?"

"Never. Hang yourself with it."

■□■

Remainder of the weekend I hide in my cell from all of them. I can't take it. I don't bother doing laps. I don't set foot inside the rec room. I skip half my meals. No appetite. I pass hours gazing out my window.

On Saturday, I take a badly needed shit.

Shortly after dinner, Sunday, I start noticing my tongue tastes sour. I try rinsing it with water from the sink, but this foul chalky taste won't go away. Throat's sore too. I lie back down. Mouth won't quit producing drool. Every ten minutes, I'm tilting over so my bottom lip is lined up with my popcorn tin. From there, I let gravity do all the work. Fourth or fifth time doing this, I realize I need to vomit out all my spaghetti. Luckily most of it ends up in the tin. I try to stand. I'd like to swish more water in my mouth, but I'm too woozy. Legs lack any strength. I flop back on the mattress, shut my eyes.

Rest of the night, I lie there watching all the pockmarks in the ceiling shifting back and forth. Longest I stay asleep is half an hour. Face is burning though no sweat has broken out as yet. Mouth still tastes awful. I vomit once more, close to dawn, then finally conk out.

It's dark again when I wake up. It must be Monday night. Somebody hosed out my tin for me. An opened apple juice is sitting on my nightstand. Marvin must've checked on me when I skipped dinner. I gulp down the apple juice and call his name, but he don't answer.

Later, I hear women whispering out in the hall. Door's cracked an inch. Rainy steps in first, balancing a bowl in her right palm. Mimi unfolds a chair for her, then helps me sit upright.

"Think you can swallow this?" asks Rainy, extending the spoon.

I nod. She gets some broth in me, some more.

"What day is it?"

"Wednesday."

"Wednesday?"

"You got puke all over you, Popsicle."

She feeds me some more broth then sets the bowl beside the pisscup on my nightstand. Mimi wipes my face and neck with a damp towel. One of them lifts me while the other peels my shirt over my head. Marvin steps into the room, shaking the house thermometer. He slides it underneath my tongue. A crowd has gathered in the hall behind him.

"What's going on?" asks Creep.

"Nothing."

"What is he, dead? Dick, you dead? Let me see him."

"Be quiet," Old Hat says, "Dick caught sick is all."

"I don't believe it."

"Somebody should bring him extra blankets."

"Do we got any?"

"He'll be fine. He needs to sweat it out. That's how I shook it."

"Be quiet. Let him rest."

"You let him rest."

Temperature is 101. Marvin orders everyone out in the hall back to the rec room. Mimi lays a wet rag on my forehead then goes out. I drift off while Rainy's smoking in the chair.

It's daylight when I wake back up. Now Mimi's in the chair. They must be alternating shifts.

It's dark again with Rainy in the chair when someone knocks loud on my door.

"What is it?" she says.

Thinker enters. A demented leer is plastered on his face. He splits the notebook open in his palms and starts to read.

"One of the causes of the downfall of Rome was that people, being fed by the State to the extent of three-quarters of the population ceased to have any responsibility for themselves or their children, and consequently became a nation of unemployed wasters."

"Go away! Can't you tell he's sick?"

"They frequented the circuses, where paid performers appeared before them in the arena, much as we see crowds now flocking to look on at paid players playing football."

"Will you get lost?"

"Football in itself is a grand game for developing a lad physically and also morally, for he learns to play with good temper and unselfishness. But it is a vicious game when it draws crowds of lads away from playing the game themselves to be merely onlookers at a few paid performers. I yield to no one in enjoyment of the sight of those splendid specimens of our race, trained to perfection, and playing faultlessly, but my heart sickens at the reverse of the medal—thousands of boys and young men, pale, narrow-chested, hunched-up, miserable specimens, smoking endless cigarettes, numbers of them betting, all of them learning to be hysterical as they groan or cheer in panic unison with their neighbors."

CHAPTER 12: MY PISSCUP RUNNETH OVER

Don't ask me how I fell near end of January. All that's important to relate is that I got myself wedged between the wall and my own bed, that I was stuck back there the better part of a day. I yelled and yelled for help until my voice box petered out completely, and Marvin only found me when I didn't show for dinner or for medications.

By that stage, I'd lost all track of time. Window had been dark for hours. Side I was lying on kept going numb in stages. A bladder can only hang on for so long. How's that old nursery rhyme go? I jumped into a box of eggs. Yellow ran all down my legs. Well, sometime after that I must've passed out from the pain because I remember snapping back awake at the sound of someone tapping on my door.

"Hey Dick...Dick...are you athleep?"

I let out the hoarsest scream for help you ever heard.

Marvin unlocked my door, yanked my bed out of the way, and dug my quad cane out from underneath my ribs. As he tried lifting me, I hissed and waved at him to stop. I knew I was hurt. He set me back down on the floor and rushed to call an ambulance. Face stung. I reached up and felt around my forehead. There was blood. Cheek got scuffed up too. If only I had tripped the other way. Least I could've braced my fall.

That was six weeks ago.

I spent two weeks in the hospital—x-rays, stitches, fluids, surgery for a busted hip—plus four more weeks relearning how to walk in the same rehab joint they shipped me to five years ago when this all started. No one there remembered me.

Last night, this social worker drove me home. Her name is Kay. She's the type I would've made a run at right until the stroke: late-thirties, brunette, with that slightly husky sort of voice I've always liked. Kay visited me twice. We talked over my whole situation. Most of these social workers are in such a hurry, they'll take one look at your file, one quick look at you, then tell you where you ought to go. Kay wasn't like that. When she asked me what I enjoyed about this place, I told her the truth. Although it may be short on niceties, I'd always figured there'd be more laughs here than in some nursing home. I've made some friends. Plus everything about those other places sounded final. Kay didn't interrupt. She heard me out, then listed all the reasons why it might be time for something better suited to my physical needs. We went back and forth on it awhile.

Second visit, she brought a brochure with her for one nearby she had in mind. Being a veteran, honorably discharged, a Purple Heart and all, I get priority. I let her put me on some waiting list to make her happy. Place looked alright. Guess I'll be shipping off soon as somebody frees a room up over there by dying.

■□■

It's Wednesday morning. I've been watching *Looney Tunes* past hour from this wheelchair Marvin dug out of the crawlspace for me. Swab is snoring on the sofa. Two gophers on the screen are balancing upon this log that's drifting down a river towards the Acme lumbermill. I can't seem to get comfortable in this seat. I decide to move again. Wheeling with one arm just makes the chair go round in circles, so I pivot round the sofa and start pushing myself backwards by the shoe.

Swab's eyes reopen. Something about the jerky way I'm moving makes us grin at one another. He shuts his eyes again, right as I pull up to that dusty bookcase near the door.

Top is covered with two easy-looking puzzles under a pair of overflowing ashtrays. Three crushed soda cans are mixed in with the books.

First row is full of funny-titled Westerns: *The Cockeyed Corpse, Saddlebum, The Vanishing American.*

Next row has those cheap leather classics, ones with the bright-colored bars along the spine: condensed *Oliver Twist*, condensed *Inferno*, condensed *Pilgrim's Progress*, condensed *Odyssey*, condensed *Grapes of Wrath*, condensed *Don Quixote*, condensed *Canterbury Tales,* etc.

Bottom row has most of a set of *Funk & Wagnalls*, Volume *C*, then *F* straight up to *V*. There's two copies of *The Thorn Birds*, several Michener novels, two more army field manuals—*FM 21-18* and *FM 72-20*—plus a black leather Bible which says *Large-Print Version: Words of Christ in Red.*

Pilgrim one sounds interesting. I stash it between my legs and push my way towards the canteen, still backwards with my head cocked to the side to make sure I don't crash into the wall. This takes several minutes, though it's hardly fifty feet.

Canteen's empty. I open the book at the far table, resting my forearm across the bottom to hold my place. I start to read under my breath.

"As I walk'd through the wilderness of this world, I lighted on a certain place where was a Den..."

I've barely finished the first paragraph when Salvy strolls in and pours himself some coffee from the urn. He snatches the paper off the other table and brings it to the seat right next to mine.

"Didn't know you were Italian."

"What?"

He points at the backrest of my wheelchair.

"Oh. That ain't me."

"Who's Modesti then?"

I shrug. He means the guy whose name is written on the backrest in thick silver magic marker. His obituary's out there on the noticeboard, slowly yellowing with all the others.

I glance at the paper he set down while he's sipping his coffee: *PA Senate OKs Welfare Cuts, Working to Get I-95 On the Move Again, Dow Soars 98.63 Points, Company Fine-tuned Nicotine.*

He flips the paper over to the Sports, coughing loudly, then squints down at yesterday's box score. "See Jordan put up 38 on us last night?"

"I saw. What's our record again?"

He squints at the page. "13 and 52."

"Christ."

Sal's hay fever's returning. Eyes look raw. He rubs his knuckles in the sockets then sniffles steadily until he's gathered something he can gulp straight down.

I return to my pilgrim book. I have to spread my fingers out across two pages at a time. When Sal rises to refill his mug, I ask him to bring me one. We sit there reading for awhile. By the time I've read ten pages, my right hand begins to cramp. Book wants to shut itself.

"Look who's back!" a voice shouts from the doorway, "The Fall Guy."

Creep pours himself some coffee and comes over. After two long sips, he bends down to examine the curved gash along the left side of my forehead.

"Still a little puffy," he remarks.

"You should see the other guy."

"What other guy?"

"Never mind."

"How many stitches that take?"

"Ten."

"Nasty. What's with the chair? Can't you walk anymore?"

"It's temporary."

"Temporary?" he repeats, patting my shoulder disbelievingly, "I don't know. Once you settle into one of those, hard to go back, Dicko."

■□■

Rest of the morning, I spend struggling to get comfortable in this chair. I do several trips along the hall. Sometimes standing up in place a couple minutes helps.

Noon comes. I scoot over to the canteen early, even though I don't feel hungry in the slightest. Some new girl's preparing sandwiches. I don't bother to introduce myself. I eat half of mine and leave. Doctor told me I looked undernourished before surgery.

After lunch, I sit through *Hogan's Heroes* and *Gilligan's Island*. Halfway through *Columbo*, I wheel myself backwards to my room. I shove my window up and sit there listening to some pigeon cooing from the ledge above me. Sound it makes is cute for a few minutes, but you let a pigeon get too comfortable, their cooing turns into this deep reverberating grunt. I grow annoyed and bop the windowsill two times to scare him off.

At 3:00, I hear the school bell dinging three blocks down the road. Black kids begin to rush along the sidewalk, all of them clowning, shoving one another. A hobo passes next with a full shopping cart.

First thing Marvin does at 4:00 is check on me. From all his cheerfulness, I sense he feels a little guilty for not finding me much sooner back in January. I let him wheel me to the canteen.

En route, he fills me in on all I've missed these past six weeks. Old Hat returned home. Peg's in the hospital again with heart trouble. Rainy got 3-0-2'd. Thinker did too after he fell apart one night. Warden upped the price of packs another thirty cents. I should be glad I wasn't here for that.

As he's locking my wheels in place beside the sink, I ask him if he's ever heard about that nursing home Kay recommended. Turns out he applied to work there twice. Never did he imagine he'd be stuck here for two years and counting. This job was only supposed to tide him over until something better opened over at the hospital. He keeps explaining while he's making dinner.

■□■

All week, I wheel along the hall. This new ceramic hip can't handle stairs as yet. At cattle call, someone appoints themselves to wheel me from the rec room to the canteen. Somebody else'll wheel me back. We watch *Jeopardy* followed by *Wheel of Fortune,* then either the basketball or hockey. Anytime a handful of us sit together lately, I keep noticing this potent odor I can't pin on anybody in particular. It's not the regular reek of smoke in all our clothes. It's muskier. Animals kept in captivity too long. Nobody can be bothered to change or bathe this time of year.

■□■

Leg's beginning to feel a little stronger. I've started doing hallway laps again. One night, I walk to dinner with my cane. Everybody looks astonished as I step into the canteen. They've already grown accustomed to me in that chair. Each day, I tack an extra lap or two onto my total. Still can't manage stairs, but I am making progress.

■□■

Day I'm feeling confident enough to venture out of doors, tail end of March, it has to piss-rain on us, four days in a row. I hear the storm drains gurgling from my open window. Cars are sloshing past. This dump sits downhill in all four directions. Longer it rains, the more the little puddles in the yard consolidate into this single filthy bog with plastic bags and twigs and ten thousand mushy butts all floating on the top.

■□■

Sunday afternoon, I'm at the canteen windows, watching this solid sheet of water pour over the gutters. Flowerbed in front of me is filling fast.

Sal comes walking in and spins the chair beside me so he can face the windows too. He's dressed in his only suit. As he takes his pinstriped jacket off, I see a dozen tiny moth holes in the back. He drapes the jacket over his chair and untucks his shirt. When he sits and extends his swollen legs, I realize he isn't wearing socks or shoes. Last two inches of his pants are soaked.

"Wish we owned a friggin canoe."

"How bad's the sidewalk?"

He wags his hand to tell me to forget it.

"I'm gonna go stand on the stoop then."

"What for?"

"I need air."

"Don't forget your life jacket."

He slides this woven piece of yellow palm out of his pocket and starts fiddling with it. I unstick my shoes from the linoleum and step around him. Lolly's two seats over, writing another letter to her cousin in Nevada. Zorro's mumbling to Rainy as she sips a mug of something.

"They gotta act like they're providing you a service. You understand I'm trying to be sensitive about this. I'm not trying to point no damn fingers at no guilty asses."

"It wasn't my ass."

"I realize."

"Don't leave out guilty dicks. You can't have guilty asses without guilty dicks."

"That's our luck."

It's six steps to the landing. They take me a good five minutes. Front door refuses to give way at first. I put my shoulder into it.

Outside, there's a small dry area below the awning, wide enough for two people, where the water only drips a little on your arm. I lean against the brick and size up my surroundings. Yard's a swamp. Some spots appear knee-deep.

Across the way, some woman I don't recognize is standing on another stoop in this ruffley red sweater and black leggings. She jams her cigarette between her lips so she can wave at me, both arms, far above her head, smiling like she thinks it's funny that we had the same idea. I wave back at her, just to be polite. After she flicks her finished butt into the bog, she cups both hands around her mouth and yells some word. Rain's too loud to make it out. I curve my hand behind my ear to tell her to repeat it. She yells the word a second time. I still don't understand, but I nod anyway. She waves goodbye and goes inside.

Ten minutes later, I see Creep ducking through the trees, clutching his coffee with both hands, hood even with his nose. He sets his coffee down and bends to roll his corduroys as high up his wide calves as they will go. He starts splashing through the filthy water, laughing to himself. He yanks his hood back as he takes the covered spot beside me. Face is round and poreless as a bowling ball. Drops of rain are bouncing off it.

"Ahoy there!"

"Ahoy."

He gulps down some coffee before telling me, "You look marooned."

"I'm waiting for McHale to pick me up."

"Who's that?"

"Nobody."

"You look glum, Dicko, how you feeling?"

"I feel tremendous."

"Tremendous! I don't believe you. How could you possibly feel tremendous?"

"Alright. I feel like you then."

"That's more like it."

"Just another soaked asshole."

He starts to giggle. "There you go, Dicko. That arm of yours working yet?"

"Fuck you."

He reaches over and tries to rub my belly. I flick his hand away. "Keep your fat paws off me."

This only makes him giggle harder.

■□■

Next day, I receive a phone call shortly before dinner. I'm waiting on the pew with Sal, rereading one of the obituaries on the noticeboard, when Marvin unlocks the door and pushes people back so he can poke his head around it.

"Dick, you're wanted on the phone."

"Very funny."

"C'mon." He waves me over.

"Yeah, yeah, April Fool's." I gesture towards the calendar.

"I'm theriouth. C'mon, I'm cooking."

I do my best to hurry between the two rows of people pressed along the walls. He locks the door behind me, rushes to the smoking oven, slides a pan of chicken cutlets out, and waves his dishtowel at them, cursing.

Receiver's waiting for me on the counter. I lift it and say hello. It's that social worker Kay. She says she's calling with good news. A spot just opened at that nursing home. We can go check it out if I'm still interested. When I don't answer right away, she asks me if I'm free on Thursday.

"I'm free til Labor Day," I tell her.

That gets a solid laugh. We plan for her to pick me up Thursday morning at 10:00.

I hang up.

Marvin stops me soon as I start walking towards the door. "Ith almoth ready," he says, "Have a theat."

Gripping the table, I glance over at the windows. Rain hasn't stopped. There's some banging on the door. Zorro's nose is smushed against the porthole. Both his middle fingers are squeezed in beside his face. Marvin keeps on stirring a big pot that smells like beans. He tips half a can of seasoning into it, then ladles some onto a plate, adds a cutlet, walks it over to the farthest spot at the other table.

I watch him repeat this process fifteen times.

As he sets mine in front of me, he goes, "You're gonna leave, huh?"

"I don't know. Guess I should check the place out. I'm not sure what to do."

"Ith way nyther there. Bet you can get PT too. There'll be more people your own age."

"That don't matter. No one acts their age here anyway."

"They'll have activitieth. I think they even have a comedian wunth a week. You'll like it."

"Doubt he's funnier than here."

He chuckles in agreement. Once he's set out all the knives and forks, he steps over to the door and lets out this dramatic exhale, several seconds long, clearly a daily ritual. Zorro's been shouting at him through the porthole this whole time. He exhales once more, then looks at me.

"Hey, Dick."

"Yeah?"

"Mind if I athk a favor?"

"Shoot."

"Could you put a word in for me over there?"

Being on this side of the door for once is interesting, witnessing what Marvin witnesses daily, the same line of idiots shuffling in, second the door pulls back, all in a hurry to reclaim their favorite seats, wolfing whatever's on their plates immediately, only to complain about his cooking while they pick their teeth.

Tonight Rainy and Sal end up on either side of me. Both reach for my plate before I've had a chance to ask for help. Rainy beats him to it. She cuts my charred cutlet into safer bites and slides it back. I sneak my fork under a piece which still has breading on it, aim it in my mouth.

All I hear now besides the exhaust fan churning is the sound of thirteen sets of jaws, moving up and down at different paces.

Sal passes me the rolls. I set mine on the table and hand the basket off to Rainy.

No games are on tonight, so I walk to my room right after *Jeopardy* to pull that brochure from my nightstand. I flip it open: Bingo, Watercolors, Memory Hour, Bridge and Rummy, Book Club, Flower Arrangement, Comedy Nite, Sunday Singalongs. Beside the activities, there's a photo of some Lawrence Welk impersonator in a powder blue tuxedo. None of that stuff appeals to me too much.

It does say I could get PT on-site. It also says a barber visits twice a week. I start recalling the good reasons Kay provided: elevators and pneumatic doors, improved food, a cleaner room, designated smoking area, emergency cords alongside every bed and toilet. Here you just yell. I could even have a motorized wheelchair if I wanted. Instead of a yard, there's an enclosed garden with these tall glass ceilings. Photo makes it look nice. There's an old couple on a bench with all these ferns and pots of marigolds around them. Her hands are resting on a metal walker. His are holding a four-pronged cane like mine. Everyone looks my age or much older in the photo of the spacious dining room beside it. I don't know. It's not like I haven't mulled this over since our conversation, but her phone call earlier caught me off guard. What I keep thinking is that some of her good reasons don't sound that good to me. What good's a wheelchair? What good's an elevator? Bad leg isn't getting any stronger propped up in some leg rest without stairs to climb.

■□■

Next two days, I don't allow myself to think about my situation. I'll go and see.

■□■

By Wednesday, yard has drained enough for my inaugural lap of spring. Afterwards, I pass two pleasant hours on my bench waiting for Crutch. I monitor the pigeons and the squirrels. Some new guy in suspendered pants approaches me, asking for fifty cents.

"I gave at the office."

He grins wryly like he understood my joke, and backs away.

Around 3:00, Ben Franklin joins me. I interrupt one of his tales to ask if he knows how Crutch is doing. He has no idea. He hasn't seen him since November.

■□■

After dinner, I sit through the Sixers game against the Pacers. We keep it tied until the half, but then the Pacers pull away.

Back in my room, I lay out my least-stained golf shirt, least-stained pair of sweatpants for tomorrow morning, making a mental note not to put them on until after breakfast. Next I walk my shoes across the hall, one at a time of course, to rinse the tops under the sink and wipe them off with toilet paper.

Right before bed, I pull out that brochure again and read it over in the hopes some detail will force me to feel one way or the other. It don't work. I hate this fucking place, but I don't want to leave. Call it penance. I don't know. Maybe I want them all to see me get rolled out of here like Bunyan on some random afternoon.

I pull the notice form out next. There's only three lines on it. Name. Move-out date. Reason for leaving. I set them both beside my pisscup on the nightstand and lie back in bed. It takes me far longer than usual to fall asleep. Last time I notice on my clock's 1:48.

■□■

A door slams loud enough to wake me in the middle of the night. Clock says 3:42. I need to piss. Level on my cup's too high to chance it, so I carry it across the hall, pour the contents in the sink, then stand the cup under the faucet, let hot water run inside while I step over to the toilet. Somebody mummified the seat again. Whoever did so also dumped a bag of seaweed in the bowl. I honestly can't tell if what I'm staring at is vomit or shit.

I flush the toilet, slide my sweatpants down, and piss.

Crossing the hall, pisscup in hand, I hear several voices talking over one another near the canteen. I set my pisscup on the nightstand and investigate. It's perfectly normal to find a sleepless smoker or two, staring off in there at any time of night, but whatever's going on sounds rowdier than that. There's lots of clapping. A cheer erupts right as I turn the corner.

From the doorway, I count twelve of them lined up along the larger wooden table with some toppled cans of beer and two-liters, spilled bags of popcorn, emptied cookie trays, and crumpled packs of cigarettes around them. Down one end, Rainy's rewinding a cassette tape in her boombox with a ciggie dangling from her bottom lip. Simon's rocking back and forth beside her. Thinker's tearing pages from some book. Mimi's stuffing popcorn in her mouth. Creep's juggling three pretzels. Sal's counting up change in his palm. Jiggles and Swab are sharing a whiskey bottle. Dot is brushing Lolly's hair. Kneeslapper's face is smushed against the table. Zorro's legs are propped beside her head. He's sounding complicated words out of some pamphlet in his lap.

"Tar-dive dys-ki-nes-i-a?"

The few bothering to listen shrug. None have noticed that I'm standing in the doorway yet.

"How about extra pyr-a-mid-al symptoms? Anybody? No? A syndrome including excessive drooling, involuntary tremors, and an inability to remain still."

"What's his name's got dibs on that one."

"An-he-don-i-a? Cat-a-ton-i-a? Mel-an-chol-i-a? Par-a-phas-i-a? Tar-dive dys-ki-nes-i-a?"

"You said that one already," Thinker reminds him. He's still ripping pages from his book. He sets one in the nearest ashtray and aims his lighter at it.

"You're right. I did. A disorder of the nervous system causing blinking, lip smacking, grimacing, teeth grinding, or other repetitive motions."

The cassette tape clicks. Rainy pushes play and begins swaying before the first keys on the piano have been struck. I don't recognize the tune until Peggy Lee starts talking about the time her house caught on fire when she was a little girl, and how she watched their family home go up in flames after her father rescued her. Rainy's mouthing all the words. She's even pantomiming what's described. She folds her arms across her chest and wriggles her bony shoulders at the part where Peggy mentions being cold out on the pavement. When Peggy describes her first trip to the circus, Rainy hops and swings her hands from side to side, mimicking a clown, then presses her right arm against her nose and swings it around just like an elephant. A violin joins the piano. A banjo's being plucked. A trumpet's tooting. A round of honks shoots from a tuba.

"Dancing fucking bears!" shouts Swab.

As Rainy shimmies past him, he grabs her right thigh. She shakes free and nearly trips but keeps on dancing.

They still haven't noticed me. Although I'm grinning, I can also feel myself becoming angry at the lot of them. What I would give to have these twenty years they are about to waste, to have my arm still work. I want to warn them, but I've learned they'll never listen.

I yell from the doorway.

All of them look over.

"Poppppppppsicle!"

"Dick!"

"Richie, join us!"

"Get in here, Dicko!"

"Sisyphus! Set down your boulder! Come join us in this foggy netherworld."

"Why aren't all of you asleep?"

"Popsicle, come have a drinkie-poo!"

"How often do you do this?"

"Do what?"

"Hey, where's his cane?"

"Sit up bullshitting all night."

"Somebody get him a cup."

"Now hold on a minute, Rich," says Thinker, pointing down the table at Zorro, "Donald was just reading to us from his memoirs. What's the title again, Donald? Those words there on the front. That's right."

"Managing Demented Individuals. I stole it from the office."

They're all grinning with anticipation like they will applaud if I take one step in the room. May as well. I'm wide awake by now. It's not like I could fall asleep again, not at this hour at my age.

Thinker is motioning for me to take the empty seat of honor in the middle. Rainy's rewinding her cassette again. Soon as I step into the room they all burst into applause.

Thinker pulls the empty chair out for me.

"The man of the hour!"

As I'm easing down, Sal glances at his palm to count the coins in it again.

"Hey Dick," he says, gripping my arm, "you happen to have a nickel? We're all outta soda."

I shake my head. "Sal, are you fucking nuts?"

"I don't know," he wonders more than asks me. "Is it nuts to ask for a nickel?"

About the Author

Originally from Delco PA, Chris Eagle has lived in Berkeley, Paris, Antwerp, Pasadena, Sydney, Berlin, Chicago, and now Atlanta, where he teaches Health Humanities at Emory University. His short stories have appeared in AGNI, Louisiana Literature, and SORTES. Chris is currently at work on a short story collection set in Delco.

About Tortoise Books

Slow and steady wins in the end, even in publishing. Tortoise Books is dedicated to finding and promoting quality authors who haven't yet found a niche in the marketplace—writers producing memorable and engaging works that will stand the test of time.

Learn more at www.tortoisebooks.com or follow us on Twitter: @TortoiseBooks.

CPSIA information can be obtained
at www.ICGtesting.com
Printed in the USA
JSHW020207250423
40763JS00002B/2

9 781948 954792